Deverell Gatehouse

Karen MacLeod

PENTALPHA
PUBLISHING
EDINBURGH

DEVERELL GATEHOUSE
Karen MacLeod
© *Karen MacLeod 2015*

Published by Pentalpha Publishing Edinburgh

The author asserts the moral right under the Copyright, Designs and Patents Act 1988 to be identified as the author of this work. All Rights reserved. No part of this publication may be reproduced, stored in a retrieval system, or transmitted, in any form or by any means without the prior written consent of the author, nor be otherwise circulated in any form of binding or cover other than that in which it is published and without a similar condition being imposed on the subsequent purchaser.

All rights reserved.

Cover design: MadCow

All enquiries to pentalphapublishing@live.co.uk

First printing 2015.

ISBN: 0-9528843-5-6
ISBN-13: 978-0-9528843-5-4

For Valerie, Anna and Dave,
who were there too.

Deverell Gatehouse

~

THE SHADOWY BEDROOM WAS COLD, but I was fine with the blankets doubled over and the mattress was comfortable enough. Once accustomed to the country silence, I felt myself drifting into sleep.

I was woken by a man singing, a line of plainchant, haunting in its sadness. No sooner had I begun to listen than it stopped. I could just see my clock. It was two in the morning.

Footsteps on the stairs. Above me, descending from the attic. Cautious, even hesitant. Whichever child it was had not put the turret stair light on; I would have seen it beneath my cracked oak door. I expected the steps to pass my room. Instead they halted outside it. I sat up, reaching for my bedside light. A knock on the door.

'Come in,' I said. My voice sounded very loud.

Nothing happened.

'Come in,' I repeated. 'It's all right. Just come in.' I switched on my light and got to my feet, throwing my towelling robe round me. There was no more sound, so I crossed the old boards in my bare feet and opened the door.

Young Jack stood there, wide eyed and shivering in his pyjamas.

'Something's in my room,' he said.

CHAPTER ONE

THE GATEHOUSE TURRET WAS UNUSUAL, its stairs made of oak instead of stone. After four hundred years the steps were uneven and cracked. Standing in the studded doorway, I could see through them up to winding infinity. As the guidebook warned, it was not a holiday property for the elderly.

There were no elderly here. My husband's nine year old niece Elizabeth ran past me and tore up the steps to explore, yelling for her brother, her long, golden hair flying behind her. I followed, somewhat daunted; this was rural Hampshire, but it was hardly going to be a quiet week.

Below me, as I climbed with my holdall and provisions, came the usual sounds of arrival, car doors slamming, luggage heavier than mine dragged across gravel, my sister-in-law Marcia loudly adamant that the provisions be kept separate from everything else. As if nobody could have thought of it but her.

The oak steps in the turret were in fact very uneven and though the walls were whitewashed the slit windows hardly brought in enough light. Lack of modern amenities was one of the attractions of places like this and despite its succession of visitors the gatehouse smelled musty, ancient. Elizabeth was screaming down from the top floor, bagging one of the two attic rooms. I wondered when she would notice there was no television.

'It's your kind of place,' my husband Emery had said. It was not his kind of place, so he had implied that he was sacrificing himself on my behalf in his eagerness to be reconciled to me. I was glad he had not arrived yet.

I reached the first floor. By floor, I mean a small stone pause in the wooden steps. There were two doorways here, one to a spacious bedroom with carved fireplace and mullioned windows, the other to a drawing room with a tiny turret kitchen off it. The property brochure had a ground plan, so we adults had agreed beforehand where to sleep. Marcia had wanted Emery to have the best room for his attempt at reconciliation, so this bedchamber on the first floor would be ours. I cast one amazed look at its sixteenth century wondrousness before dumping my holdall and taking the provisions through to the drawing room.

The grand, rectangular drawing room, which was above the gatehouse archway and therefore its entire width, had large triple windows on either side. One side overlooked the bumpy track connecting Deverell to the outside world. The other had a side view down to the mossy roofed manor house itself, which the guidebook told us had been occupied by the family for centuries. Both drawing room views were heavily restricted by trees in summer foliage. Had it not been for the late afternoon sun it might have been gloomy. The little turret kitchen with its arched windows was charming. I had never seen curved worktops before.

'Let's see the kitchen then.' Bob Weightman, my sister-in-law's husband, heaved in more food and looked round. He was in his mid forties, greying, small, compact and friendly. I liked him and often wished him a less dominating wife than Marcia, but he seemed unable to imagine anything else. Some men get like that.

'It's nifty.' Bob opened cupboards, typically determined to cover any awkwardness, for until lunch today I had not seen Emery's family since Christmas. He found serviceable but good quality china and plenty of teapots.

'It's lovely,' I said.

Bob beamed at me, then shot out again as Marcia called him sharply from outside.

One of the kitchen windows overlooked the manor house lawns, elegantly kept. Perhaps they had peacocks. A middle aged man in tweeds with thick, iron grey hair was throwing a stick for an elderly chocolate Labrador. As I opened the arched window, I heard him encouraging it, evidently trying to keep it fit as long as possible. It ambled about to please him.

'Mum thinks we'll starve,' Jack said, arriving with more food bags. He was Elizabeth's brother, two years older, with his father's friendliness and none of Elizabeth's selfishness. I think he would have said more had Marcia herself not steamed into the little kitchen, tall, blonde and vigorous, and begun organising it within an inch of its life. I made my escape. Pointless arguing over such trivial matters as the arrangement of cereal boxes.

I explored further. Marcia and Bob would sleep in the large ground floor room directly below ours. Known as the guardroom, it had four windows and its chimney was vast with iron cooking implements still *in situ*. Pieces of armour hung above it. Steps inside the guardroom led down to the gatehouse's rear entrance, which was firmly locked and to which we had not been given a key. The furniture here as elsewhere was oak, basic and solid.

Since I could now hear Elizabeth shouting outside, I climbed to the attics. Both rooms were small with steeply sloping beams. It was oddly cold up here, even in August, but the views of the rolling hills beyond the gatehouse were spectacular. The gentleman in tweeds still exercised his dog on the lawn. He glanced up, saw me, smiled and waved. I waved back. In theory we had no contact with the Deverell family – an agent had met us with the keys – but he must be used to visitors invading part of his ancestral home.

We had a makeshift tea at the long dining table in the drawing room, bacon rolls, salad, cheese and fruit. The children were restless, particularly Elizabeth. Since one of Deverell's advertised attractions was its remoteness from the modern world and lack of television, Marcia had gone further and decreed this a technology free holiday. She had confiscated all her family's phones, including Bob's (she generally treated him like a third child and Elizabeth consequently had no respect for him). I could see what Marcia was driving at, though I wondered how long it would last. Meantime I kept my own phone out of sight.

I was growing edgy myself with the prospect of Emery's arrival. Get through the week and stay calm, I told myself. I now half regretted agreeing to it. But if it did not work out, it would be easier to split permanently afterwards because we had at least given our marriage another chance.

'We'll need to think about tomorrow,' Marcia said. Ever organised. Never spontaneous. 'The weather's to be fine again. What do we want to do?'

I said nothing. I suppose one has to be organised when one has children, but she still grated on me.

'I'm easy,' Bob said, saving face since his opinion would not count. He looked at me. 'Imogen?'

'I want to phone Chloe,' Elizabeth pleaded.

'No phones on this holiday.' Marcia lifted a pile of tourist leaflets from the sideboard, dumped them on the table. 'There's lots to do. We won't get through half of it in a week…'

I avoided the discussion which followed by volunteering to do the dishes. Then I went for a stroll, to retrieve my camera which I had left in my car.

Outside, rock roses scented the air and it was markedly warmer than in the gatehouse, though cypress and pine shaded the walk from gatehouse to the grassy area set out for cars. The sun was dipping below the rolling horizon as I walked towards my little bronze Volkswagen. The car windows glowed blood red, almost blinding me, then grew clear once more as I drew nearer and blocked out the sun. I saw a second head reflected in the passenger window as I reached to open the door. I turned instinctively, but there was no one there.

CHAPTER TWO

THERE was no one there. The sun's blood red reflection on the car window must have affected my sight. I opened the passenger door and lifted the camera, then continued my stroll in the cooling dusk.

The track leading to the B road and the outside world was long, surrounded by cattle, with a grid at its end. Not a country girl, but an accountant from London, I felt faintly nervous about the cattle, but they did not approach me. When I had gone some way from the gatehouse, I turned to view it at a distance. With the track curving, it was almost all obscured by trees, but I could see the many chimneys and gables of the manor house now, built at right angles onto the gatehouse which guarded it. The manor house was probably Elizabethan, perhaps Jacobean, certainly newer than the gatehouse, but presumably built on top of an earlier house. I must look up the guidebook, I thought, before becoming aware of a car engine behind me.

Emery. My heart beat faster. He would attempt to charm me. He would charm Marcia – her younger brother was her blind spot – into trying to persuade me to go back to him. I must make my own mind up, I told myself, turning to face the car.

It was not Emery. If he had bought another car since February it was unlikely to be an old brown estate. The man driving it was taller than Emery. He raised a hand to thank me as I stood aside, then drove slowly level with me. The driver's window was open. I saw a long, tanned face with chestnut hair and beard. I frowned, wondering whether I had seen him somewhere before. He stopped the car.

'Are you staying in the gatehouse?' he asked. He was in his thirties, about my age, and wearing t-shirt and corduroys. His hazel eyes were the most melancholy I had ever seen. He seemed to be forcing himself to speak, to go through the motions of politeness to a guest, albeit a paying one. Noblesse oblige, I thought. I had the impression that something very sad had happened to him recently.

'Yes,' I said, smiling to show I was grateful for the effort he had made. 'It's lovely. It's going to be a wonderful week.'

He smiled back. 'The weather should hold for you. Enjoy.' He raised his hand again and drove on.

I continued my walk as far as the cattle grid. The dusk was deepening. It occurred to me that Emery might not arrive tonight; reliability and punctuality were not his style. He might have found a party to attend in London instead. I might get one night to myself in my Tudor bedroom.

Back at the gatehouse, Marcia had organised a jigsaw on the drawing room table. There were quantities of games stored in the sideboard to compensate for the lack of technology. Elizabeth was flagging and bored. Just as I entered Marcia was sending her off to bed.

'Can't I phone Chloe and Louise?'

'No,' Marcia said.

'Just once, mummy, please…'

'No.' Marcia kissed her briskly. 'I'll come up and see you soon.'

Elizabeth left, dragging her feet. Marcia turned to Jack. 'You too. It's been a long day. And remember, no running on those tricky stairs.'

Jack heaved a sigh, but went.

I found the property's guidebook, sat down by the window to read it. My guess had been right. The gatehouse, built by the Deverell family in the late fifteenth century, was older than the manor house, which had been built in the late sixteenth century to replace the fourteenth century manor house. The Deverells' past did not appear especially colourful, but like all the best Tudor families they could boast of a representative in the Tower. A son and heir had been implicated in the Duke of Norfolk's rebellion against Elizabeth I.

'Has Emery been in touch?' Marcia asked me.

Bob, one of nature's jigsaw completers, kept his head down.

'No,' I said.

Marcia grimaced. 'Oh, Imogen, you've not fallen out already, have you?'

'We haven't been in touch to fall out,' I said frostily. It was none of her business. 'If he doesn't turn up, that's his choice.'

'You should get in touch with him,' Marcia said. As if it was my fault. Where Emery was concerned, it would always be my fault.

'It's up to him, Marcia.' I stood up, guidebook in hand. 'I'm having an early night, if you don't mind.'

'We've decided to go to Winchester tomorrow,' she called after me.

'Fine by me.' I was thirty two years old so refrained from slamming the door.

My bedroom soon soothed me. The carved ceiling and splendid fireplace, I read in the guidebook, were Jacobean, the rest Tudor. The white bed cover and whitewashed walls made the most of what brightness there was and when I closed the wooden shutters on both windows it was as snug as possible in a naturally cold building. I was filled with admiration for the toughness of medieval people. What must it have been like in winter?

I had a reasonably modern en suite bathroom, two uneven steps down into a whitewashed turret with an enormous locked chest. I lay in a hot bath in this curious circular bathroom, delving into the guidebook again. It said nothing about the Deverell family today, referring only to 'the present owner'. Soon sleep began to overtake me – it had been a long drive from London – and I went to bed, opening the shutters again to catch the moonlight.

It was now nearly eleven. The shadowy room was cold, but I was fine with the blankets doubled over and the mattress was comfortable enough. I heard Bob and Marcia go down to the guardroom. Each wooden step creaked loudly beneath their feet. Presently, I heard Elizabeth scamper down from the attic, past my door and into their room. There was no bathroom on the attic floor, so the children had to descend two floors if they got up in the middle of the night. Much as I appreciated my room, I decided I would volunteer to exchange it for the guardroom tomorrow, then they would only have to come down one floor to use their parents' bathroom. I cared less about Emery and I having the most splendid room than Marcia did. And he might not turn up at all. Hope was rising in me. Once accustomed to the country silence, I felt myself drifting into sleep.

At first I was surprised when I heard the man singing. I knew Bob sang – he was allowed out to a choir once a week and I had attended some of their concerts – but I had not expected him to do it here. I had never heard him sing at home and could imagine Marcia's indignation if he had woken her up. It was the sort of music his choir performed, though, a line of plainchant, haunting in its sadness. No sooner had I begun to listen, however, than it stopped. I could just see my clock. It was two in the morning. Would Bob have been singing at two in the morning? Well, I could always ask him, when Marcia wasn't around. I turned over and shut my eyes again.

Then came the footsteps on the stairs, descending from the attic. Cautious, even hesitant, unlike either of the Weightman children. I expected the steps to pass my room. Instead they halted outside it. I sat up, bemused, reaching for my bedside light. A knock on the door.

'Come in,' I said. My voice sounded very loud.

Nothing happened.

'Come in,' I repeated. 'It's all right. Just come in.' I switched on my light and got to my feet, throwing my towelling robe round me. There was no more sound, so I crossed the old floorboards in my bare feet and pulled open the door.

Young Jack stood there, wide eyed and shivering in his pyjamas.

'Something's in my room,' he said.

CHAPTER THREE

'WHAT do you mean, something's in your room?'

Jack's eyes grew wider. 'I can hear it.'

I tied my robe round me, more to give me time to think than anything else. I had no idea what to do. I wasn't his mother, I wasn't anyone's mother and he had come to me. I did not relish the idea of going up to the attic floor at dead of night, which was evidently what he wanted me to do.

'What did you hear?' I asked. 'Singing?'

He shook his head. 'A pulling sort of noise.'

'Pulling? Describe it.'

He frowned. 'A scratching noise, I suppose.'

'Mice overhead,' I said, relieved.

'And grunting. More grunting than scratching.' Jack found inspiration. 'Like that time I got my arm stuck in a railing. I was pulling and grunting, trying to get it out. Elizabeth took a picture,' he added crossly.

I realised I was staring at him and came to a decision. He was eleven years old, cold and shivering. He had come to me because he was worried. I had to help him.

'Okay,' I said, 'I'll come up.'

He had left his light on, so the creaking wooden steps grew easier to see the higher we climbed. His room had two single beds with red covers. It was untidy and freezing. He had piled the bedclothes from the unoccupied bed on top of his.

'First things first. Put on your dressing gown,' I said. 'It's cold up here.' He did as I told him to. 'Okay, where did the noise come from?'

I was uneasily aware that it was not what Marcia would have done. She would have told him it was his imagination and settled him back into bed. Perhaps that was why he had come to me instead.

'There.' Jack pointed firmly to the space in front of the window at the foot of his bed. 'It went on for ages. There's no bedside lamp, only the wall switch, so…'

It was probably the closest he would get to admitting he'd been frightened to get up because he would have to go close to the noise. I would have given him a cuddle, but I didn't think boys his age appreciated that.

'Any other sounds?' I asked.

'It sounded like a man,' he decided. 'Must have been a …'

He didn't actually say the word I was dreading. I didn't believe in ghosts. Who ever heard of an accountant who believed in ghosts? But at that moment, in that dim room, at two in the morning, under those old, steeply sloping timbers…

'There are no such things,' I said, Marcia-like. Jack shot me a shrewd look. He could see whose benefit I'd said it for.

'Why did you think I'd heard singing?' he asked.

I was saved from answering by footsteps on the stairs. We both turned. I think Jack stepped nearer me. But it was Marcia. She came in quietly so as not to wake Elizabeth across the landing, but even her whisper was full of command.

'What's going on? Jack, why have you got Imogen out of bed?'

He hesitated. It was obvious he didn't want to admit to being afraid. It might get back to Elizabeth. I came to his rescue. 'He heard mice in the rafters.'

'Rats more like,' Marcia snorted, unafraid of either species of rodent. She shooed Jack back to bed like the capable mother she was. I slipped down to my own room. But I kept my bedside light on until dawn.

Dawn was hazily sublime, promising another fine day. Marcia had the household up early, but I had been up earlier still, walking the full distance to the cattle grid this time.

Although my disturbed night had left me tired, that was the only indication it had happened at all. It seemed bizarre in the extreme and I wondered whether I had been dreaming. The plainchant in particular must have been a dream. I saw no point in asking Bob about it. Life bemused him enough.

As I began to walk back to the gatehouse, a little white Fiat came towards me. The window nearest me was down and the driver – a slim, fine featured woman in her forties – smiled and waved to me as she passed. Perhaps the wife of the grey haired man on the lawn.

The noise of the Weightmans round the drawing room table at breakfast put an end to any speculation about the Deverells. Neither Marcia nor Jack mentioned last night, but Marcia buttonholed me all the same.

'Imogen. Have you heard from Emery?'

I shook my head. I had not checked for texts. Marcia looked impatiently at me. She must have suspected my determination not to reconcile, my reluctance to see her brother again. 'He'll probably meet up with us in Winchester,' she said.

'I expect so.' I concentrated on fruit salad and cereal.

'You can't have more toast,' Elizabeth squawked at Jack. 'You've had three slices already. You'll get fat, you'll get fat…'

Neither child had ever been anything but active and thin, so Jack, who was growing fast, just pulled a face at her and went on buttering. He made no mention of last night and I certainly wasn't going to remind him.

'Less noise, both of you,' Marcia said. 'Bob, go and put more toast on…'

We drove in convoy to Winchester, headed for the mediaeval cathedral.

It was busy yet vast, echoing yet hushed, and awe-inspiring. Grey stone now, when it must once have been madly colourful, but the smell of sanctity had survived the tourists.

It was a grim sanctity in places. 'That's horrible!' Elizabeth recoiled from Bishop Gardiner's cadaver tomb, the writhing stone skeleton contrasting with the fine carving around it.

'It was the fashion,' Bob said, as if Elizabeth was listening, 'a reminder of what you came to.'

'People weren't soft in those days,' Marcia sniffed. 'Different now.'

'Just as well,' Bob said. 'Some of the things they did…'

But Elizabeth had long since made herself scarce.

I managed to make myself scarce too and lose the Weightmans in the vastness of the cathedral. I walked round, craning my neck to the height of the splendid ceiling and marvelling at the altar screen crowded with row upon row of stone saints. Memorial tablets to members of prominent local families covered the walls and aisles. I saw none to the Deverell family. Camera flashes and a huddle of tourists betrayed the whereabouts of the cathedral's most famous occupant, in the north aisle of the nave. An admirer myself, I went there too, looking down at Jane Austen's black marble slab and the inscription which made no mention of her books.

Someone caught me round my waist.

'Knew I'd find you here…'

Estranged husbands ought to be cagey, or sheepish, or anxious. Here was Emery as breezy as if we had never separated. He was blue eyed and fair, like his sister Marcia and her children, and thickening in his thirties only slightly, his charm his outstanding characteristic.

'Well, hello again,' he said.

I detached myself from his arm. 'Hello.'

'Oh, the icily polite look. Okay.' He smiled again, held out his arm. 'I've just arrived. Take me round.'

'I don't know it well. I've never been here before.'

'Then let's explore it together.'

He might lack the purposefulness of his sister, but he had the knack of making me feel, and probably appear, churlish. He was not putting it on either; he was good natured in private too. I knew others wondered why we had separated, particularly those of my own sex. Lots of women like shallow charm.

'All right.' I took his arm and we began to stroll round the cathedral.

'So,' he said, 'how have you been?'

I suppose it was a bad place to meet up again. I wanted to explore our surroundings. Emery was no more interested in history than his niece Elizabeth.

'I'm fine,' I said brusquely.

'No better than fine?'

'What else would I be?'

'You might be just dandy, Imogen.'

'I'm just dandy then.'

He was steering me away from a crush of Japanese tourists snapping cameras a few steps above us. I resisted. This was one part of the cathedral I had read about; it was well known for The Miracles of the Virgin, a sequence of medieval wall paintings which had survived the Reformation. 'That's the Lady Chapel,' I said.

'Too crowded.'

'I'd like to see its frescos.'

He let go. 'Okay, okay, but you'll not get near them…'

I went up the steps. I didn't understand why he thought I wouldn't get near the paintings, for the Lady Chapel was all but empty and winter dark, lit only by candles on an altar. A boy of Jack's age stood there, alone, wearing mourning black and sobbing his heart out. I had never seen a child in such anguish and went towards him, holding out my arms to him. He saw me and ran to me.

'Ow,' Emery said, hopping about comically. 'My foot…'

'What?' I was dazed. It was light again, and crowded, cameras flashing. The boy had gone.

'You stood on my foot.' Emery grinned. 'Never saw anyone so keen to see a picture. Are you all right?'

I wasn't. I was growing more dazed by the second. What had happened? Had I imagined the boy? I had seen clothes like his before, in Tudor portraits. I looked around. It had been night, or at least winter. Now it was August.

'Think you should sit down.' Emery led me to a bench over against the wall. I eyed the renowned frescos behind their glass screens without taking them in.

'I'm all right,' I said.

'You sure?'

'I'll find Marcia.'

Irritation helped me. 'I don't need Marcia.' I stood up and walked from the Lady Chapel without attempting to view the frescos up close.

CHAPTER FOUR

'PENNY for your thoughts,' Emery said, smiling and leaning over the wooden table towards me.

Having left the cathedral, we lunched outside at a pretty riverside restaurant, a large canvas umbrella shading the six of us from the midday sun. I think Marcia had wanted Emery and me to have our own table, but I stuck resolutely to the wider family and he did not object. I was very quiet indeed. He must have thought it was because of his arrival.

In fact, I was doubting my sanity. I was intelligent, educated, respected at work and trusted with other people's money. I had a routine, responsible life. My only impulsive act had been to marry Emery six years earlier and I intended to put that right as soon as possible. So a second face in a car window, monastic singing in the night and a Tudor boy in a candlelit chapel in broad daylight had to be my imagination, as the scratching, pulling sound in Jack's attic had been his. Why we should take to simultaneous flights of fancy was a mystery. I couldn't answer for Jack, but it was untypical of me. If it wasn't my imagination I wasn't sane. But the Tudor boy's grief haunted me. And if I had seen him, he had seen me; he had run towards me...

'Come back to us, Imogen…' Emery waved a hand in front of my eyes. Elizabeth, who adored him and sat next to him, did the same.

'I'm fine.' I gave myself a mental shake.

'So, Chawton Cottage?' Marcia said, eyeing me curiously.

Jane Austen's house. I felt unutterably relieved, and not just because I had always wanted to go there. The woman who had mocked flights of fancy so brilliantly in *Northanger Abbey* would come to my rescue.

I loved bright, homely Chawton, every item in the rosy bricked house speaking to the useful and sensible if limited lives lived there by Austen, her mother, sister and friend. Even Austen's neat and elegant handwriting suggested a serenity which someone who had lived her life could not always have felt. It was not simply genius which marked that house, but strength of will.

'Fancy buying a cottage like this?' Emery asked, stealing up behind me in the garden. 'Get you out of London…'

'No.'

'You hate London.'

'Who doesn't? It's where my work is.'

Emery didn't work, much. He came from a wealthy family and called himself an artist. He liked the party side of the artistic life. He was like Austen's George Wickham, but with money. He would have hated living in the country, so why suggest it?

'All right.' He sighed, addressed his feet. 'Moody Imogen. Thought Chawton might cheer you up. I suggested it for you.'

It depends who you visit it with, I thought, but didn't say this. It probably hung in the air unspoken. 'I'm going for a drive,' I said instead. Incredibly, even Jane Austen had not been able to shake off my sense of dread. 'I'll come back to the gatehouse tonight. Tell Marcia to start dinner without me if I'm not back.'

Emery looked at me. 'Sure you're all right?'

I saw genuine concern in him and it touched me. I realised there would be moments like this throughout our week at the gatehouse. One cannot forget six years easily. I wasn't entirely certain yet that I wanted to.

'Yes,' I said. 'Really, I am.'

So there I was, all right, driving back to Winchester and the cathedral on my own. I had no idea what compelled me. I told myself I only had to walk into the Lady Chapel in the twenty first century in bright August sunshine. If that happened I would be fine. I simply needed to know anything else had been my imagination.

I walked up the aisle of the cathedral as quickly as possible. It was busier than ever. Many of the visitors would be staying for Evensong. I could see the Lady Chapel as I approached. It was not in darkness. Stay like that, I thought, getting nearer with every step. Nearer. Still August in the twenty first century. Still bright. Nearer. Bright. Nearer. Bright. At the steps into the chapel now. Still bright. Lots of tourists in twenty first century dress milling around the wall paintings.

I was in the chapel now. No darkness. No candles. Around me chatter and camera flashes. My relief was intense. Smiling to myself, almost laughing aloud, I tried to forget where the grief stricken Tudor boy had been standing. But I could still recall the spot and went there. The relatively modern inscription beneath my sandals told me I was standing above a tomb believed to be that of Bishop White of Winchester, who had died in 1560.

I thought, how curious they're not certain whose tomb it is, as late as the sixteenth century, then turned my attention to the renowned wall paintings. They were magnificent. Ironically, one of them told the story of a dreaming woman. In her case it was a celestial Candlemas celebration, rather than a distraught boy whose clothes would have fitted 1560. I shivered, then took a grip of myself. I quickly left the cathedral before imagination got the better of me again.

In my haste, I all but stumbled into a tall, bearded man in smudged, faded overalls who was taking leave of an elderly priest in a cassock. The brown estate car was presumably parked somewhere nearby.

'I beg your pardon,' he said, though it had been my fault rather than his, then recognised me from my stroll yesterday. He put his head to one side, less melancholy today. 'Hello again.'

'Hello,' I said. The priest gave me a twinkling smile, the very image of Anglican benevolence, and went back into the cathedral.

'How's the holiday going? Is the gatehouse comfortable?' My tall, bearded man in smudged overalls was well spoken, with a neutral accent, his voice pitched neither too deep nor too high.

'It's very comfortable.' It was, in daylight. If I said it was alarming at night he would think me ridiculous. I settled for the obvious, 'It's got lots of character.'

'You can say that again.' I didn't like to ask what he meant. He was taller than Emery, but his overalls hung on him, perhaps borrowed from a heavier man. He carried an old tool bag, saw my eyes go to it. 'I've been up in the rafters,' he explained.

'The cathedral rafters?'

It didn't surprise me that his family were involved in the preservation of the cathedral. But I had not expected such a hands-on approach. He must have seen my surprise; he smiled and lifted a shoulder deprecatingly. 'I get plenty of practice at home.' Even with the gatehouse rented out, I supposed the manor house cost a fortune to maintain.

'I'm Nicholas Deverell,' he said, extending a long, sunburned hand.

'Imogen Webb.' We shook hands. His palm was warm, dry and calloused. We stood there in the shadow of the great cathedral, surrounded by tourists, the clack of many tongues in our ears, neither of us at ease, yet I sensed he was as unwilling as I was to end the conversation. To prolong it I said, 'We went to Jane Austen's house this afternoon.'

He seemed pleased. 'You've seen her grave here?'

'Yes. No mention of the novels.'

'I saw you in the Lady Chapel,' he said, 'looking at the murals.'

The Tudor boy sprang back into my mind to embarrass me. I had been so relieved to find the Lady Chapel in daylight, had it been obvious to others?

'There's a bishop buried there who might not be buried there,' I said. Anything to steer the conversation away from myself.

'I think you mean Bishop White,' Nicholas said. 'He arranged his own funeral brass in the chapel at Winchester College where he was Warden, then Queen Mary Tudor made him a bishop. So they can't be certain where he's buried.'

I was impressed. 'You're very knowledgeable.'

'Hardly.' Nicholas shook his head. 'You happened to pick a period I know about. An ancestor of mine was in his service as a page.'

A page. A boy. I stood there, my heart beating unpleasantly fast. I seemed to see the dark, candlelit chapel again. The boy was mourning him, I thought, he was mourning Bishop White. He was standing over the grave.

'Queen Elizabeth disliked White because he opposed her on religion,' Nicholas added. 'She deprived him of his bishopric, so the funeral wouldn't have been grand enough for any records of it to survive. It might even have been furtive.'

'He's buried in the Lady Chapel,' I said, before I could stop myself.

'Probably, yes.' Nicholas looked at me seriously, as well he might. My brain was absorbing the implications of what he had told me. The Tudor boy had really existed. I had not imagined him. He had been Bishop White's page. How could I have known about him?

How could he have seen me? But I kept outwardly calm. It had been mortifying enough to feel light headed in Emery's presence.

'What was your ancestor's name?' I asked.

'Dominic Deverell. He went to the Tower as a young man for conspiring against Queen Elizabeth.'

'Was he guilty?'

'Probably. He was in the Duke of Norfolk's service by then.'

'As mentioned in your gatehouse guidebook. Of course…'

He smiled. 'You've been reading.'

'I like history.'

I could not have had this conversation with Emery. But I had been aware for some time now of the broad gold band on the wedding finger of Nicholas's left hand. I suspected he was no Emery, light hearted in fidelity, but I had no intentions of tempting him. I knew the heartache such things could cause.

Did he pick up on my thoughts? He coloured, turned away slightly. 'I'd better leave you to it,' he said. 'Your family will be wondering where you are.'

Marcia had been wondering, evidently annoyed that I had detached myself from her brother and that he had not tried to stop me. Although I had said to go ahead with the evening meal if I was not back in time, she had delayed it anyway.

'Where were you?' Elizabeth demanded. 'I'm hungry…'

'Sh,' Marcia said, no doubt delighted I was getting the general blame. 'Don't be rude to Imogen.'

'You could have started dinner without me,' I said.

'Rubbish. I don't approve of all this separate eating.' Marcia sniffed. 'Trays here, trays there, slouching in front of televisions. A family should gather round a table at least once a day.'

'There's no television here.' I did not disagree with her and I was weary, knowing she was challenging me to declare that I was no longer part of Emery's family. She was prepared to wreck everyone's holiday and hold me responsible.

I looked round the gatehouse drawing room. All seemed tranquil. Bob was trying to build a model airplane he had bought on the journey down yesterday, watched by a patient Jack, who would probably have to take over and repair it in due course. Emery was sketching Elizabeth in the window seat. I wasn't going to fall for Marcia's bait and bring disharmony to the scene.

'All right then,' I said, assuming a smile. 'Let's eat.'

CHAPTER FIVE

Emery and I allied over dinner to persuade Marcia and Bob to swap our bedroom for the guardroom on the ground floor. This would mean the children would only have one flight of stairs down to their parents' bathroom. Elizabeth applauded our efforts. Jack looked sheepish; perhaps he thought I was trying to avoid a repetition of last night's little adventure. I sent him a smile of reassurance. He immediately looked even more sheepish.

Marcia agreed in the end, thanks to Emery's siding with me. He might be her beloved brother, but he sometimes took pleasure in aggravating her. Having given in, she countered by suggesting that he and I go out for a drink in the nearest village; Bob could drive us there. Bob was willing, he could hardly be anything else, but Emery demurred, explaining that he wanted to finish sketching Elizabeth, who was excited at the prospect of appearing on canvas in an exhibition.

So it was a quiet evening at the gatehouse. I sought for history books among the shelves in the drawing room and found a general one, which confirmed that Thomas Howard, fourth Duke of Norfolk, had been beheaded for treason in June 1572 after two risings against Queen Elizabeth, having also sought to marry Mary, Queen of Scots. Politically unwise to say the least.

There was of course nothing about any of the gentlemen in Norfolk's service. Why would there be? Only the very wealthiest in the land had left a trace of their lives in the sixteenth century. I thought of the furtive burial by night of a former bishop, whose wealth had been stripped from him, and of his grieving page, last to leave the chapel, perhaps having to be dragged away before officialdom came.

Presently, with sunset, I went out for a stroll. Instead of going down the track towards the B road, I turned without thinking much about it towards the manor house, though I wasn't sure that visitors were supposed to go there. Like the gatehouse it had been built on to, the manor house was of grey stone, but instead of round turrets it had stepped gables and mullioned windows.

I was no builder, but I could see that it needed work done. The roof appeared to be mossy and the paintwork peeled in places. In other places new stones and tiles showed that work had begun. No lights were on, but I peered into a ground floor window and glimpsed a large room, presumably the former Hall, set with wooden tables. It felt lonely and unloved. The pillared front door appeared firmly shut. If Nicholas and his family were at home, perhaps they had apartments round the back, away from the prying eyes of people like me.

'Boo,' someone said softly.

I actually cried out in fright. I turned, expecting to see Emery and give him a piece of my mind, and saw

Nicholas standing there in the dusk. Since I probably wasn't supposed to be here, I couldn't give him a piece of my mind.

'Forgive me,' he said. 'I didn't think you were the startled type.'

'I'm not, usually,' I said, thinking, if you only knew the half of it, you should have been here last night...

'You got me wondering about Dominic today,' he said. 'I've been doing some digging.' It seemed an unfortunate turn of phrase, but that evidently hadn't occurred to him. He must be at home in his dark, ancient grounds. He held up a white envelope. 'I was going to slip this under the gatehouse door for you.'

I was very glad now that I had bumped into him. I could imagine Marcia's curiosity and the construction she might put upon it.

'That was kind of you,' I said, taking the envelope.

He smiled. 'I find it interesting too. It looks like Dominic survived the Tower, which is more than Norfolk did, and lived another ten years at least. It's not exactly clear how...' He caught himself up. 'Well, you'll see it all in the envelope.'

'No,' I said, 'go on.'

But something padded out of the dark and came up to snuffle my hand. It was the chocolate Labrador I had seen on the lawn yesterday.

'He likes you,' Nicholas said.

I stroked the dog's warm, furry head. He sat down, leaning heavily against me, enjoying the attention.

'He answers to two names, just to confuse,' Nicholas added. 'He started off as Walnut, but my brother-in-law calls him Madogany.'

I laughed. The brother-in-law was presumably the older gentleman in tweeds I had seen with the dog on the lawn. I had liked his genial smile.

'I think I saw him yesterday, on the lawn.'

'Yes, that would be Alistair. He told me you waved back.'

We heard a creaking sound as the gatehouse door opened away to my left. Light from the turret staircase spilled out onto the gravel drive. Emery emerged. He switched on a torch, swung its beam around and stopped in surprise on seeing us.

'Oh,' he said. 'There you are.' He approached, smiling, and held out his hand to Nicholas. 'How do you do? I'm Emery Webb, Imogen's husband.'

Nicely done. Civilised, even friendly, but letting it be known that I was off limits. Had I been another kind of woman, had I wanted to be off limits, I might have appreciated it. But I wasn't and I didn't, and I was also surprised. Until now I had not been sure that Emery wished to stay married to me. But I didn't want to cause a scene, so I concealed my feelings for the moment.

'Nicholas Deverell.' Nicholas shook hands, friendly also, but I could see in his eyes that he got Emery's message. 'I hope you both enjoy your stay.'

He clicked his tongue to Walnut/Madogany and turned about, heading away into the darkness. Emery gave me one of his breezy smiles.

'Thought you'd got lost,' he said. 'Marcia despatched me, a one man search party. Spooky out here at night.'

'I wasn't lost,' I said.

'So I noticed,' Emery replied amiably.

Exasperated, not wanting Nicholas to hear us argue in the still night, I went into the gatehouse and up the few steps to the guardroom. Emery followed me in and closed the door. The guardroom was tidy; the super efficient Marcia had already packed up her things and Bob's, ready to take them upstairs.

'You didn't lose much time,' Emery said, still amiable, but wary now.

'Sorry?'

'Do you want a divorce? Is it because you hate my guts, or because you've met a handsome widower with a house dripping in history?'

'Widower?'

It explained the melancholy I had seen in Nicholas.

'I looked him up before I came here,' Emery said. 'He lost his wife and child in an accident a year ago. Don't tell me he never said.'

'Why would he? I hardly know him.'

'But you want to know him better.'

'Why not, Emery? You don't own me. We were talking about history, as it happens, as if I need to justify myself.'

Emery shrugged. 'Well, as I said, with a house dripping in the stuff, he's off to a flying start. What a good way to get to know you.'

'That's...'

'It's what I'd do in his shoes, Imogen. I must say, you have to hand it to him. It seems to be working.'

I was stunned. 'I don't think this is your business,' I said eventually.

He laughed. 'We are still married.' He folded his arms. 'Shall I drive off into the uncertainty of the black night now?'

I had not anticipated this reaction from Emery and it felt very odd. I had never hated his guts, in spite of what he had said.

'No, it would upset Marcia. Don't be dramatic. Anyway, you're her brother. I should be the one to drive off.'

Emery laughed. 'But you don't want to, do you?'

I thought ruefully of my reluctance to come on this gatehouse holiday. 'I don't think we should spoil things for everyone else.'

'Oh, very sophisticated. Suppose I don't want to watch my wife mending another man's broken heart?'

'That's rich, coming from you!'

'I never did it under your nose.'

'That makes it all right, does it?'

He smiled. 'Don't let's quarrel, Gen. It doesn't suit us.'

In a strange sort of way he was right. We had never been one of those fighting couples unfit for a calm. A semi detached sort of marriage, my friends said, envying me Emery's looks and easy ways. I had never let on how much semi detached could still hurt. And here I was, by the mere fact of agreeing to this week in Hampshire, letting him know that I could consider a reconciliation. I was suddenly determined that there would be nothing of the kind. On the other hand, I had no desire to leave early. As Emery had discerned, Deverell and its owner intrigued me too much.

'I'm not quarrelling,' I said. 'You know I like history. I'll talk to anyone about it. No need to make an issue of it.'

'How true.' He laughed. 'You realise he won't come near you now that he knows you're married? I know his soulful type. He'll avoid you like the plague and reckon his bad luck rumbles on.'

'He doesn't feel sorry for himself,' I said. 'He works hard. He fixes roofs, for heaven's sake.'

'But in the evenings, when there's nothing to do in this dark, godforsaken countryside…' Emery shrugged. 'Sorry, I didn't intend to criticise. It can't be easy for him. I'd be out of here.'

Yes, you would, I thought. But Emery was in effect offering me a truce, a chance to see the week out. I turned away from him ungratefully. 'We'd better move our stuff down from the bedroom upstairs,' I said.

It didn't take long to swap rooms. Marcia directed the whole thing like a military operation. The guardroom was bigger than the room we had left. There was a double bed in one corner and a single in the other. By mutual, unspoken consent, Emery quietly took possession of the single. Overhead the old floorboards creaked as Marcia and Bob settled in upstairs. Elizabeth was running up and down between their room and the attics, as Dominic had perhaps done before he was sent away from his home to be Bishop White's page, probably at a younger age than she was now. I slipped Nicholas's envelope into my handbag. I would open it later when there was peace.

CHAPTER SIX

THE guardroom had a turret bathroom similar to the one above it. Here, trying to relax in the bath, I opened Nicholas's letter. His writing was striking, something between italic and spiky.

> *Dear Imogen,*
>
> *I've been into the family records in search of Dominic. There's not too much about him, but this is what is known. He was born here in 1548, only child of William Deverell and his wife Catherine Cobb. Catherine died in 1551 and William married Anna Mervyn. That marriage produced three daughters. So Dominic was the heir and only son. In 1556 he began his education in Bishop White's household and when White lost his bishopric in 1559 he transferred to the Duke of Norfolk's service. In 1570 William died. Dominic inherited Deverell, but was imprisoned in the Tower with Norfolk the next year. Queen Elizabeth gave Dominic's lands to*

his elder uncle, Clement, who had become a Protestant. Dominic must have been out the Tower by 1573, the date of his marriage to Isabella Raymond. He had three sons and in 1584 his eldest son John inherited Deverell Manor because Uncle Clement had died childless and the younger uncle, Francis, was a Catholic priest on the run. Either Dominic was still under a cloud in 1584, and as far as we know he remained Catholic, or he was dead. There's certainly no record of his contesting his son inheriting. There's no record of where or when he died, either, but that's history for you. You'll be glad to hear we're a boring lot nowadays compared to our ancestors.

Best wishes,

Nicholas.

I read it several times, fascinated. Although I could not help recalling what Emery had sneeringly implied, that Nicholas was using his family history to get my attention, I was pleased to see no sign of this in the letter. I wanted Nicholas to be straightforward, a man of integrity, so unlike his detractor, Emery. It seemed to me that Dominic, too, had been a man of integrity, holding to his religious convictions even though they brought him such misfortunes. I thought of the twinkling Anglican priest outside the Cathedral today and thanked heaven English Christianity was a less violent faith in my own time.

'Imogen.' Emery knocked on the old, oaken bathroom door. 'Have you drowned? May I come in?'

Here was the downside to my own time with a vengeance. I didn't want Emery damaging the antiquated metal bar which passed for a lock. 'Wait,' I called, 'I'm just finishing.' I stepped resentfully out the bath, put on my towelling robe, thrust the letter into one of its pockets and unbarred the door. Emery was still fully dressed, a glass of red wine in his hand.

'Are you all right?' he asked.

'Of course I'm all right.'

'Imogen, what on earth's the matter with you? You look…like a ghost.'

'I've never had colour,' I snapped, which was true.

'Yes, but… You really are acting oddly, you know.'

'Thanks for the compliment.'

'Imogen…'

'There's nothing wrong with me a little peace and quiet won't fix.'

'Peace and quiet to dream of Nicholas?'

He was so provoking. 'I'm not having another discussion, Emery. We agreed not to quarrel for the week. So let's say as little as possible, shall we?'

He held up his hands and backed away, smirking. 'Okay, okay…'

Night. Emery snored softly in the single bed, having made no attempt to come near me in the double. The guardroom was darker than the bedroom upstairs, being more overshadowed by trees. Moonlight scarcely entered. Branches touched the unshuttered window to my left. Wide awake, not warm, I re-read Nicholas's letter beneath the blankets by the light of a mini torch. I wondered whether he lay awake too, remembering his wife and child.

Someone or something banged on the guardroom's locked external door to which we had no key. Heart thudding, I sat up in bed. Emery didn't stir. He was a sound sleeper. But suddenly I was grateful for his presence. I waited anxiously for another bang on the door. When none came I lay down eventually. Perhaps it had been my imagination. Again.

Of course, it didn't help me to sleep and when I heard footsteps on the turret stairwell which did not stop at the room upstairs I was up and in my dressing gown, two seconds away from running to Emery and shaking him awake. The door opened very slowly. My shaking torch beam swung at the intruder. It was Jack.

'I can hear him talking,' was all he said.

You can't. It's your imagination. Don't be silly, Jack. You're eleven, too old to be silly. What would Elizabeth think? She would laugh and giggle at you. She would laugh and giggle at me. None of these words came out. I don't know which of us made for the other first, but we ended up huddled into each other and shivering on the guardroom threshold, talking in whispers.

'I don't want to go back up there.'

'What's he saying?'

'I don't know. I think it's Latin.'

'Is it part of a conversation?'

'A conversation with God,' Jack answered. Such a strangely formal phrase for a twenty first century boy to use. I shuddered.

'You mean, praying?'

'I don't think so.'

Find some guts, Imogen, I lectured myself. Jack's only a child, but you're an adult. You've got to set him an example if nothing else. Tomorrow, if I survived the night, I was going to confront Nicholas Deverell and demand the truth about his blasted gatehouse.

'You stay here,' I whispered. 'I'll go up.' Jack's face was aghast in the torchlight. 'You'll not be alone. Uncle Emery's over there. Look.'

But Jack came with me, and I was secretly glad he did. We creaked up those ancient stairs together, his hand clutching my wide sleeve. His bedroom light was on, so, like last night, the going became easier going as we went higher.

'Where was the voice ?' I looked round Jack's attic, which was much as it had been last night. Blood galloped in my head, but again I saw nothing unusual. 'Was it from the same place as the scratching?'

'Yes.' Jack shivered. 'He's desperate. I think he's going to die.'

Because he heard pounding on the guardroom door, I thought. They came for him in the night. Whoever he was, they came for him in the night. That's what the pulling, scratching noise was. He had been tied up in Jack's attic and was trying to get free before they reached him…

'It must be prayer,' I said to Jack. 'Maybe they sounded different when they prayed in those days.'

He nodded. 'Maybe.' He was forlorn. 'I don't want to sleep here any more.'

'What will you tell your mum?'

He shrugged, the smallest trace of sheepishness stealing into him. I was glad to see this and gave him what passed for a game smile.

'It – he – won't harm you,' I said. 'He doesn't know you're there.' I remembered that the boy in the Lady Chapel had known I was there, and hurriedly added, to reassure myself as well as Jack, 'You're not in his time. It's just a… recording, if you like, of something long ago.'

Jack nodded, recovering somewhat.

'Just keep your light on all night,' I said.

'How did he die? He's not at peace, is he?'

He was too intelligent to accept a lie, had I been able to think of one. I shook my head. 'But remember, he doesn't know you're there. He can't see this modern furniture, or you, or any of the visitors who come here.'

'But if he saw us, it might help him,' Jack said. Unlike his sister, he had inherited Bob's kind heart. I was stumped.

'Perhaps, if you keep your light on, he doesn't suffer,' I said.

It was a ludicrous notion, of course, but we both wanted to believe it, and Jack nodded. 'Are you going back to bed then?' I added, patting the crumpled red counterpane. He nodded again, climbed into bed slowly. I drew the heavy heap of covers over him and kissed him. He reached up, put his arms round me, hugged me for a moment, then let go and turned over. Eventually he slept. I watched him for a while. Nothing moved in the room. No sounds came. Then I left, leaving the light on.

It grew darker on the turret stairs as I descended. Barefoot, I grew painfully aware of the rough unevenness of the oak steps. Soon, as Jack's light grew distant, I clung to the circular plaster wall. My fear returned with the dark. The small beam of my torch was inadequate; the whitewashed walls seemed to absorb rather than reflect it. My steps faltered, the timber growing more uneven. I formed an idea that my toes would catch in the cracks, causing me to tumble and break my neck.

By the time I got down to the guardroom I was shaking with cold and dread. The door was ajar as I had left it. I pushed it further open slowly, trying to prevent the old oak creaking, and crept in, shutting it slowly behind me.

Emery was still fast asleep. The moon seemed a stronger presence than before, but its light didn't reassure me; it allowed me to glimpse the shadow moving in the huge fireplace. Before I could even cry out, it left the fireplace and assumed height, as though a man had been hiding in it and now emerged to stand up in the guardroom.

I saw him clearly. He was about Emery's height, but with darker hair and a beard. Some sort of jerkin covered him loosely. He moved rapidly and something glinted in his hand. I knew him, of course. It was the boy from the Lady Chapel grown up, the round face thinner, the jaw harder, the eyes fierce.

I think I froze. I would have recovered, said his name, stretched out a hand to him, but he gave me no chance, for he didn't notice me this time. He ran past me and out the guardroom, as though, then, the door to the stairs had been open.

CHAPTER SEVEN

Someone was screaming. It was a woman's scream, not high, but anguished. It was me, I was certain of it, and baffled why Emery did not wake and jump out of bed in alarm. Then my senses recovered and I realised the screaming was upstairs.

Jack, I thought. Oh God, he'll be terrified…

I dragged open the guardroom door and sprinted up the turret steps, dropping my torch in my haste. Jack's light was still on and I didn't notice the curving steepness in my panic. I must have got there in seconds. As I ran into his attic he was just sitting up in bed, staring at me. I realised at once that it was me who had woken him.

And not only Jack. My mad flight had disturbed the gatehouse. Elizabeth appeared on the landing, bright eyed and curious. Marcia charged upstairs demanding to know what was going on. Going on now, to be exact. Bob appeared behind her, anxious in blue pyjamas.

The only person who still slept was Emery.

What could I say? I was lost for words. I couldn't meet anyone's eyes. It was one of the trickiest moments of my life.

Jack, wonderful Jack, tried to rescue me. 'I was having a bad dream. I must have been shouting in my sleep.'

Wonderful, but unrealistic.

'And Imogen heard you when we didn't?' Marcia was scathing. She turned her fire on me. 'What the hell's wrong with you?'

I had never heard her swear before.

'A nightmare,' I said. 'I dreamt something terrible was happening up here. Perhaps I ran up in my sleep.'

She ignored me, turned back to Bob. 'Go and wake Emery.'

He left at once.

'Marcia, there's no need to wake Emery,' I said. My voice trailed away. She wasn't listening.

'Elizabeth, back to bed now. Jack, stop gawping and lie down. There's nothing for you to be worried about.'

She sent Elizabeth back to her own room and ushered me out, switching off Jack's light and shutting his door. The main turret light was on now, so Marcia and I had no difficulty descending to the drawing room.

'Sit down,' Marcia said. 'I'll make us a cup of tea.' Her voice was kind, for her, which was far more worrying than her vigorous scorn. Knowing she deserved an explanation, I sat down in an armchair. She disappeared into the tiny, round kitchen to make tea. Presently, Emery appeared, sleepy but concerned, and Bob shot into the kitchen to join Marcia.

'What's up?' Emery came to crouch beside my armchair. 'Come on, Imogen, you'll have to talk about it. We're all worried about you.'

It might have been more considerate to let me be for a few minutes, as Bob had done by scampering into the kitchen, but I was beyond caring about my husband's motivation. My brain was working frantically. I should have been trying to invent a story which would not suggest I was losing my mind – I had not believed in ghosts myself until I came here – but I could think only of what I had experienced tonight. It seemed to me that Dominic had not been the prisoner held in the attic, pulling and trying to get free before his jailers reached him. Dominic had been hiding in the guardroom fireplace and had gone to the other man's rescue. There had been a woman somewhere, too, who had screamed...

'Brandy?' Emery wafted it in front of my nose.

'I'm all right.'

'Just take it.' Emery was losing patience. It brought home to me how exasperating I was being, not to mention strange, and I took it to avoid further arguments. I was secretly glad of its warmth.

'Here's some tea.' Bob came through from the kitchen, holding a mug. 'I've put lots of sugar in it for shock...'

It wasn't possible to be angry with such anxious kindness. I gave him a wan smile and accepted the tea. I longed to tell him that his son needed him too, but knew Jack would not have wanted me to, lest Elizabeth find out. I could only hope he had found the courage to cross the floor to switch on his bedroom light again.

'Well?' Marcia emerged from the kitchen, plates of toast aloft. 'You've got to tell us what's wrong, Imogen. We're worried sick about you. And if there's something the matter with Jack, we're his parents and need to know.'

She meant well, she always did, but I heard the sharpness in my voice as I answered her. 'Jack's fine.'

'Has he been having nightmares?' Bob asked. 'He's always had such an imagination.' He smiled self deprecatingly. 'This gatehouse gives me the creeps at night too. I thought I heard a man singing tonight before you woke us up.'

I nearly dropped my tea in surprise, then winced for him. Dear, guileless Bob, laying himself open to Marcia's scorn, which descended upon him instantly.

'So we're haunted now, are we? A big help you are, Bob Weightman!'

He looked flustered. 'I must have been dreaming.'

She had already turned back to me. 'So if Jack's fine, what's with the matter with you? Have you looked at yourself in the mirror lately?'

As it happened, there was a mirror above the sideboard. I glanced involuntarily at it and saw a white, frightened face. My dark brown, shoulder length hair looked black and was awry, as though it had been standing on end.

'This week's a bit of a strain for Imogen, that's all,' Emery said, unexpectedly coming to my rescue.

I didn't know whether to feel patronised or relieved. Marcia looked to be on the point of believing him, too, when we heard childish screams from upstairs.

'Elizabeth!'

Marcia bolted from the drawing room, followed by Bob. Emery cleared his throat and helped himself to toast. 'The place does have a certain atmosphere,' he murmured.

But even as he spoke, Elizabeth's screams turned to crowing laughter.

Breakfast in the drawing room.

Jack, found out by his younger sister, was subdued and embarrassed. I was silent, exposed as the irresponsible adult who had encouraged his fears instead of making light of them, not to mention being frightened myself. Elizabeth sniggered periodically. By feigning fear last night, pretending to scream, she had well and truly sewn the pair of us up. She must have overheard Jack and me talking.

To her credit, Marcia had suppressed mention of the whole thing, which was the reason Elizabeth did no more than snigger. But the damage had been done. I worried for Jack. He was not an unduly sensitive child, but I sensed how upset he was behind his stoic silence. And he had no likelihood of getting out his attic room now; I knew he would not even ask. Even the prospect of today's trip to Portsmouth, to see Nelson's flagship, the Victory, could not cheer him up.

As it happened, I had seen Victory before and Henry VIII's Mary Rose. No one else round the table had. Which gave me the perfect excuse not to go with them.

'Just come for the day out,' Bob said. 'I'm sure it's worth seeing again. Have you seen the Warrior? One of the first Ironclads.'

The dockyard certainly was worth visiting again, but I felt demoralised.

'I'll just potter about here,' I said.

'Potter?' Marcia said. 'What do you mean, potter?'

Why ask? Why must she be so tactless? Did she not realise that I wanted to be alone, that I felt awkward and out of place with most of Emery's family? I felt, in fact, that I had gone from awkward-in-law to madwoman. But tacit acceptance of a situation was never her strong point.

'This and that,' I said, knowing how evasive I must appear.

Elizabeth turned to Emery. 'You'll come with us, won't you?'

He smiled easily. 'Of course I will.' And sent me a shrewd glance. Unlike Marcia, I think he knew exactly how I felt.

The two of us had a brief word in the guardroom after breakfast.

'I wish you'd try harder with the family,' he said, 'or at least be honest. If you've arranged to meet Nicholas, I won't punch his nose. We're grown ups.'

'I haven't arranged to meet anyone,' I said.

He shrugged, began to gather his stuff for the Portsmouth trip. Sunglasses. Guidebook. Sketchpad and crayons. Car keys.

'I don't think Marcia particularly wants me around,' I said defensively.

'No, Imogen, get it right. Portsmouth was Marcia's idea. You didn't want us to go somewhere alone. Just the two of us doesn't seem to appeal to you.'

'I know, but maybe she's changed her mind…'

He laughed. 'She hasn't, Imogen. Marcia believes in couples staying together. I trust her judgement, as it happens. I don't think you're judging anything well at the moment, do you?'

It was a lightly unkind remark, but how could I deny the truth of it after last night? 'You admitted the place has a certain atmosphere,' I said.

He laughed. 'Of course it has. It's old. What did you think I meant?'

I nearly gave up at that point. I wondered whether it would be better to leave Deverell while everyone else was in Portsmouth, but that seemed cowardly and deceitful. I didn't want to put myself in the wrong.

'Have a nice day, pottering,' Emery said and left the guardroom.

Soon they had all gone. The gatehouse was silent. I was alone in it for the first time. Standing in the drawing room, I felt a frisson of unease, but it was bright morning. I tried not to remember that the Lady Chapel had been in bright morning sunshine until it turned to candlelight.

I went down to the guardroom to find notepaper, and sat at the little wooden table to write a note to Nicholas.

Dear Nicholas,

Your information about Dominic was fascinating. He must have been a very brave

man. If you find out more about him, I'd love to hear it.
Best wishes,
Imogen

Short but friendly. Now, how to get the letter to Nicholas? I could always post it, of course, but I set off on a walk around the grounds with it, while I decided what to do with myself for the day.

My luck was in. I practically ran into his brother-in-law Alistair, he of the tweed jacket, who was talking on a mobile and throwing a ball for Madogany right outside the gatehouse door.

'Bars for the east gym,' he was saying in a warm, plummy voice. 'They need replaced. We can't go another year with the ones we've got.'

He saw me and beamed at me. He was stocky, with an aquiline profile and long, crinkly eyes to match his thick, untidy, crinkly grey hair. I felt at ease with him immediately. 'Must go,' he said on the phone. 'Got a visitor.'

I had begun to walk away rather than eavesdrop, but he called to me.

'Imogen Webb, isn't it?' He held out his hand. 'How do you do? I'm Alistair Sievewright. I hope you're enjoying the gatehouse. The weather's held for you all right.' He seemed a quintessentially polite English gentleman, yet I sensed a genuine friendliness behind the good manners.

'It's a remarkable place,' I said.

'Not too uncomfortable, I hope?'

'Not at all.' His warmth gave me courage to offer him my letter. 'I wondered, could you give this to Nicholas for me, please?'

His thick eyebrows shot up as he took it. 'Of course. But you're not leaving already, are you?'

After the sideways looks at our tense breakfast his friendliness was almost too much for me. I did not tell him that I had considered leaving.

'No, I'm here for the week,' I said.

Alistair twinkled. 'Excellent.'

At that moment, Madogany presented me with his slimy red ball. I threw it and he ambled away for it gamely.

'He's getting a stiff old dog,' Alistair said, 'but the vet says he isn't in pain, which is the main thing.'

He was no longer smiling. It seemed to me that the words he's a companion for Nicholas, a last link with his wife and child floated unspoken in the soft air. Sadness could never have been far away at Deverell Manor.

'How old is he?' I asked.

'He's ten.'

'That's a good age for a big dog,' I said.

'Yes, it is.' He smiled again as Madogany positively trotted back and dropped the ball at our feet. I threw it again. 'Could you tell me,' I asked, assuring myself that I was changing the subject for Alistair's benefit, 'is the gatehouse haunted?'

Alistair chuckled. 'Sometimes we wish it were,' he said. 'It would be very lucrative. Why do you ask?'

'Probably just my imagination.' And my husband's nephew's, I thought, and my brother-in-law's, since Bob had heard singing too.

'Really?' Alistair looked intrigued. Well, he was too polite to look sceptical. 'Do tell me more,' he said.

'No, it's just silly.'

'Surely not.' He stooped as Madogany brought back the ball. As he did so, I heard vehicles coming down the drive. In the same moment Madogany began to growl. Alistair straightened up and frowned. 'Damn,' he said. 'Damn. They're back again. Excuse me, my dear. Not all visitors are as welcome as you.'

He stomped away to confront the newcomers.

Two vehicles were drawing up, both black with blacked out windows, one a four wheel drive, the other a Jaguar. I think my jaw must have hit the ground as several men in dark glasses got out the four wheeler and stood guard beside the Jaguar. It was like a scene from a film. Who were they? They seemed utterly out of place here. But then I guessed. I was an accountant, after all, with clients in similar situations and such things were happening all over rural England. Someone with a great deal of money, unlikely to have been gained honestly, was pressing to buy Deverell Manor.

CHAPTER EIGHT

I SHOULD have disappeared back into the gatehouse. It was none of my business. But I was uneasy. I compromised by walking away some distance, picking up Madogany's ball and pretending to clean it. The Labrador, meanwhile, stood beside Alistair, growling, hackles raised. The Jaguar drew up alongside man and dog. The window whirred softly down. I glimpsed a heavy face with pale eyes.

'My brother-in-law isn't available,' Alistair said, no longer the genial, bumbling English gentleman. He was clipped, authoritative, in command. It occurred to me he might be a former soldier. The reply was too quiet for me to hear. 'I repeat, my brother-in-law isn't at home,' Alistair answered. 'If you want to see him, I suggest you have the courtesy to make an appointment.'

The men in dark glasses were exchanging glances. I began to be worried for Alistair – these did not look like people to get on the wrong side of and Madogany's growls were growing louder – but he appeared unconcerned.

It worked. Perhaps pale-eyes reckoned he had made his point. He leaned back in his seat and the window whirred smoothly up. The men got back in the four wheel drive. The convoy turned solemnly and made its exit, Madogany padding after it, determined to see it off the premises until Alistair called him back.

I realised that I was shaking and my heart was thumping. Alistair turned and smiled at me. 'Sorry about that,' he said.

'It doesn't matter.'

I longed to ask questions, but it would have been rude.

'Anyway…' Alistair waved his hand, as if dismissing pale-eyes, and threw Madogany's ball. 'Ghosts are much more interesting. Why don't you come in for a coffee and tell me about them?'

The offer took me by surprise. I wondered how many of the gatehouse guests were invited to the family quarters and suspected it was very few. I couldn't help hoping I owed the privilege to Nicholas. 'Thanks very much. That's kind of you.'

'Not at all.' Alistair smiled.

I went with him round the corner of the manor house, past mullioned windows, where flower borders brightened battlemented but faded Elizabethan splendour, and then into a little renovated courtyard on the left hand side. French windows led into a huge, homely kitchen with walls the colour of watermelon, an old dresser and a large pine table covered in maps. A percolator chugged on a red Aga.

'We camp out here, really,' Alistair said, seeing me look round. It was the sort of kitchen I had always dreamed of. Not a reality in central London. He swept the maps into an untidy pile and plonked a flowered mug of fragrant coffee in front of me. Then he sat down opposite me, Madogany at his feet, and listened.

I told him everything, beginning with the second reflected face in the car window and ending with my glimpse of Dominic emerging from hiding in the chimney last night. It was a tribute to Alistair Sievewright that considering that I was telling a pretty unbelievable story, I didn't feel too stupid. He didn't laugh once.

'And it's Jack you're worried about?' he asked when I had finished.

'Yes.'

'Boys are very resilient,' he observed.

'I suppose so.' I thought of good natured Bob. Jack was similar in some ways. I didn't like to think of him meeting another Marcia.

'It's just a matter of finding something he's particularly good at, to build his confidence again,' Alistair said, as if reading my thoughts. He spoke with such easy certainty that I must have seemed surprised. 'I have a boys' school,' he added, by way of explanation. 'And for what it's worth, I do believe your story. I think the gatehouse must be haunted.'

'You do?' I was both surprised and grateful.

'Oh yes, you seem quite sane, my dear.'

I laughed in relief. 'What about the manor house itself?'

'There are stories of a Civil War widow.' He beamed. 'Here's Nicholas.'

I turned. Nicholas stood in the French windows, looking surprised, as well he might. Alistair got to his feet. 'There's more coffee.'

'Thanks.' Nicholas stepped into the kitchen, very tall and cautious compared to his stocky, exuberant brother-in-law. He wore a pale green t-shirt and blue jeans with splashes on white paint on them. There was a dab of it above an eyebrow. He smiled at me. 'Hello, Imogen.'

'Hello.' I suddenly felt abominably shy, unsure of what I was doing here. I had noticed something else in the kitchen by now too, on a little corner ledge, as if it had become a shrine – a photograph of a lovely, fair haired young woman and her little daughter whose hair was darkening to Nicholas's colour.

'Vaganov was here again,' Alistair murmured, handing Nicholas a mug of coffee. 'And Imogen has been telling me about life in the gatehouse,' he added more loudly. 'It's quite a tale. You might like to hear it.'

He contrived to leave at that point with Madogany in tow, murmuring something about the Labrador needing more exercise. It was very blatant. Nicholas smiled wryly and sat down opposite me.

'Tales from the gatehouse?' he prompted.

I hesitated. 'I think I saw Dominic's ghost.'

'What?'

'It was the boy from the Lady Chapel grown up.'

'The boy from the Lady Chapel?'

I realised that I was not telling this properly second time round. I ought to begin at the beginning as I had with Alistair, but I felt so self-conscious. 'I saw a boy in the Lady Chapel in the cathedral,' I faltered. 'It went from daylight to darkness, with candles. He was standing over Bishop White's grave.'

Nicholas did not look at me. His long fingers gripped his coffee mug. 'The Lady Chapel went dark, in broad daylight?'

'As though I had gone back in time, to when it was night, yes.'

Nicholas said nothing. Here, painfully, from a bereaved man with this Vaganov to worry about, was the scepticism my story deserved. Yet Alistair had genuinely seemed to believe it; surely it hadn't just been his good manners.

'It doesn't matter,' I said, standing up. 'I won't waste your time any longer.'

Nicholas stood up too, obviously embarrassed. 'You're not wasting my time, Imogen…' But he still didn't look at me and I saw distress in the way he held himself.

'Oh God, I'm so sorry,' I said and fled the kitchen.

I ran towards the gatehouse, my steps uneven on the gravel, then squelching and slipping. I almost fell, teetering for a moment, putting my hands out to regain my balance. I looked down into mud.

There's no mud here, I thought idiotically. There's gravel which continues under the gatehouse arch and up the drive. But I could not see any gravel now, only the mud, which reeked of horse dung. I raised my head and saw that the gatehouse stone had brightened and sharpened. The bushes and the shed where we hid the front door key had disappeared. There was nothing but mud and, further off, trees.

'No,' I said aloud. 'No…'

But a black eyed, elderly woman in a black gown and white coif was walking towards me with a small wicker basket over her arm. I guessed she had come from the manor house. Not a servant, for the black gown was of fine wool with a little white ruff and an ebony crucifix above it. She walked smartly for someone her age, expertly avoiding the mud with outdoor clogs. She didn't see me as she passed me and continued on towards the gatehouse. There, she rapped sharply on the same door I had recently come out of, which suddenly gleamed with wax, and waited.

Had I been less miserable, this imperceptible transition would have frightened me more. As it was, though my heart thudded, I think I was in shock. I managed to feel curious, glancing over to the manor house. It was brand new, there was no moss on its roof and it must just have been completed. Smoke rose from one of its chimneys. Though the day was as warm as in my own time, they would still have needed fires for cooking. Chickens clucked some distance away, perhaps beyond the trees.

The elderly lady rapped again impatiently. Who was she? I wondered. She was of an older generation than Dominic. Her face was lined and I suspected she had few teeth, but her bone structure remained. She must have been beautiful once. A dark haired beauty, for her skin tone was sallow. As she waited, she glanced in my direction, but evidently saw nothing.

The gatehouse door opened. Not the heavy, grating creak with which I was familiar, but well oiled and easy. A stooped man in a dirty jerkin and greasy hat stood behind it. I glimpsed the guardroom door behind him to the left of the turret stairs, which were less worn than in my time. He bowed slightly on seeing the woman and held out his hand for the wicker basket.

'I would see him,' she said sharply.

'Ain't allowed, mistress,' he said.

'He's my brother-in-law, as you well know.'

'Ain't allowed, mistress.' He put an ill shod foot in the door lest she try to shove her way inside. It was presumably beneath her dignity to argue with a serving man, far less wrestle with him. She pursed her lips and thrust the basket at him.

'Make sure he gets it all.'

Then she turned away and walked towards the manor house. I think fascination compelled me to follow her. The manor house front door, without the pillars of my own time, was ajar. She went inside and I followed. Here, in the Hall, I glimpsed more people. They seemed to be setting up the long tables I had seen from outside. But it was a glimpse only, for they were less clear and now they were fading, as was the elderly lady who had been my guide. Suddenly, I stood in the Hall in the present and the front door was shut up and locked.

The place was magnificent, with wood panelling, decorated plaster and high, grand ceiling, but, as I say, shut up. There were two sets of internal double doors, intricately carved. I tried them also, in panic, but they too were locked and the windows were jammed. The family must come here only rarely. What use had they for it now, when they camped out in that homely kitchen? I was trapped without even my mobile to summon help.

CHAPTER NINE

THINK, I told myself. Think, don't worry, someone will pass the windows soon. I only needed to bang on the little square panes to effect rescue, though it was the kind of attention I could do without. But all I could think about was that I had walked through a locked door. It simply was not possible. How was I going to explain without being carted off to an asylum? It was one thing to see and hear the inexplicable. That could be set down to an overactive imagination. But this...

It was ridiculous. Was I actually here at all? I pinched my arm dubiously, felt the nip all right. Don't be daft, I muttered, where else would you be? I walked to the mullioned windows. Motes of dust dallied there in the morning sunlight. I felt the heat on my face. Twenty-first century heat. But it had been hot in that other world too, about the same time of year. That other world was never there, I told myself, but if not, how had I got into this locked Hall? How – I sniffed and looked down – had mud got onto my feet and sandals? My thoughts buzzed in vicious circles.

From here I could see out into the gravel drive, but not the gatehouse, which was to the right. I guessed that what was now the front door, with pillars, by which the old woman and I had entered the Hall, had not been the front door then. I vaguely remembered another door amid the Elizabethan splendour round the corner, near the little courtyard where Nicholas and his family had their sanctuary. There must have been a reception area, perhaps with a grand staircase, beyond the Hall I stood in. But it made no difference to my plight; I was only speculating to keep my mind off my own situation because its practicalities were dawning on me. Though I was young, with a strong bladder, eventually I would be in a predicament. The humiliation of it didn't bear thinking about.

Time to start yelling.

In that other world, who had the elderly woman been? He's my brother-in-law, as you well know. So she was the sister-in-law of the gatehouse prisoner, the man they had later come for in the night. The man who was probably not Dominic, because Dominic had hidden in the guardroom chimney, then gone upstairs to help the prisoner. So the prisoner could be anyone, but he had a sister-in-law who was a gentlewoman. She was too old to be Dominic's wife Isabella Raymond, so she must be some sort of dowager. The obvious candidate was Dominic's stepmother, Anna Mervyn. And Anna Mervyn's brother-in-law, Francis, Dominic's younger uncle, had been a Catholic priest on the run. Which might account for the plainchant Bob had heard as well as myself. And Dominic was a staunch Catholic and a brave man, who would try to help a captured priest.

It all fitted. I felt a sense of achievement. It might be time to start screaming, but I hadn't done it yet. Speculation had averted panic.

But why would Francis Deverell, Dominic's uncle and renegade priest, be imprisoned in his own family's gatehouse? His older brother, Clement, who owned the manor, would surely not have countenanced it. Anna Mervyn's disapproval had been evident. But with the Queen's spies everywhere, perhaps Clement had had no alternative. Only recently turned Protestant, perhaps he had had to prove his loyalty to keep his lands. Or perhaps he and Francis were no longer on good terms; perhaps religion had torn Dominic's uncles apart.

It was horrible either way. I stood at the Hall's mullioned windows in the bright sunlight and shivered. Nicholas's old brown estate car was parked almost opposite the windows; the grassy area further down the drive, where I had seen the second face in the car window, was for guests only. An old green Rover stood beside the brown estate, presumably Alistair's since Nicholas's sister drove a white Fiat. Nothing stirred out there, so I turned to examine the portraits on the wall.

If I had hoped to find likenesses of Dominic or his family I was disappointed. The oldest portraits were from the Restoration period, a century later, and most were from the eighteenth century, a hundred years after that. Nothing distinguished them from the usual portraits to be found in a stately home. In my anxiety, my need to keep a look out for activity outside, they did not hold my attention and I turned back to the windows.

I glanced at my watch. I had been here half an hour. I opened my mouth to call out, then shut it again, perplexed. What on earth was I going to say to explain how I had got here? It was too ludicrous for words. I followed one of your ancestors into the Hall on a visit to the sixteenth century. But Anna Mervyn wasn't even Nicholas's ancestor. She was Dominic's stepmother. The fact that such a detail could even occur to me almost made me laugh aloud. I was, finally, definitely, going mad. But even if I was going mad, how had I finished up locked in here?

At last, I heard a sound. A car was approaching. I actually ducked, the natural instinct to hide, since I wasn't supposed to be where I was. It was the white Fiat. It stopped beside the green Rover and Nicholas's sister emerged, slim and elegant in a lilac suit, pearls at her throat. The one member of the family I had not yet spoken to, of course, just to make matters as awkward as possible.

She shut the car door and turned to walk away. I gritted my teeth and rapped on the window, praying the old glass would not break. She heard me immediately, turning with a frown. She saw me and her hand went to her mouth.

It was more than surprise. It was shock, I was sure of it. Then she recovered and walked towards me, summoning a polite smile. I had to admire her sang-froid.

'I'm locked in,' I yelled. 'I'm sorry, but I'm locked in…'

She wouldn't have the keys on her, of course, but instead of running for them she nodded and took a mobile from an elegant shoulder bag. I saw her make a call. God knows what she said. She smiled, giving me the thumbs up, then she disappeared from my view.

Within five minutes, I heard the key in the lock of one of the internal doors. It opened and Nicholas put his head round it, his face pale and strained.

'So it's true,' he said.

'Yes,' I said. 'I'm here. I'm sorry. It wasn't my fault…'

I practically stammered, but he didn't even appear to be listening. I saw terrible grief in his eyes and looked away. When I looked back again, he had gone.

I made my way out my grand prison, down a panelled corridor. To my surprise I found myself in a large stone entrance hall with eighteenth century proportions, black and white tiles and imposing staircase. Doors which looked down to the lawns stood ajar and it was filled with sunlight. Alistair emerged from a door at the end.

'Are you all right? How did you get in there?'

He was worried, sympathetic and curious. I almost wished I was one of those women who burst into tears easily.

'It's hard to explain,' I said desperately. 'You'll think me insane…'

'Of course I won't. Tell me. '

I pushed back my hair, half turned away from him. 'I went back in time. The Hall door was open then and I followed an old woman through it…'

It took even Alistair aback. Then his eyes widened in fascination. I realised he believed me, I couldn't think why, and felt gratitude again. 'Have you any idea who she was?' he asked.

'Anna Mervyn, I think.'

He shook his head, evidently less familiar with the history of the Deverells than Nicholas. 'How did it happen? What else did you see?'

'There were people in the hall, but they vanished, and I was left…' I broke off as Nicholas's sister approached us.

'Yes, this is Imogen,' he confirmed, as if she had spoken. 'Imogen, this is my wife, Meta.'

Meta Sievewright smiled, shook my hand. 'How do you do? I'm so glad I was on hand to rescue you.' She spoke as though there must be some reasonable explanation for the circumstances under which we had met. What she thought I could only imagine. I suspected she would not have believed my story and wondered what Alistair would tell her. She was the epitome of the cool, collected English lady. The shock I had glimpsed in her seemed a figment of my imagination.

'I can only apologise,' I said.

'Oh, it doesn't matter in the least,' Alistair said. 'I want to hear more when we get back. Alas, Meta and I have to be somewhere else quite soon…'

Which was a courteous way of saying I had held them up. I quickly backed out the entrance hall into the sunshine and escaped to the gatehouse. The green Rover came past almost immediately, Alistair at the wheel.

Shaken, I made a cup of coffee in the turret kitchen and took it through to the drawing room. The morning's experiences were catching up with me. I was frightened and incredulous. Past and present seemed to blur as I sat there, staring at the blue and white mug in my trembling hands. I ought to get away from Deverell and go somewhere my sanity was not in doubt, but did not trust myself to drive.

Nicholas's words perturbed me too. So it's true. What had he meant? What was true? I hadn't told him anything, I hadn't had the chance…

Presently, before my thoughts made me ill, I went to the sideboard and rootled among the board games and jigsaws there. One of the jigsaws had a picture of the Tower of London. I hastily shoved it back and opted for a glitzy rooftop view of New York at night.

The change of scenery evidently did the trick. I must have become absorbed in the jigsaw because when someone knocked on the oak door downstairs I nearly jumped out of my skin. I looked about, but the drawing room was as it had been when I began the jigsaw. What a state I'm in, I thought wryly, never certain which century I'm supposed to be in now…

Legs like jelly, I went downstairs, turned the great iron key in the lock. I don't know what I expected, but it was Nicholas standing there, strained still, his hand resting on the door jamb, Madogany sitting beside him.

'I'd like to talk to you,' he said.

CHAPTER TEN

I LET him in. I could hardly refuse. The gatehouse was his property and I was worried for him. He followed me up to the drawing room. I wondered what he thought of our occupation. Elizabeth's pink cardigan lay higgledy-piggledy across one of the chairs, Jack's mini telescope lay on the coffee table and a set of Emery's crayons stood on the bookcase.

'Coffee?'

He shook his head. 'No, but thanks.' Eyes anywhere but on me.

I sat down where I had been, at the head of the table. He took the seat at right angles to me, on the other side of the jigsaw. I was grateful for the presence of Madogany, who leaned against my knee and gazed up at me appealingly as I patted his thick, warm coat. His tail thumped on the carpet.

'Did you want to know how I got into the locked hall?' I asked, when I could bear the silence no longer.

Nicholas seemed to brace himself. 'Yes.'

'You won't believe me. You didn't believe I saw Dominic's ghost.' They seemed harsh words, so I said them as softly as I could.

'I might,' he replied. 'If I was rude to you, forgive me.'

'There's nothing to forgive. Everything's mad. To tell the truth, I feel as if I'm going out of my mind.'

At last he looked at me. 'I can identify with that.'

Another silence, less awkward.

Toying with part of the Empire State Building, I said, 'After I left your kitchen this morning, I found myself in the sixteenth century. There was no fanfare, no preparation. It just happened. Suddenly, that's what was around me. I saw an old woman who might have been Dominic's stepmother Anna Mervyn. She was trying to get into the gatehouse to see a prisoner she referred to as her brother-in-law. It struck me that he might be Dominic's uncle Francis, since he was a Catholic priest and priests were hunted at the time. The guard refused to let Anna into the gatehouse and she went into the Hall. I followed her and then the twenty first century came back.'

Nicholas had begun frowning. He was intent on my face now, likely checking me for honesty. I felt myself crimson as I went on and could only hope he saw it was embarrassment rather than lies.

'I can't believe it myself,' I ended, 'but how else could I have got into the Hall? It was locked and no one let me in.'

Nicholas practically interrupted. 'Who else did you see?'

'The guard Anna spoke to at the gatehouse and some servants setting the tables in the Hall.'

'What did the servants in the Hall look like?'

'I don't know. They vanished quickly.' Suddenly I thought I understood. 'Why? Have you seen them too?'

He shook his head. 'No, I've never seen anything.'

'But someone else has?'

I could have bitten my tongue off when his strained look reappeared and he turned away. I realised I had understood nothing.

'My daughter did,' he said quietly. 'I didn't believe her. Why would I? She was six years old.'

So it's true.

I knew now why he had said those words when I had been discovered in the Hall. I was aghast, afraid to move, my eyes on the New York skyline until he turned round. He was dry eyed, half smiling.

'Now I know. At least I pretended to believe her.'

I imagined him with his little daughter whose hair was the colour of his own, walking with her round the Hall, hiding a smile as she pointed to the places she had seen the sixteenth century servants.

'I'm so sorry,' I said. 'What was her name?'

'Freya. She called them the funny people.'

'She thought you believed her,' I said. 'That's what's important.'

'Yes.'

'Did she see them more than once?'

'Twice. The second time on the day she…They…' He broke off.

I wanted to take his hand, but I didn't. If we had been in the manor house I would of course have left. As it was, I sat there, wretched, feeling movement would jar, while he struggled with himself. Madogany tilted towards him, evidently sensing his misery, and he put his hand on the large, amiable, chocolate head.

'I'm sorry.' He looked up, attempting a smile. 'As you can see, I'm not great company these days.'

'It doesn't matter,' I said. 'I understand.'

I was conscious as I spoke that I didn't understand. I was fortunate enough never to have known bereavement. But it was all I could think of to say. He smiled again, in control of himself once more. 'Thank you,' he said.

He stood up, walked to the window which overlooked the side of the manor house. He was very lean standing there, long hands on hips, with a clear, sunburned profile. 'It's odd what you've told me. It does rather suggest one particular family tradition might have some truth in it.'

'What tradition?'

'That Francis Deverell was hanged, drawn and quartered at Tyburn. Being a Catholic priest later in Elizabeth's reign meant he risked treason. If his brother Clement was involved in his capture and he was held here first, it might be why we have no record of how and when he died. Clement would want it all forgotten as soon as possible. I suppose any trial might be on record somewhere in London, but as far as I know no one in the family's ever tried checking it out.'

'I'm surprised. That's a story for your guidebook.'

Nicholas nodded. 'Makes you wonder, doesn't it? As if some memory of Clement's betrayal lingers and no one wants it confirmed.'

'You have no record of how and when Dominic died either,' I pointed out. 'If he died trying to help Francis, Clement would suppress that too...'

Nicholas nodded. 'Logical.' He smiled wryly. 'Maybe I should let you tell me about Dominic's ghost.'

So, still sitting at the table, I related every incident which had happened in the gatehouse since our arrival. Nicholas listened intently again, and this time I sensed that he believed me. When I finished, he even whistled.

'Well,' he said. 'I think you ought to get a discount on your holiday.'

I burst out laughing. 'A refund, I was so scared last night.'

'Were you really?' He crossed to me, put his hands on my shoulders, half laughing too, half serious. He smelled of fresh paint. 'Oh, Imogen, I wish I'd been there for you...'

'Me too.' I covered one of his hands with my own and felt the strength in his fingers. 'I'm fine, honestly,' I added because he now looked genuinely concerned. He nodded, moved away with what looked like reluctance, back to the window. What was it Emery had said? I know his soulful type. He'll avoid you like the plague now he knows you're married and reckon his bad luck rumbles on. I wished I could show Nicholas he was wrong, but dreaded to intrude on his grief. I hesitated even to tell him Emery and I were estranged.

He might think less of me because I did not appreciate the fact my husband was still alive.

'You're painting?' I asked eventually, into what was becoming a silence.

'One of the outhouses,' he said. 'I should get back to it, if you're all right.'

'Of course I am. I'm going away for the afternoon. Maybe to the coast.'

We looked at each other.

He said, 'About Dominic and Francis…'

Thank God for the past. It had become our link, something we could talk about without complications.

'…I've a friend who works in the British Library. He might point me in the direction of someone who knows where to look. There must be records of all the priests who died at Tyburn. I can't think why I've never wanted to know before.'

Because it's a sad story and you were happy, I thought, with your wife and daughter. But all I said was, 'You're too busy trying to keep the manor in one piece, that's why.' Which was surely true also.

Nicholas smiled. 'You're not wrong there.' He left the window, came towards me, then passed me on the way to the door and the turret staircase. 'I hope you enjoy your afternoon at the coast.'

Feeling more normal, less guilty, I drove south, to Portsmouth in fact, and managed to catch up with the others buying ice creams in the dockyard after lunch. They had been to the Victory and the ironclad Warrior in the morning and were about to visit the Mary Rose. I was pleased to see that Jack looked happier. The cold, quiet, thick-walled gatehouse seemed another world as the six of strolled through the busy, noisy dockyard in the warm sunshine.

'You've cheered up,' Emery remarked to me.

I had. He had no idea why, of course. I pulled away lightly when he tried to take my hand and he did not pursue it.

I was glad to see the Mary Rose a second time. Even Elizabeth stopped giggling and stared with awe at the great wooden hulk which had been pulled from the sea and preserved with such dedication. Her dark, glistening timbers seemed to exude an unfathomable power.

'I can almost see and hear the men still on her,' Bob whispered to me. 'She's like a time machine.'

I knew what he meant. And Marcia was further down the viewing gallery, so this was my chance. 'Tell me about the singing you heard,' I whispered.

Bob checked Marcia was out of earshot, whispered back, 'English plainsong. Sixteenth century.'

Since his choir specialised in early music I could trust his judgement. 'The sort of thing a Catholic priest might sing?'

He nodded. 'Oh yes, I should say so. If I'd heard more I could be more specific about it.' Then he looked alarmed. 'For goodness sake, don't tell Marcia. She'll think I need a psychiatrist.'

'I won't tell her.' I could have kissed his round, anxious face. I was happy to believe him, because Nicholas had believed me.

CHAPTER ELEVEN

It was another glorious evening. We ate outside at a picturesque restaurant which had been a coaching inn. Because the courtyard was crowded, Emery and I were obliged to have our own table, to Marcia's not so secret satisfaction.

'So,' Emery murmured, working his way through a large seafood platter, 'what did you do with yourself this morning? Did pottering amuse you?'

His tone was very civil, but the question nettled me, as I guessed it was meant to. The implication was that I was either a deceiver or a half wit. But I was determined he would not ruin my fragile new serenity.

'Of course it did,' I replied.

'But you came and joined us.'

He meant, didn't you get anywhere with Nicholas?

'Making an effort with your family,' I said. 'You asked me to, remember.'

He couldn't say anything else. He smiled, raised his Pimms to me, and carried on with the meal in silence.

Dusk was falling by the time we reached the gatehouse. As I got out my car, I tried to imagine what this grassy area would have been like in that other time. There might have been tenants' cottages here, or farm buildings, for the manor would have had to be self sufficient. That face I had glimpsed in my car window, had it been someone hiding in such a building? Francis Deverell, perhaps, shortly before his capture by his brother Clement's men?

A firefly startled me with its swiftness and beauty. It was gone before I could follow where it went. Meanwhile, Elizabeth, who had come home in Emery's car, which had led our convoy, ran down the path to get the key from the shed before Jack. She was therefore first into the gatehouse. She ran back to the rest of us, waving something white and whooping with glee.

'Letter for Imogen!' she shouted. 'Letter for Imogen!'

Emery whistled and laughed. Marcia immediately turned an accusing face to me. I practically snatched it from Elizabeth; she might be only a child, but she was such an annoying child.

'Who is it from?' Marcia demanded.

'That's none of your business,' I snapped back. So much for my serenity.

'But it's Emery's business,' Marcia hissed and stalked off into the gatehouse, hustling Bob and Jack with her.

'Getting on with my family, are we?' Emery mocked at my elbow.

I ignored him, moved away to read the letter in peace. He did not try to follow, but went on into the gatehouse, leaving me standing alone in the dusk with the letter. It was from Nicholas.

> *Dear Imogen*
>
> *I hope you enjoyed your trip. Ranald has got in touch with an Elizabethan specialist. He's just emailed me back. Francis was hanged, drawn and quartered at Tyburn on 17 October 1582 aged 48. Most such men were Jesuits, but he was just a former parish priest. His first parish was in Southwark, where the Bishop of Winchester's palace was, which might be why Bishop White took his nephew Dominic on as a page, or why Dominic's family were in a position to ask for the parish. There was presumably some connection there.*
>
> *Best wishes,*
>
> *Nicholas*
>
> *P.S. Alistair and Meta would like to hear about your adventures this morning. If it's convenient come and see us if you're not back too late.*

I glanced at my watch. It was after nine. Too late for a social call. Blast. I wondered how long that letter had been waiting for me. I did not even have Nicholas's mobile number to inform him by text that I couldn't make it. I made a mental note to exchange numbers at the first opportunity.

I re-read the letter, taking it in properly. If Francis had been held in the gatehouse around this time of year, he had been a prisoner for two months before his execution. He might have been tortured. At best his conditions of imprisonment would have been ghastly. I longed suddenly for modernity, electric light, even Elizabeth's screeches, and went into the gatehouse.

Marcia was making cocoa for the children before they went up to bed. I watched Jack growing tense, but he said nothing. I was in a quandary. Eventually, when he was taking his mug back to the kitchen, I followed him and spoke hurriedly.

'If you hear any more noises, don't worry. I've found out who the man was. He was a prisoner, but they didn't kill him there and he was a priest, a good man. So he'll not harm you.'

Jack listened in silence, then nodded. I thought I saw relief in his eyes, then Marcia appeared and looked at us suspiciously. Jack went straight past her without a word. 'Well?' Marcia said. 'What are you putting into his head now?'

I lost my cool. 'I'm helping him. Which is more than you've done, even though you're his mother.'

'Excuse me?'

'Aren't you worried about him?'

'Of course not! There's nothing wrong with him!'

'He was frightened,' I said.

'Only because you put ideas in his head.'

'He came to me first, Marcia. This gatehouse has history and it's time you acknowledged it.'

At that moment Bob popped his head round the door. I saw alarm in his face and realised that in my anger I had been on the verge of telling Marcia that he had heard plainchant. 'Do either of you fancy Scrabble?' he asked.

'Yes,' I said. 'Yes, of course.'

Marcia assented too. Even she must have known that an all out row with me would be detrimental to her brother's chances of repairing his marriage. So we four adults buried the tension under the game, which was still under way when we broke up after eleven. Emery was winning. He often did. He had gone through life under-using his brain.

'So,' he said, as we descended the spiral stairs to the guardroom, 'what adventures will befall the fair Imogen tonight?'

'Nothing you need worry about,' I retorted.

'You're very secretive.'

'You don't believe me.'

'Try me.'

'No. You think I'm off my head.' I escaped into the circular bathroom and turned on the bath taps. I wondered, as I had wondered throughout the game of Scrabble, whether to write a note to Nicholas and leave it outside his kitchen windows. There was no likelihood of rain and they would find it in the morning. It would be more polite than not answering his note at all, though it would mean venturing out alone in the dark again.

My mind made up, I turned off the bath taps, came back up the steps to the guardroom and sat at the wooden desk.

'U-huh,' Emery said.

'Leave me alone.'

Dear Nicholas

We were too late back for me to come round tonight. I'd be glad to come round another time, whenever it's ok. Got your info about Francis. Horrible.

Best wishes,

Imogen.

'And now she finds the torch,' Emery said, as I stood up. 'And now out she goes to meet Nicholas.'

'I'm not meeting him. That's why I'm writing a note.'

'He'll be heartbroken.'

I ignored this last jibe and went down the two steps from the guardroom to the front door. I turned the great heavy key. The door creak seemed very loud. I could imagine Marcia running downstairs, but I didn't care. I moved out into the dark, fragrant night and turned left for the manor house.

I kept my torch's beam steady, ahead of me. An owl hooted. The stars were out, a marvellous show never seen in London. I passed the front door where in that other time Anna Mervyn had led me into the Hall and walked on as quietly as I could, approaching the corner.

The place was silent. I suppose I had half expected to see one of the family on the lawns beyond, giving Madogany final exercise for the night. I rounded the corner. My eyes were adjusting to the dark, enough to see the Elizabethan battlements, appearing unnaturally high. I moved into the little renovated courtyard. The kitchen's French windows were in darkness.

I glanced up, saw a light on above the windows. Grey blue curtains. Nicholas's bedroom, perhaps. I stood looking at it, biting my lip, wanting to be with him. Full of regrets, I left my note in front of the French windows and turned away.

For the first time since I had come to the gatehouse, my night's sleep was undisturbed by the past. As to the present, Emery again remained in the single bed on the other side of the guardroom.

I woke after six, feeling rested, and stole out for an early stroll up the drive to the cattle grid. The cattle flicked their tails lazily at me. Haze lay on the rolling hills beyond Deverell; it was going to be another hot day. The manor house looked as it must have done in that earlier time, except there would already have been fires lit.

On my return I met Jack, still in his pyjamas. I think he had been watching for me. His eyes shone with excitement.

'I heard him praying,' he said, 'so I prayed with him. I think he heard me. But I wasn't afraid. I wasn't afraid…'

'Wait a minute, he heard you?'

'Yes, he must have, because he slowed down for me.'

'He did what? Was he praying in Latin?'

'Yes, but he started to pray in English when he heard me. You know, Our Father and all that. We sometimes get it at school. And we go to Carol Service at Christmas. Mum always sings the descants.'

I was stunned. And then I felt happiness. 'You helped him, Jack,' I said. 'You must have helped him. He wasn't alone any more.'

CHAPTER TWELVE

THE Weightmans were going pony trekking in the New Forest today. They were cheerful at breakfast, or perhaps they seemed that way because I was cheerful myself. If I thought about it, the idea that a man dead for centuries had been given some brief comfort because of our visit was lunatic. But I was past thinking about it.

Did I want to go pony trekking too? Marcia asked. All eyes turned instantly towards me. Emery looked at me coolly. I could not decipher his expression, but could hardly have cared less about his wishes. I longed to see Nicholas and talk to him about Francis Deverell. On the other hand, I saw Jack nodding enthusiastically at me; he had conquered his fear of the attic and I was his co-conspirator. Besides, Nicholas would have work to do and I did not want to hold him back. And the idea of riding appealed to me in a way it would not have done before I had come to the gatehouse; it was another link to the past, something Dominic and Francis and Anna Mervyn would have done without giving it a thought.

'I'll come,' I said.

I even risked going in Emery's car instead of my own, committing myself to the Weightmans for the day. Elizabeth wanted to go with us, but Marcia nipped that in the bud, rather obviously determined that Emery and I be alone.

'You look better,' Emery said, driving his classic open topped Mercedes with a recklessness I ought to have remembered. 'All you needed was a good sleep.' He was even more reckless than usual. I thought he showed off. He shot past Bob's careful Volvo, arriving at the pony trekking centre fifteen minutes in advance.

'This is nice.' He gestured towards the ancient, wooded landscape shimmering in the morning heat. In the holiday season it was not quite as tranquil as the brochures suggested; we would not be getting these dappled lanes to ourselves. 'Mm, I could draw all this. Do you think I'll manage to draw in the saddle?'

He must have said much more, but his flow of mildly humorous remarks went over my head. Compared to Nicholas, he never shut up. I tentatively patted the nose of an attractive chestnut horse, not a pony, which wandered towards us, stuck its head over the fence and snorted to us. It tried to eat my sleeve.

I wondered what Nicholas had made of my note. I visualised him reading it over a rushed breakfast in that delicious, informal kitchen, perhaps putting it aside after a glance at his dead wife and daughter's photograph, before hurrying off to resume his painting work. It seemed as though he did most of the manual labour himself. There might be staff somewhere, but I had not seen any. Nicholas did not have time for inconsequential chatter.

'Hey,' Emery said, brandishing his sketchbook. 'Hold it, Gen.'

I did, as anyone who has lived with an artist does automatically. It becomes part of life. There is an inherent blackmail in the process; few people would deliberately sabotage another person's efforts in any field and art is no different. So I maintained my pose until the Weightmans turned up. But I wouldn't have bothered to look at the result had he not insisted on showing me later; a preoccupied brunette in t shirt and jeans leaning against a fence with a horse trying to eat her sleeve.

'Does that horse go trekking?' Emery asked a passing groom, who shook his head and replied that it belonged to one of the guides. Soon the stable owner Caroline greeted us. She was young, coppery haired and attractive, but she ignored Emery's attempts to flirt with her.

It was me she turned to, while expertly detaching the determined chestnut, whose name was Artus, from my sleeve. 'You're the party staying at Deverell Gatehouse, aren't you?'

'That's right.' I was unsurprised; she would have been given contact details with our booking.

'Artus must have thought you're taking him back.'

'Back to Deverell?'

She nodded. 'He came from there.'

I wanted to know more, but did not know how I would have framed any questions. With the Weightmans arriving, Caroline swung into a brisk introductory talk. She was equally brisk with Elizabeth's screeches of delight on being given a sweet little white pony, reminding her quite sharply that she would frighten the horses.

We were six in a party of twelve. My horse was a placid brown mare called Amber. I had been pony trekking once before, on a childhood holiday in Cornwall, so once I got accustomed to it again, I was able to saunter, as it were, through those improbably lovely lanes. Amber knew where she was going, clopping along with minimum direction from me. We had two guides, the younger one a brunette like me, but more curvaceous; Emery discovered he could sketch on horseback. I didn't care one jot, though I sensed the annoyance of Marcia, who was luckily too far engaged in a battle of wills with her grey mount to interfere.

As I rode, Amber's narrow, arched neck nodding between me and the ground, I mused on priest Francis, taken all the way from Hampshire to London. Perhaps Hampshire had still been too Catholic, or the Deverell name too well known, for Elizabeth's officials to risk a local trial. Perhaps Clement had asked it as a favour. Had they made Francis walk all the way, or carried him in a litter hidden from view? Or had he simply ridden, but between guards and with bound hands to prevent escape? Was Dominic by then dead?

There must be some way of finding out. But Nicholas's contact at the British Library would have told him if there had been more in the records. There was of course another way. I wondered whether it would happen to me again. There seemed no means to bring it on. So far everything that had occurred had been unpredictable. And did I really want to go back in time again? It might be unbearable. I felt haunted enough already. Why was it that in this peaceful, glorious landscape I could not get terrible suffering out of my mind?

We encountered some of the wild, shaggy New Forest ponies with their barrel bellies and long tails. Elizabeth tried to attract their attention, but they shied away from her, startling her own white pony. One of the guides was quick to intervene, taking the pony's reins for a while until it was settled again.

Amber moved alongside Bob's black mare. Bob glanced back, but he was safe to speak. That wonderful, head tossing grey was still engaging Marcia's attention, to the perplexity of our guides, who insisted that it was usually good tempered. 'I didn't hear any singing last night,' Bob murmured. 'Did you?'

'No.' I said nothing about Jack and his prayers.

'What do you think is going on?'

'Ghosts,' I said.

Bob glanced over his shoulder again. 'I saw a ghost once, when I was a little boy on holiday in Scotland. I didn't tell anyone, of course. My grandmother claimed to be psychic and the other side of the family thought she was off her head…'

I thought of Nicholas, who had not believed Freya and had lost his child. Perhaps Bob did not appreciate how lucky he was.

'You could stand up for Jack about it more,' I said, the words out of my mouth before I could stop myself, even though it was none of my business how Bob and Marcia brought up their children. Bob of course looked guilty and I felt awful.

'We'll see,' he said. 'I'll have a word.'

I knew he wouldn't, but I had already overstepped the mark.

We were on a full day's trek, so we dismounted rather stiffly, let the horses drink, then tethered them and munched chicken legs, fruit and biscuits beside a clear, bubbling stream. Everyone was happy in this blissful place except Marcia. That grey deserved a medal. Having failed to engage the interest of the curvaceous guide, Emery strolled upstream and sat down on a rock to sketch us as a group.

'Imogen, isn't it?' It was the older guide, a slim, well spoken, blonde woman, the one who had steadied Elizabeth's white pony. She held out her hand. 'I'm a friend of Meta Sievewright. I help out here with the horses in the summer months. How do you do? My name's Grace Raymond.'

Two things astonished me, that Meta Sievewright must have told her friend about me, and that this woman had the same surname as Dominic's wife, Isabella. Perhaps she was a descendant of Isabella's family.

'How do you do?' I shook hands. For this woman to approach me so directly suggested Meta had spoken of me with approval, or at least wanted to find out more about me.

'We get lots of riding parties from Deverell in the summer,' she said. 'Are you enjoying staying there?'

'We are.' I was sure Meta would not have mentioned anything supernatural, so refrained doing so myself. 'Do other people like it?'

'Everyone does. And it's a good base to explore Hampshire.'

So far, so innocuous.

I was conscious of Emery making a mobile phone call from his rock, and recognised his flirtatious expression, but felt no interest. I was wondering how to ask Grace Raymond about Nicholas. She must know him well.

'Caroline said that chestnut horse came from Deverell,' I said carefully.

Grace smiled sadly. 'Yes, Artus belonged to Sophia. He was the horse she was riding when it happened.'

Grace evidently assumed I knew more than I did. I thought rapidly. Sophia must have been the name of Nicholas's wife and she must have died in a riding accident. I realised I had supposed it a road accident, with six year old Freya in the car also. Perhaps Sophia had been giving Freya a ride on Artus and they had both tumbled. She must have been an experienced rider, so maybe something had startled the horse. I could not bring myself to ask. But I did not wonder at Nicholas's giving Artus to Caroline. He would have been a painful reminder of a double loss.

'It was a terrible tragedy,' I said. Banal, but what else could one say?

'Yes, and it goes on. It'll never end, not until…' A spasm of pain crossed Grace's features, then she recovered. 'Well, I dare say we ought to get moving again. We can't take the horses too fast in this heat.'

She moved away, capable and energetic, calling to everyone to pack up their lunch boxes. I obeyed too, wondering what she would say about me to Meta, and filled with curiosity. Nicholas's wife and daughter were dead. What had Grace meant when she said his tragedy had not ended?

CHAPTER THIRTEEN

'THAT was a pleasant little jaunt,' Emery remarked to me when we were alone in the guardroom once more. Marcia had decided that everyone was stiff and tired and needed to go home immediately for a rest and a hot bath, though the children were fine and Emery and I were not too bad. I suppose she was right. We would all be stiff in the morning. Marcia was often right. It was just the way she said these things.

'It was pleasant,' I agreed with Emery now.

He unbuttoned his shirt. 'I'm, er, going out tonight,' he said. I had guessed as much, seeing him making calls earlier. He would probably try to sneak out without telling Marcia. With any luck, he would home in on a party and stay there overnight, something he had done regularly in the last year of our marriage.

'I'm not your keeper,' I said lightly. I went into the bathroom and began running hot water. He followed me in.

'Listen, Gen, it's something in London I can't miss…'

The big, baby blue eyed, little boy look. The I'm-sorry-I'm-unfaithful-but-I-don't-mean-to-hurt-your-feelings look. Emery was not hard hearted, but he had always wanted to have his cake and eat it.

'Do what you like,' I said. 'It doesn't feel like my business any more.'

He went back into the guardroom.

He made it out without detection. Marcia blamed me, of course; I must have driven him away by my coldness to him all week. The fact that he had gone without even saying goodbye to the children did not seem to occur to her. Elizabeth had been hoping for another portrait session.

'It's your fault,' Marcia hissed at me, having briskly dismissed her daughter's wails. We were gathering in the drawing room before the Weightmans went out for a late tea; I had decided to make my own. 'Don't think I didn't see you refusing to take his hand at the dockyard yesterday.'

If she had known I had another note from Nicholas, she would have brought that up too, but Jack had been first home tonight and he had kept it secret, pressing it into my hand behind both our backs like the gallant little conspirator he was. I kept it close until the family had gone, then, with the gatehouse to myself, I read it.

> *Dear Imogen,*
>
> *I don't go to bed until late, so it would have been all right to come round and knock on the kitchen windows. Meta and*

Alistair will be out tonight. If you'd like to risk my cooking, I can make supper.
Best wishes,
Nicholas

It certainly surprised me. I don't know when I have ever been happier to have Emery proved wrong, for this did not fit his theory about Nicholas. So much for his being wary of another man's wife. I stood in the little turret kitchen, half laughing, half nervous. Not for one moment did I consider turning him down.

It was eight o'clock. I had put on a pale blue and white summer dress. I shivered in the thin cotton in the guardroom, but the manor house kitchen had been warmer, so hoped I should be all right. Just in case, though, I reached for the least casual sweater I had with me, of fine grey wool. But I froze in the act.

He was singing Latin plainchant again.

Despite the daylight, I think I cried out with fright. Then I remembered my words to Jack. He was a priest, a good man. So he'll not harm you. And he had not harmed Jack. But Jack had not been alone in the gatehouse as I was.

Shivering with more than cold now, I pulled my sweater over my head and looked up at the turret staircase through the open guardroom door. The plainchant was two floors above me. Two floors I would have to walk up slowly, towards a sound growing louder, a sound not being made in my own time. I longed for Nicholas's phone number. Absurd that we had not yet exchanged numbers...

A baritone, I thought, analysis keeping decision at bay. Quite a good voice once, I reckoned, though Bob would have known for sure. I heard no fear in it, but Francis Deverell had been braver than me. That did it. All I had to do was walk up a circular oak staircase in broad daylight and listen. The last steps he had taken, above jeering crowds, had led to an agonising death on the gallows.

So I began walking, clutching the handrail and hunched over with dread, not daring to look above me lest I glimpse something through those fearful cracks. I passed the drawing room, then Bob and Marcia's bedroom, and the singing continued. He was still there. Oh God, he was still there. He was ill; I was near enough now to hear him wheeze between the exquisite phrases.

Up I went, the oak creaking beneath me. There were no windows from now on. I prayed Jack and Elizabeth had left their attic doors open to give me daylight. Luckily, both were ajar. I slowed as I reached the top, my shaking hand over my face. I looked right to Jack's room, seeing through my fingers the red covers on the two single beds. So I was still in my own time; Francis was visiting mine. Somehow, I made the final steps. I was standing on the threshold of Jack's room looking in.

I saw nothing but a boy's untidiness. Clothes strewn on the bed and chairs. Bob's model airplane, now finished, standing on the little round table. A Mary Rose banner Emery had bought Jack from the dockyard shop dangled from the overhead lamp. Francis was still singing, but I heard him weakening. Some sort of chest infection was hindering him badly now; it sounded like pleurisy. Perhaps he had been hiding out in wet weather before he was caught. Jack's window was open behind him and I felt an impulse to close it.

Pity had taken the remnants of fear. I walked forward, keeping my head down beneath the beams which slanted to the floor on my right. I stretched out my hand, felt intense cold. The singing was almost a whisper now. I think he was near to losing consciousness.

He had heard Jack; he might hear me. How did one address a priest in the sixteenth century? Were they called 'sir', the spiritual equivalent of a knight? If I ever knew I had forgotten.

'Father Deverell,' I said. 'Father Deverell.'

My first two words sounded normal. The third and fourth echoed oddly, as though I were no longer in a stuffy attic. I realised why; they were following him, back into his own world. He was still in the attic, but time has its own echoes.

Nicholas met me at the kitchen's French windows, which were open to catch the balmy evening air. He took one look at my face and drew me in, his arm round me.

'What happened, Imogen?'

Close to tears, I buried my face in his broad, bony shoulder. 'I heard Francis singing in Jack's room. I went up. He's ill….'

Nicholas held me tight and stroked my hair. 'It's over for him,' he said. 'It was over for him a long time ago.'

'But he's not at peace.' I looked up wildly. 'If you'd heard him, you'd know. He's not at peace. You must do something!'

'You mean exorcism?'

'Yes!'

'All right, I will. Hush, Imogen, we'll give him peace…'

He was soothing me as if I were a child, not the attractive, independent young woman I hoped he had thought me until now. I made an effort to control myself, pulling away from him. Madogany was looking up at me worriedly from a large basket on the other side of the kitchen.

'I'm sorry,' I said. 'It overwhelmed me, that's all.'

'I don't blame you,' Nicholas said.

Madogany put his great head down and snoozed again. Calmer, I looked at Nicholas properly. He too was out of jeans, in light shirt and trousers for summer. They hung on him a little – he had probably lost weight after his bereavement – but were of good quality. He had an understated elegance I had not noticed before. He saw my appraising glance and moved closer again. He lifted my hand and held it to his lips.

'You look lovely,' he said softly.

I caught my breath. 'Thank you.' It was a long time since Emery had said or done such a thing. Had he ever meant it when he did?

'But…' Nicholas added.

'But?'

'I think you need to get away from here for a few hours. If you don't want to risk my cooking, I could take you out. We can't be too late, or Madogany will be crossing his paws, but there's a good little restaurant just down the road.'

I didn't give my marriage to Emery a second thought, but this was turning into an evening of surprises. Nicholas and his family must be known for miles around. If we were seen out together, if he made an effort to put his loss behind him in the company of a married woman, it would be public knowledge instantly. I would be compared to beautiful, golden, dead Sophia, probably unfavourably, since that is how gossip works. What had altered his attitude? Emery was too shrewd to have been completely wrong about him...

'On the other hand, if you don't want to go out,' Nicholas added, with a touch of his old diffidence, 'I can rustle something up quickly.' He gestured towards the Aga.

'No, you need a break from work.' I smiled, allowing happiness to touch me, and went to the French windows. 'Let's go out.'

He smiled back. 'In that case, let's be practical and take Meta's car. It's not covered in dog hair...'

CHAPTER FOURTEEN

'So, Imogen Webb,' Nicholas said, 'as the old cliché goes, tell me about yourself.'

We had ordered salads, venison to follow and wine. The restaurant was delightful, ten minutes drive from the gatehouse, in what had been a medieval almshouse. The staff evidently knew Nicholas. Though we had not booked, they found us a table in a corner of the cobbled courtyard, which gave us privacy. The ancient, arched buildings around us were filled with character and mellow in the softening evening light.

'I'm not very interesting,' I said. 'I work in London and currently rent a studio flat high above the city. It has a fabulous view of St Paul's, but it's nothing like Deverell, I'm afraid.'

'It sounds good,' Nicholas said. 'Where are you from?'

'I was brought up in London, in St John's Wood.'

Nicholas leaned forward. 'Okay. Tell me more, though. Tell me everything about yourself.'

So I recited, 'I graduated in Economics from Cambridge and trained as a chartered accountant. My father was an engineer, my mother a GP. They retired to Cornwall last year to do some painting and sailing. I have an older brother called Charles who is an engineer and who lives with his family up in the Peak District, and a younger sister called Sue who went to art school, sculpts and is currently on a three year project in the Australian outback.'

Sue was also the reason I had met Emery, at one of her parties; he had been two years ahead of her in art school. I ought to have known better at the time; parties were not really my thing, and the chances of my meeting the love of my life at one were very slim. However, I had no intention of dragging Emery into the conversation tonight – a husband ought to feature more in a summary of one's life – and Nicholas was delicate enough not to mention him.

'Do you like living in London?' he asked.

I shook my head. 'The work's there, that's all. Not many people who live in London actually like it. It's pretty inconvenient, actually.' I took a deep breath. 'So that's me. Yourself?'

'Me?' Then he nodded, accepting the obligation politely. 'I trained as an architect, specialising in old buildings, for reasons which are presumably obvious.'

'That must be quite a help.'

'Yes and no.' He smiled wryly. 'Very much yes and no.' He broke off to thank the waiter who brought our salads. I had already noted his politeness with the restaurant staff; having been a waitress in my student days I noticed such things, which were a telling mark of character. To do him justice, Emery was always polite too.

The salads tasted as delicious as they looked. The waiter returned to light the candles in their little stained glass holders on the table. It was growing dark.

'Tell me more about yourself,' I prompted Nicholas.

'More?' He considered. 'Well, you know where I live. I was working in Vienna when my father died four years ago. I'd met my wife Sophia there so Freya had dual nationality. We all piled back to Deverell and my mother moved to an old cottage in Alton which is still in the family. The actual Dower House was sold off decades ago to pay taxes. Meta is my only sibling. She and Alistair live near Wells in Somerset. Their children are at university. Meta's a family law solicitor in Wells and Alistair has a boys' school. They're busy people, but they've been very good to me this last year. I don't know what I'd have done without them. Would you like water?'

I recognised the little diversionary tactic and held out my glass. He poured water for us both.

'Have you plans for Deverell?' I asked.

'Sort of. We obviously lease out the gatehouse and if I can get the manor house up to scratch I think I have to go down the dreaded wedding venue route. Just stopping it falling down means one damned thing after another, never mind getting it up to venue standard. I don't know how long I can go on at Deverell, but after seven hundred years I don't want to be the one to give it up. Meanwhile, I talk nicely to my bank manager and it helps to have a solicitor in the family.' He smiled. 'Is that enough about me?'

No mention of Vaganov. I didn't blame him. It was his business and why spoil this lovely evening? I was holding back myself. My family had always liked history and I knew that as engineers both my father and brother would have been interested in Deverell's maintenance. They could give advice at a distance, they had contacts… But, again, it wasn't my business, I didn't want to raise Nicholas's hopes and he must have had contacts of his own. Meanwhile, it would have helped him to have had an accountant in the family too. I wanted to offer my professional advice for free. Meta would have recommended a good accountant, but he presumably paid for the service and it sounded as though he could hardly afford to. But I didn't like to be presumptuous or officious. And he might be too proud to accept. I simply didn't know him well enough to risk it.

'I hear a friend of Meta's was taking you pony trekking today,' he said. 'Did you enjoy it?'

'Yes, I did. Is Grace Raymond from the same family as Dominic's wife Isabella?'

'Probably. Raymonds have been round here for centuries. Grace has been a good friend. She bought Sophia's horse. Did she tell you that was how Sophia died?'

'I think she assumed I knew,' I said carefully. If he wanted to talk about it, it was up to him. I was ready to listen.

'It's name was Artus.' He spoke steadily, with less emotion than when he spoke of Freya. 'I couldn't look at him after that day. And he was Sophia's anyway. She was the rider. I couldn't have afforded to keep him.'

It sounded as though Sophia had been wealthier than Nicholas, with sources of income which were not tied up in an ancient building. It struck me that her death might have been a financial disaster for him as well as a personal one. The ongoing work on the manor house would quickly swallow any legacy…

I was thinking like an accountant again. I gave myself a mental shake, just in time, for Nicholas spoke again, less steadily now.

'Sophia was a fine rider,' he said, 'but she went down first. They don't know how Freya clung on to Artus for so long. I suppose it means she would have been an even better rider.' He looked down, then up again. 'I am so sorry, Imogen. You must be sick of my wife and child.'

'Of course not,' I said indignantly. 'A year isn't much time to get over loss, if you ever do..'

'But I meant to stay off the subject tonight at least.' He reached for the water jug again and poured me more, then did the same with the wine. 'Change the subject for me, please.'

'If you're sure,' I said. He nodded, so I told him that Francis Deverell had heard Jack praying alongside him and switched from Latin to English. He was as dumbfounded as I had been.

'It shows adaptability,' he said at last, 'that he wasn't one of those diehards who kept insisting on Latin the people couldn't understand. But what does it mean for Francis himself? We know Jack will remember hearing him. But would Francis have remembered hearing Jack?'

It was an eerie thought. Had Jack altered a man's memory and thus altered history? Was it possible that anguished, tortured man had even remembered Jack's comfort on the scaffold at Tyburn, for who else would have had the chance to comfort him between then and his final ordeal?

'Oh, Christ,' Nicholas said under his breath. I realised the same possibility, that we had altered history, had occurred to him.

'Are the Deverells still Catholic?' I asked.

Nicholas looked faintly ashamed. 'No. Once Dominic's direct line died out, they became Anglican in the late seventeenth century. I assume that James the Second being kicked off the throne was the last straw.'

'I'm not Catholic either,' I said. 'It makes me even more helpless. How can we give Francis peace if we're not of his faith?'

Nicholas nodded. 'That's how I feel too.'

We sat there, half fascinated, half afraid, in the busy yet intimate twenty-first century restaurant. The darkness above brought the ancient stone arches of the almshouse into stark relief, just as the Elizabethan battlements of the manor house had appeared higher last night.

'You work on the Cathedral roof,' I said. 'The Anglicans will know a priest you can contact. It's all very ecumenical these days.'

He nodded. 'Yes.' He tried to smile. 'My contact in the British Library's going to try to find out more about Francis. Hey, I could host ghost tours. They bring in cash. I wouldn't be the first posh beggar to go down that route.' The smile faded. 'But somehow, I couldn't. Not now.'

I knew what he meant. It had become too personal.

He paid for dinner. I didn't like to protest since it had been his idea and it might hurt his pride.

We drove back to Deverell wrapped in a delicious silence, my grey jumper unused on my lap, cats' eyes on the country lanes glowing in the headlights. A fox darted across the road. At some point Nicholas reached for my hand, and I gave him it. He kept it, steering the little Fiat with his right hand, changing gear smoothly with my palm beneath his. Once he raised my hand to his lips and kissed it.

Did he know that Emery had gone to London? How could he know? To ask him would break the spell.

Finally, he swung left, the car juddering on the cattle grid and spoke for the first time. 'Do you fancy a grand tour of the manor house?'

'Yes, please.'

He smiled. 'I'll have to let Madogany out first. Though he's a gallant old mutt, hasn't had any accidents so far.'

I gathered from this that Alistair and Meta would not be back yet. I suspected they would discover a reason to stay out very late indeed. I think Nicholas had the same suspicion. He slipped his arm around me as we bumped down the track towards the gatehouse and I leaned into him.

Approaching the archway, our headlights caught three figures standing outside the gatehouse. With abominable timing so far as I was concerned, the Weightmans had returned. They turned towards us, though they would have been blinded by the headlights. As we drew nearer, a fourth figure scampered across from the shed and began to unlock the door.

'Want to duck?' Nicholas asked, laughter in his voice.

'No. Want me to?'

'Can't say I do.'

So we braved it out, driving past the gatehouse door exactly as we were. I glimpsed Marcia's horrified expression.

'Oh dear,' Nicholas said in a droll voice. 'Oh dear, oh dear, oh dear.'

He swung right, turning the Fiat into its usual position opposite the manor house front door. We undid our seat belts. I watched in my mirror as Marcia herded her family inside and shut the door and the turret light disappeared. Thank heaven she had not stormed over to us.

Then, the silence of suspense between us.

'This is where we talk about it,' Nicholas remarked presently.

'Yes.'

'Your husband's in London. Christ knows why, but he isn't faithful to you.'

After everything, my face still burned. 'How did you find out?'

He held me tighter. 'I've been debating with myself all evening whether to tell you. I'm afraid Grace overheard him making arrangements on his mobile today.'

It hurt. Even now, it hurt.

'I don't love him,' I said tightly.

'Not loving doesn't always help,' Nicholas answered. I stared at him, wondering at his words, then a childish scream ripped the silence.

'What the...' Nicholas let go of me, jumped from the car.

Another scream. I recognised Elizabeth's shrillness. Knowing she had played a trick before, I would have ignored it. But Nicholas sprinted towards the gatehouse. Frantic, he threw open that heavy door and disappeared up the turret staircase. With the door now ajar, I heard the commotion for myself.

It was Jack. Jack had fallen downstairs.

CHAPTER FIFTEEN

HE HAD fallen awkwardly, between drawing room and guardroom. He was half upright at an angle to the ancient wooden steps, whimpering with pain in his right shoulder, trying not to cry. Blood streamed from his forehead and both knees. An adult would have jammed sooner in that narrow, circular space, but he must have fallen a long way down.

Elizabeth was wailing, hindering matters. As Nicholas and I arrived, Bob was picking her up and carrying her upstairs out the way.

'How many times have I told you not to run on those stairs!' Marcia ran down them herself with bags of frozen vegetables. I took some from her, applied them to poor Jack's head while she dealt with his knees. With his left hand he clutched at me. He tried to form words silently, but I couldn't make them out.

'Hush,' I whispered. 'You can tell me later.'

Bob brought down the gatehouse's first aid kit, but our options were limited. We dared not try to move Jack ourselves. He screamed when we touched him and his shoulder looked odd beneath his t shirt. Nicholas was already on his mobile for an ambulance. I could only imagine his turmoil, but his voice was calm.

'Yes, he's bleeding from his head and his shoulder's damaged... We've got iced bags... He fell downstairs ..He's ten...' No calling up to Marcia, just guessing Jack's age so as not to waste time.

'I'm eleven,' Jack managed, shuddering with pain.

'Don't talk!' Marcia hissed. None of us were doctors. For all we knew, his lungs were pierced.

Nicholas came back up to us. 'Should be ten minutes,' he said. I saw the awkwardness in his eyes.

'Thank you.' Marcia was cool but polite. I admired her in that moment. Another mother might have brought up the difficulty of the stairs. Another sister might have mentioned her brother's marriage.

'Can I do anything else?' Nicholas asked.

She shook her head.

'Soldiers,' Jack said feverishly.

Nicholas and I exchanged horrified glances. Suddenly, I realised why Jack had fallen downstairs. He had encountered the soldiers who came for Francis in the night. Perhaps he had tried to stop them coming upstairs. It was spreading, this spilling over of time. It was out of control. I saw the same realisation in Nicholas's face.

'There are no soldiers here,' Marcia soothed Jack, oblivious.

The ambulance arrived in eight minutes. So as not to impede them, everyone except Marcia went upstairs. We heard poor Jack scream as the paramedics worked on him. Nicholas turned away from the rest of us, shoulders hunched. I went to him, slipped an arm round his waist. He turned and looked down at me, dry eyed and tormented, caught my hand and squeezed it.

'It's not me you should be worrying about,' he whispered. But he lifted my hand and rested it briefly against his face.

Elizabeth sobbed in Bob's arms. Though she was only nine and had had a fright, it seemed unusual; she was not that kind of child and she generally took her cue from Marcia and ignored Bob. I wondered whether she had witnessed Jack's fall, and what she had seen, but I did not dare ask.

I did what I could, texting Emery, though I doubted he would notice until the morning, finding pyjamas and toiletries for Jack for hospital, then making a flask of tea and sandwiches for Marcia, who would have to go with him. It might be a long night for her. Nicholas helped me. Both of us were silent and subdued. I was fighting to keep fear at bay and guessed he was too. Everything was escalating. Who knew what might happen next? Our intimate evening in the cobbled courtyard of the almshouse seemed a long time ago now.

As it turned out the estate gates with blue lights flashing, the ambulance passed Alistair and Meta, who were returning home to the manor house. They came round to the gatehouse at once. Bob, who was taking Elizabeth up to her room, said a brief, anxious hello, and disappeared.

Nicholas, Meta, Alistair and I sat sombre and tense in the drawing room, lamps lit against the dusk, and I related what had happened to me yesterday with Anna Mervyn, then what Nicholas and I suspected had happened to Jack tonight. Alistair and Meta showed sincere sympathy for Jack, especially Alistair, but they stayed calm. I suspected very little would have made them panic – they were strong, practical people – and events had moved beyond incredulity.

'I have some Catholic boys in school,' Alistair said. 'A priest comes to hear their confessions and so on. Father John Draycott. He's a good chap. I don't know whether he's ever done any exorcism, but I'm sure he'd be willing to help.'

'He's quite chatty,' Meta said, soignée in cream silk and pearls. 'He would need to keep it secret. The last thing we want is talk.'

Alistair sent her a reassuring glance. 'Where his faith's concerned, he's a different man.'

She nodded, turned to me. 'I made sure the agency has responsibility for the gatehouse visitors. What are the Weightmans like?'

The question surprised and secretly pleased me. Meta seemed to be taking it for granted that I had a future with Nicholas, an impression she could only have got from him, and that if it came to law I would take his side against Emery's family. She must think she could trust me. She was a solicitor. A little boy had been hurt, but it was her job, her instinct, to consider the distasteful legal implications and she was doing it crisply, though both Alistair and Nicholas looked uncomfortable.

'They're not the litigious type or publicity seekers,' I said. 'They came here knowing what kind of property it is. There are enough warnings on the brochure and website to put anyone off.'

'But they didn't know it's haunted.' Meta shrugged elegantly. 'Trying to prove it in a court of law would be entertaining....'

'They wouldn't try. Besides, Marcia doesn't believe in ghosts. Ergo, ghosts don't exist.'

'I don't see how we can prevent talk,' Nicholas said. 'We can hardly ask the family to keep quiet and these things get out sooner or later anyway. Nothing's private now with social media.'

It was true. We were silent. 'In that case, it's up to you,' Meta said eventually to Nicholas. 'You could capitalise on it. The level of supernatural activity here in the last few days must be unusual anywhere.'

'I don't want to capitalise on it,' he answered almost angrily.

'Well, whatever you decide is for the future,' Alistair said. 'First things first. I'll phone Father Draycott in the morning.' He stood up, came over to me and patted my arm. 'We'll say goodnight, my dear, and hope for better fortune in the morning.'

'It'll work itself out,' Meta said, standing up herself. Soon she and Alistair had gone, suspiciously quickly in fact, leaving me alone with Nicholas. We went downstairs slowly and stood beside the great oak door below the guardroom steps. He reached out for me. I moved closer and his arms circled my waist.

'I am sorry,' he said. 'What an end to the evening.'

'It's not your fault.'

'The agency doesn't own the gatehouse. I do.'

'Which doesn't make it your fault. They were soldiers from the past.'

'Christ, I even got Jack's age wrong. Freya was so tall for her age…'

'As if Jack's age matters…'

I ached to go back to the manor house and stay with Nicholas tonight. He had enough on his plate without worrying about Jack too. But he had Alistair and Meta there, while Bob and Elizabeth might need me. Trust Emery to be absent in an emergency.

Madogany padded up out of the dark and whined urgently at us, sensing something wrong.

'It's all right, old boy,' Nicholas said. He bent his head and kissed me softly on the lips. 'I'll be over in the morning,' he whispered. 'If you need help in the night, just call. No matter the time.' Then he let go my waist and set off into the darkness, turning and raising an arm in farewell. Madogany went with him.

I stood watching them at the gatehouse door. Nicholas looked back before he rounded the corner and waved again. Presently, I went back into the gatehouse and shut out the sweet, balmy night, turning the huge key in the lock.

I went upstairs, hovering uncertainly between drawing room and attic, wondering how to help Bob and Elizabeth, but not liking to barge in. I could hear Elizabeth crying inside her room, but the sobs seemed to be lessening. Soon Bob emerged, anxious as ever.

'How is she?' I whispered.

He shook his head. 'She says Jack hurled himself downstairs.'

'What?'

'She couldn't have seen right. Jack wouldn't do such a thing.'

'Of course she didn't see right. Bob...He might have collided with...'

Bob looked at me. I saw dread in his face. That brought me up short. His son was in hospital and his daughter was distraught. The last thing Bob Weightman needed was a theory which would have sounded unbalanced even to someone with knowledge of the gatehouse history and he had none. But I was conscious that this was the coward's way out, for Jack himself had been trying to tell me the truth.

'Collided with what?' Bob whispered.

'It's not the moment to go into it,' I said, acutely aware that I was bungling the situation. I should either have mentioned nothing or told him everything. My feelings must have shown in my face. Bob, hypersensitive to such things and evidently trying to spare me, merely nodded.

'Have you heard from Marcia yet?' I asked.

'No, not yet.'

'Can I do anything?'

'No, no, it's fine.' He tried to smile. 'I was just about to fetch some lemonade for Elizabeth.'

'I'll bring it up,' I said.

'Okay.' He disappeared back inside. I went through the drawing room into the kitchen, poured the lemonade and took it up. Elizabeth's room was a mirror image of

Jack's, with a little girl's untidiness instead of a boy's. She was sitting on the bed, tear stained and hiccoughing, but she took the lemonade eagerly.

'I'll be in the drawing room,' I whispered to Bob and left.

Jack's room door was ajar, the chest drawers still open where I had rummaged for clean pyjamas. I went in to close them and paused to look out the window in case Nicholas and Madogany were on the lawn, but saw nothing in the darkness. The room was silent; no plainchant now.

I went downstairs, heading for the drawing room, but I thought I heard a knock on the front door. It was surely too early for Emery, assuming he came back at all, but it might be Nicholas. I passed the drawing room and almost ran down the rest of the staircase to turn the great key in the lock.

No one there. Imagination, I told myself. But it was colder down here and I shivered. My grey jumper was in the guardroom, where I had flung it as I ran upstairs to the injured Jack. I went in for it now, but did not see it.

I saw other things, a torch burning in a wall bracket, a stack of weaponry where Emery's bed should have been, and a great oak chest where mine should have been. I smelled stale sweat and urine and beer. The windows were smaller. And on a fire, in a smaller fireplace than the modern day one, a guard was stirring a pot.

CHAPTER SIXTEEN

SURPRISE, then fear, held me rigid.

'It'll pass,' I told myself. 'It's just a glimpse.'

The guard – I realised he was the stooped man I had heard speaking to Anna Mervyn – had his back to me. He was stirring a dark, lopsided pot. Somehow, I managed to move backwards, glancing behind me desperately, but the circular staircase was in murky darkness, only the lowest steps lit by the guardroom torch. I dared not go upwards into that black sixteenth century night, so I stood just out the guard's view, my heart hammering, waiting for my own time to return. No sound came from above.

As my eyes grew accustomed to the torchlight in the guardroom, I made out other details. The walls were of bare grey stone; no trace of the modern whitewash. Anna Mervyn's basket lay on its side on a table in the centre of the guardroom. I doubted any of its contents had reached Francis. The guard grunted as he went on stirring the pot. The smell of vegetables mingled with the reek of the room. The guard's dirty jerkin was torn beneath his armpits. It was surely too late for supper. Perhaps he kept late hours – my watch showed nearly midnight – but more likely the evening was not as far advanced here.

This had already lasted longer than my encounter with Anna Mervyn. Summoning courage, I put out my hand and touched the guardroom wall, just inside the threshold. I made contact. The wall was cold. I was here all right. I might be visible. I might be audible. I put my hand over my mouth lest the guard hear my frightened breathing. Somewhere in this gatehouse were Bob Weightman, a decent family man, and his little daughter who was addicted to technology. I would have given anything to see them now. So much for my fascination with the past.

Someone banged on the front door. The guard grunted again, got to his feet and reached for the torch. I fled up into the circular stairwell. The stairs were less uneven than they had become in the twenty-first century, but they still creaked. I winced at the sound, though the guard did not seem to hear it. He had come out the guardroom. I noticed the door was not locked but barred. He tossed aside the heavy plank and opened the door. Then he bowed and stood back to give entrance to the newcomer who wore dark hat, doublet and breeches.

I could not see his features beneath the hat, but I guessed who he was, even by torchlight. He was middle aged, taller and heavier than the guard with an air of authority. The guard had bowed to him. It could only be Francis's newly Protestant brother, the lord of Deverell Manor, Clement.

'How is he?' he demanded. The voice was deep and the accent was so strong I barely made it out. The guard mumbled something incomprehensible to my ears. They're going to pass me on the stairs, I thought, terrified. I slithered further up, my chest so tight I could hardly breathe, my spine shrinking from the icy wall. Then I heard the guardroom door close.

I dropped onto the stairs in my relief, burying my face in my hands. Come on, I thought, that's enough. I need to go back to my own time now. But no electricity came on in that murky staircase. My own time was gone. My mind filled with the horror of never getting back there.

I must stay practical, I thought, I must stay practical. I could creep down, unbar the door and run away from the gatehouse. Or I could creep upstairs and hope to find somewhere empty. But both options risked noise. A wooden bar. Creaking, wooden stairs. Clement might hear me or come out the guardroom at the crucial moment. And all the empty rooms might be locked, leaving me exposed at the top of the stairs; I was certain that the only occupants of the gatehouse at present were the prisoner and his guard. Petrified, torn by indecision, I sat where I was, close to tears, longing for Nicholas's arms around me.

Plainchant.

Its sweetness filled the space above me. That was when I realised what in my self-obsessed panic I had forgotten. Francis Deverell's plight was worse than mine. I was in danger, but he was doomed. So, shakily, his voice giving me hope, I forced myself to my feet and begin to walk upwards as I had done earlier this evening. This time, I would surely see him...

The guardroom door opened.

I froze in terror, cringing against the wall.

'Stop it!' Clement's bellow.

I heard fear and desperation in that bellow. Francis continued singing. The staircase turned from darkness to shadow, from shadow to torchlight as Clement thundered upstairs. I bolted up ahead of him. On the middle landing drawing room and bedroom doors were shut. I dared not stop to try them, fleeing on up to the attic, already half lit by Clement's torch. Jack's door was ajar, but I couldn't see in. Elizabeth's door was wide open. I hurled myself in there and, with no time to close the door, crouched out of sight. Moments later, Clement was in Jack's room.

'Papist! Papist traitor!' The sound of blows and of a man groaning under them, coughing and gasping for breath. The plainchant had stopped. 'Bilson!' Clement shouted down for the guard. 'Bilson! Stop his mouth!'

Bilson toiled upstairs, presumably with a gag. I heard Clement's voice again meantime. 'I warned you, brother. D'you think they'll let you blaspheme in the Tower? Do you think to sing at Tyburn?'

No answer. I heard contempt in the silence. Then Bilson arrived and there was scuffling as the gag was applied. More bellowing. It was my moment. I slipped from Elizabeth's room like the craven I was, tears streaming down my face, fled down the stairs, unbarred the door with trembling hands and stumbled out into the black night and stinking mud. I ran and kept on running until I fell.

The sky had grown pale. On which world did the sun rise? I sat up, looked about me and saw trees above my head. There were trees in both worlds. I remembered running into a wood last night and tripping over a branch, lying on the ground with the unbearable knowledge of my cowardice. Then, far off, I heard a cock crow and despaired. I had heard no hens at Deverell in my own time.

I stumbled to my feet, stiff from the pony trekking yesterday. The heel had come off one of my sandals. My blue and white dress was ruined. These were the least of my troubles. With dawn and the manor house full of servants, I stood no chance of avoiding discovery. No matter how far I managed to walk, there would be villages populated by people unused to strangers. My shoulder length hair was too short for a peasant woman's, too straight for a gentlewoman's in 1582, and either way should have been covered. As for my clothes, my watch… I was close to hysteria.

I would have given anything to be sitting at the breakfast table in the drawing room, with Marcia's pointed remarks, Elizabeth demanding her mobile back and Emery's unreliability. I wondered what Bob and Elizabeth thought had happened to me. Nicholas would guess. Nicholas, whom I might never see again…

Voices dragged me back to what was now my present. The voices of young children. I peered through the trees and saw four of them coming my way, dark haired, barefoot and wearing ragged gowns. But for the difference in hair length, they could have been either sex; I knew that boys wore gowns until they were breeched at five or thereabouts, and I couldn't see any of their faces. They were collecting firewood. I had no intention of letting them get any closer, so I decided to run for it. At which point I discovered that when I had tripped I had gone over on my ankle more seriously than I had realised.

I could have yelled in frustration, on top of the pain, but there was no time. I hobbled to a tree and hid behind it. Children having sharp eyes, I could only hope the mud had dimmed the white in my dress. At least two of them were talking as they approached. I failed to make them out, their accents were so strong. One of the boys began showing off, putting down his burden of wood and turning cartwheels. I silently blessed him for the distraction. Another child tried to imitate him and fell down to much laughter.

A fifth child appeared in the distance, taller than her companions, her hair covered by a dirty white scarf. Not quite part of the group, though sent out on the same errand, she gathered her wood silently without coming closer, as if avoiding the others. Her height suggested she was older than they were. Perhaps some disability kept her back, still doing the job normally assigned to the youngest children.

They all moved away. I breathed again, if only for the moment. I glanced at my watch. It was still nearly midnight. It seemed a suspicious moment to need a new battery and I had renewed it last month. Oh God, would this never end? Would I never go back to my own world? To exist in the sixteenth century for the rest of my life would be a waking nightmare. Would knowledge of my own world fade? Would I forget antibiotics, electricity, anaesthesia, mobile phones? Would I alter our own past if I remembered them, anticipated them by some word or deed? Would I be hanged or burned as a witch?

Nicholas...

Galloping hooves behind me. I spun round, found myself in the path of a tall, black horse crashing through the undergrowth. I was so disorientated I had no idea whether it was coming from the manor house or approaching it. All could do was turn my back and hope the rider didn't notice me. It came close, swerving at the last moment as if chasing me. I screamed and flung myself out the way.

A red car whizzed past me with inches to spare.

I looked up. I was lying on the grass verge of a road. A proper road with tar and white lines. The car was disappearing into the distance. I began to cry with relief.

'Imogen!'

I looked round, saw Alistair Sievewright running towards me across the cattle grid. I was just beyond the turn off for the Deverell estate. I stood up and hobbled towards him like a madwoman.

CHAPTER SEVENTEEN

'Why Imogen?' Nicholas asked. '*Why?*'

It was almost ten in the morning. Meta had already left to fulfil a charity commitment when I turned up, but the men of the household were coping heroically. I sat at the table in the manor house kitchen in warm sunshine, close to tears and trying not to show it, wearing Meta's yellow bathrobe after my shower, my ankle strapped up, hot, sweet tea at my elbow, Nicholas's arm around me and Madogany anxious at my feet while Alistair cooked me breakfast.

They had insisted I stay and I had not argued. To return at once to the gatehouse in the state I had been in would have increased Elizabeth's distress, not to mention her curiosity afterwards. Nicholas had gone round there, explaining to Bob that I had taken an early morning walk and turned my ankle. Which was at least a version of the truth. Bob had heard from Marcia at the hospital. Poor Jack's shoulder had been dislocated. It had been put back in without the need for an operation, but he had a sling and must rest. Meantime they were keeping him in for the morning at least, taking no chances with his head injury.

'Has nothing like this happened to you before?' Alistair asked me. He was a dab hand at a fried egg.

'No.' I shook my head. 'No, definitely not. It started my first night here, when I saw the face in the car window. But there's nothing wrong with me, or with any of my family. We're normal. I'm normal, or I thought I was…'

I was conscious that I was babbling. My teeth still chattered. I felt terror of being alone, in case there was a re-occurrence. I might not come back the next time. And though I had not said so, the implications of my experiences were not lost on me. I was too frightened to stay here, but I could not expect Nicholas to leave Deverell. We had no future together.

'You're perfectly normal, my dear,' Alistair said. 'You're simply visiting an old building with a terrible story. We'll see what Father Draycott says. He'll return my call soon. If he can't do anything he'll know someone who can.'

'It's escalating,' I said. 'It began with almost nothing. I might have imagined that face in the window. It's growing bigger, as though we're under siege. At least, that's how it feels,' I added, conscious that this sounded melodramatic.

'Yes, something's happening,' Nicholas said quietly. 'There must be a reason why it's you.'

'Jack and Bob to a lesser extent,' I reminded him, 'and Freya.'

Alistair nearly dropped his fork. '*Freya?*'

I looked at Nicholas in surprise. It had never occurred to me I might be the first person he had told. Hearing Freya's name, Madogany whined. Nicholas bent to soothe him. 'She told me she saw people in the Hall,' he explained to Alistair. 'I didn't believe it until Imogen saw them too. It must have been the servants setting for a feast, probably on the same day.'

The ebullient Alistair seemed lost for words. He nodded, turned back to the frying pan. I studied the photograph of Freya and Sophia on its shelf. Freya wore a red dress with white edging. Six at most when the picture was taken – I did not like to ask exactly when – she looked older than most six year-olds did. Any puppy fat she had had was long gone. She must have inherited Nicholas's height and the chances were that the Austrian Sophia had also been tall.

Alistair plonked a vast breakfast in front of me. 'Get that feast into you, my dear.' His old fashioned belief in the efficacy of a hearty breakfast touched me. I could hardly eat at first, but then discovered I was hungry. It was delicious. Madogany sat up with intent and I sneaked him the end of a sausage.

Alistair's mobile rang. 'That'll be Father Draycott,' he said. But it wasn't. It was school business and he disappeared out into the sunshine.

'Can I pinch a sausage too ?' Nicholas asked, taking it anyway. I pretended to object. Madogany begged again. I gave in to his soulful eyes a second time. Outside Alistair strolled back into view, laughing at something on the phone, looking down at his feet. It was a wonderful, easy going morning at Deverell – or should have been.

'I'll have to return to the gatehouse,' I said to Nicholas. 'Bob needs me.'

'I know.'

'I'm scared.'

'I know. I'll walk you round.' He put both arms round me and kissed me. 'We'll get this sorted out, Imogen. Don't worry.'

'Suppose we don't?' I tried to laugh. 'Suppose it gets worse? Suppose I meet myself in the past? What would that signify?'

'We have to sort it out.' Nicholas pulled a face. 'God, I'd find it hard to live with Uncle Clement otherwise.'

Bob fretted sympathetically about my ankle and asked no questions; he had not noticed my disappearance until the morning and had no reason to question my story. Elizabeth was back to her old, self-centred, noisy self. There had been no word from Emery, naturally. My husband, a rock in a crisis.

The three of us piled into Bob's car and set off for the hospital.

'Jack fell down the stairs, Jack fell down the stairs,' Elizabeth chanted, bouncing onto his bed by way of greeting.

Her brother was one of three occupants in a multi coloured, four bed children's ward. Despite his sling and head bandages, he was not in the least sorry for himself. Looking at his resolute face, it struck me how close I had come to self pity in my new horror of the sixteenth century.

Getting information from Jack was going to be difficult. I knew he would refuse to talk about his fall in Marcia's presence and she had taken up residence at his bedside. I think she guessed I wanted to ask him what had happened. Even she must have realised by now that this was turning into no ordinary family holiday, but she was evidently loath to admit it. Meanwhile, she hauled Elizabeth off Jack's bed.

'He fell,' Elizabeth smirked, dragging up a chair instead. So much for her previous story about her brother hurling himself downstairs. 'Jack's hurt his shoulder, Jack's a silly boy…'

'Don't make such a noise!' Marcia hissed. 'Look!' She nodded towards a yellow faced girl asleep on the other side of the room with a drip in her arm. Elizabeth had the grace to look ashamed of herself. Presently, she drifted over to another little girl, who was awake and playing with a games console.

'I don't see why the rest of you can't do the Isle of Wight as planned,' Marcia said, looking meaningfully at Bob. 'If they let Jack out this afternoon I'll take him back to the gatehouse. He'll need to rest anyway.' I saw Jack bite his lip and knew he didn't want to go back to Deverell, but he said nothing.

'Okay,' Bob said. He turned to Elizabeth. 'The ferry will be fun, won't it?' She curled her lip, displaying her customary disdain for his weakness in the face of Marcia's strength.

'Maybe I should wait for Emery,' I ventured.

Marcia rewarded this blatant hypocrisy with a glare.

'Or you go to the Isle of Wight,' I added, determined not to be a Bob. 'Emery could join you there. I can stay with Jack.'

'I'm his mother,' Marcia said.

'I don't need anyone to stay with me,' Jack put in.

'They might discharge you,' she snapped.

'The nurse told me they wouldn't,' Jack said, 'when you were in the loo.'

Marcia looked irritated. 'Bob, go and ask the nurses what's happening.'

Bob went. Normally she would have gone herself. It showed how determined she was to prevent Jack conferring with me.

I had wondered whether Jack had fibbed, but it turned out that one of the junior nurses had indeed mentioned the possibility of his being kept in for another night. In the ensuing heated debate and general confusion at the nurses' desk, in which Marcia ultimately could not resist taking a major part, I got details of what had happened to Jack last night.

'I'd rushed upstairs to be first to the attic on coming home,' he said. This had become a point of honour between him and Elizabeth, though they subsequently came back down and delayed bedtime for as long as possible.

'I was gloating and Elizabeth put out her tongue at me and went into her room. I started running back down again. Then I saw a lot of men with swords and pistols. They were filthy and dirty and coming upstairs, tramping, like this.' He moved his feet and winced with pain in his shoulder. 'Tramp, tramp, like that. So I ran back up to my room to warn Francis, if he was there, which he must have been if they were. I didn't see him, of course – I never have – but I called out anyway because he heard me before, when we were praying. Then I rushed back to the stairs and tried to stop them, but they vanished as I put out my arms and I tumbled downstairs.'

'You're a brave chap,' I said.

'No, I felt so sorry for the singing priest.' He looked at me with an obstinacy worthy of his mother. 'What happened to him? You never told me. The soldiers came, but you said he didn't die in the gatehouse.'

'He died in London,' I said.

Jack's eyes narrowed. 'What did they do to him?'

'They executed him. People were much harder then.'

'I know. You don't have to protect me.' He grinned suddenly. 'I imagine him like Nicholas.'

'Maybe. He was probably bearded too.'

I tried to conceal my disquiet at Nicholas being compared to a man who had come to such an agonising end. But Jack's grin grew broader. Realising what the little monkey was up to, I spun round. A bunch of red grapes in his hand, Nicholas was approaching the bed.

'How are you?' His smile was nearly as big as Jack's. He was making a big effort to be cheerful, though the sight of sling and bandages must have hit home. Even being in a hospital must have distressed him. It occurred to me that he had never told me whether Freya had died instantly or lingered. I wasn't going to force him to talk about it. It was up to him.

'I'll be out soon,' Jack said, gamely. 'I heard my shoulder pop back in. It was quite a loud pop. They didn't need to push much.'

I could have sworn Nicholas blanched, but he nodded. He inspected Jack's bandaged head. 'Did you get stitches?'

'Five,' Jack said proudly.

'I had ten when I was your age,' Nicholas said.

Jack looked suitably impressed. 'How?'

'Oh, I was cycling with a friend on a beach and crashed onto shingle. There were skid marks on my leg...'

'Wow...' Jack would have said more had Marcia not stalked back to us. I suppose the nurses at the desk were picking themselves up and dusting themselves down. She nodded coolly to Nicholas.

'They've spoken to the doctor,' she announced. 'Jack's to get another scan in an hour. If that's okay, he can leave here. So there's no point in anyone else staying with him. He'll not be able to go to the Isle of Wight. I'll take him straight back to the gatehouse in a taxi. Bob!'

Bob arrived hurriedly, having doubtless appeased the nurses by making them feel even more sorry for him than for themselves.

'You can go to the Isle of Wight,' Marcia informed him. 'I've just had a text from Emery,' she added to me. Back to Bob. 'Emery will meet you at the ferry. At least Elizabeth's day won't be ruined completely.' She looked at me, challenging me. 'Will you be going too?' The words Emery is still your husband remained loudly unspoken. I felt Nicholas tense by my side.

'No,' I said. 'I'll go back to the gatehouse now and get things ready for Jack.'

CHAPTER EIGHTEEN

It was a longer drive back from the hospital than it had been from the restaurant last night. Nicholas again held my hand when he could.

'Jack seems a great little lad,' he said.

I nodded, appreciating the effort; he must have been thinking of Freya too. 'He's got Marcia's guts and Bob's nature. It's a good combination.'

'Father Draycott rang us after you left this morning. He's coming down this afternoon, or this evening, depending on traffic.'

'Thank goodness.' My relief was intense. 'What did he say?'

'He was intrigued. Turns out he's done an exorcism before, in a Cornish hotel, which seems to have worked all right. But I think he's bringing a colleague along, this being rather a dramatic case, as Meta pointed out. I suspect at some point we'll end up in a compendium of ghost stories.' He shook his head wryly. In the bright sunshine we were both more relaxed than we had been last night. 'Anyway,' he added, smiling, 'did I tell you Ranald says you're the toast of the British Library?'

'I am?'

'They've been digging around about Francis, and discovered more about him than they knew still existed.'

'Why, what have they found?'

'The records of his interrogation and that of other priests.'

'Oh.' I was no longer smiling.

Neither was Nicholas. 'Seems in London he came face to face with one of Elizabeth's most sadistic interrogators, name of Topcliffe. '

I was sure I had heard that name before, in connection with Mary Queen of Scots and the Babington plot. It boded ill for Francis Deverell. I shuddered.

'Hey.' Nicholas put his arm round me, kissed the top of my head. 'It's all over for him, remember. And if it isn't, it will be soon.'

I thought of what Grace Raymond had said, that Nicholas's suffering was not over, but still I could not bring myself to ask him what she had meant.

'Did you have lunch?' he asked, swinging the old brown estate through the gates and rattling over the cattle grid. 'Fancy rosti and salad? How about that tour of the manor house I promised you?'

Of course I said yes. I could prepare for Jack's return later. I had no intention of doing everything; Emery could move his own stuff down to the middle bedroom which Marcia and Bob would vacate to be in the guardroom with Jack. And even in the sunshine I dreaded being alone in the gatehouse now.

He smiled at me. 'You won't regret it. My rosti's all right. That's one good thing to come out of Vienna.' It seemed to confirm what I had already suspected, that his marriage to Sophia had not been the happiest. I kept silent.

'Alistair and Meta will be out,' he remarked, as we bumped along the track towards the massive, forbidding turrets of the gatehouse and slowed to go beneath its cavernous arch. 'They'll have to leave next week. They've spent too much time here already. I can't have them give up any more…'

His voice tailed away. He must have seen Alistair before I did, standing grim faced on the gravel drive.

'Alistair's not out,' Nicholas said. He had gone white.

What's happened now? I don't think I actually said the words. In any case, Nicholas had already driven through the archway, pulling up and getting out almost as fast as he had when we heard Elizabeth scream last night.

Vaganov, I thought. He's found some way to force a sale. He's leaned on the bank. He's inside with his goons, rampaging through that glorious house …At which point I realised that, although there was a visitor's car parked alongside Meta's, it was not Vaganov's black monstrosity. It was a prosaic little blue Renault.

Nicholas must have seen my bewilderment as I got out the car. 'It's Freya,' he said, dull eyed and stunned. 'They've found her.'

'What?'

But Nicholas had already turned away, towards Alistair, whom I now realised was not alone. A pleasant faced, middle aged woman was going round the other side of the Renault, as though she were only just arrived and had been speaking to Alistair first before getting stuff out her car.

Alistair went to Nicholas, put a protective hand on his arm. 'It's all right. If it's the worst, we'll do everything. It's all right…'

If it's the worst. What did that mean? And then it finally became clear to me, several days too late. Sophia was dead, but Freya was only presumed dead because she was missing. This was what Grace Raymond had meant.

I stood there in the drive, aghast, angry with Emery, whom it had never occurred to me might have got the details wrong, and with myself, for being so credulous. It was only by the grace of God that I had not made some unintentional but unforgivable remark to the Deverells. Perhaps I had. I searched my memory feverishly.

'Imogen?' It was Alistair, concern in his face. I saw that Nicholas was going round the corner with the middle aged woman who must be a police liaison officer.

'I didn't know,' I said. 'Oh God, I didn't know…'

'How could you?' Alistair said. 'Nicholas finds it hard to talk about. He may need you, Imogen. Do you want to come inside?'

Feeling useless, hating my stupidity and the fact that Nicholas had turned away from me instead of seeking comfort, I shook my head. 'No, better not. I'll be in the gatehouse if he needs me.'

'Are you sure?' Alistair looked perplexed. 'My dear, he's fond of you. I think he'll want you there…'

'It's still not my business. I'm not family.' I was already walking backwards towards the gatehouse door. 'Just tell him I'll help any way I can. He knows where I am if he needs me…'

Alistair nodded reluctantly and turned away towards the manor house.

So, finally, alone in the gatehouse drawing room in the armchair nearest the little turret kitchen, I did what I had thought unnecessary and obtrusive before; using my mobile phone I checked out Nicholas's tragedy on the internet.

There were plenty of references. It had happened fourteen months ago, on an evening three weeks before Freya's seventh birthday. The timing explained why I remembered seeing nothing on the news; Emery and I had been on our last, unsuccessful holiday abroad. So how Emery had come to hear of it I had no idea, but what I read on the internet, from several sources, confirmed that he had picked up the story inaccurately.

Sophia had been out riding Artus. Freya, got ready for bed in a little white linen nightdress by the housekeeper, had run out to meet her and beg for a ride. Despite the housekeeper's protests, Sophia had scooped her up into the saddle in front of her and galloped away with her. Soon after, Artus took fright, no one knew why.

Sophia had fallen quickly. Freya had last been seen by the occupants of a tour bus half a mile away across the countryside, clinging on to Artus, her white nightdress flying against his brown neck. Artus had been discovered five miles away next morning, cropping grass, saddle askew but unharmed and placid. Nicholas himself had been in Winchester that evening, at a fundraising event for the cathedral, an event cut abruptly short as the dreadful news from Deverell came through. He must have blamed himself ever since for being away that night. I imagined his tortured reasoning. If he had got Freya ready for bed instead of the housekeeper, she might not have wanted a ride. A bed time story might have been enough. He might have been able to stop her running downstairs, stop Sophia from scooping her up...

There were pictures of him with haunted eyes at Sophia's large funeral, almost hunched over with grief. Despite intensive, widespread searches of fields, woods and rivers, nothing of Freya had ever been found. There was no way of knowing that Artus had not gone further than five miles, then started to make his way back home. So the searches had grown wider and wider, until they were reluctantly scaled down. Finally, it had become a matter of waiting.

I sat shivering in the gatehouse drawing room, despite the sunshine outside. How did one identify a six year old who had been dead fourteen months? DNA? Nicholas and Meta had presumably already donated samples for comparison. Dental records? Freya might not have had any fillings. There might never have been a need for an x-ray. Would a dentist be able to remember her mouth? Don't be stupid, I thought, her dentist would have been asked immediately for as much information as was possible to provide. And if she had been losing baby teeth Nicholas or the housekeeper would have known. But I had heard that prior to puberty it was difficult to tell the skeletons of boys from those of girls. The poverty stricken sixteenth century children in the woods came into my mind, tousle haired girls and boys alike in dirty, ragged gowns which probably crawled with lice.

A knock on the door.

I started, remembering how Clement had banged on the door, but I was still in my own time, the picnic hamper still in the corner beneath the standard lamp. A few feet away in the kitchen the breakfast dishes for three still stood washed in the racks where I had left them before going with Bob and Elizabeth to the hospital. So I stood up and ran downstairs.

It was Nicholas, ashen faced.

'It's not her,' he said.

I don't know what I felt. Would it not have been a relief finally to know? The end of false hope was surely to be welcomed. Yet there would have been such anguish first. I could only hold out my arms to him. He stole into them, put his arms round me hard and his face in my shoulder.

'It was a necklace,' he said, 'a little red and blue necklace with glass beads, round the neck of a little body in a wood forty miles away. They showed me a picture. Oh Christ, she's somebody else's child, and I'm happy she isn't mine…'

'It's natural to feel like that,' I said. 'Don't feel guilty.'

'They'll do tests anyway,' he said, 'but it'll be quickest if they start with the family who recognise those little beads…'

He was terribly distressed. I walked him upstairs to the drawing room, his head still buried in my shoulder, and sat down with him on the sofa. I rocked him as though he were a child. Eventually his shuddering lessened.

'You didn't know,' he mumbled.

'I didn't. I'm sorry, I'm so sorry.'

'No, I should have told you…'

'It doesn't matter. You weren't ready to talk about it.'

He looked up at last, red eyed, exhausted. 'That's the second time,' he said. 'The first time was after four months, a pair of muddy pink slippers. They belonged to a child kidnapped in Lancashire.'

That too was horrible. What he had been dealing with was so much worse than I had imagined that I almost broke down myself. To every day expect a knock at the door to have his dread confirmed, the wound reopened…

'Who knows how long she survived?' he said. 'She might have lain for hours. And it was cold for the time of year. Perhaps she was only slightly injured but died of hypothermia, wondering why I never came to help her…'

I could not deny either of those possibilities, but I tried. 'She was only a little girl. She wouldn't have survived falling off Artus. He was a big horse and he was galloping. Nicholas, it would have been quick.'

I could tell that he wouldn't believe me, that Meta and Alistair must have put the same arguments to him over and over in vain. Why should I be any different? It would always be hopeless, something that would have to be accepted as part of a relationship with him. Freya would always be there, haunting him.

Perhaps he read my mind. He took my hand, rubbed my fingers against his own absent mindedly. 'I'm sorry. I told you I'm not good news.'

'It's part of who you are now,' I said. 'I can't make it any worse for you. I would hope to make it a little better.'

It was in effect a declaration, which I only realised after I had made it. He looked at me sombrely. 'No pity,' he said.

I was taken aback. Had I expected a declaration in return? 'Nicholas, I wouldn't be human if there wasn't some pity, but that's not...'

He put his fingers tenderly over my lips. '...a basis for a relationship.'

I dashed his fingers away indignantly. 'I was going to say pity isn't important. There's more to you than...'

It sounded, of course, as if I thought Freya unimportant. Looking back, I realise that he was right; it was still much too soon. He stood up, gently, self deprecatingly, apologetically, but he stood up.

'I'd better get back round there,' he said. 'I'll let you know when Father Draycott arrives.'

CHAPTER NINETEEN

At the time, of course, I had no hindsight, but I tried to be rational. Perhaps Nicholas's pride had been wounded; he had broken down on my sofa, after all. It hadn't made me think less of him at all, but I could not blame him for thinking it might. Some women would have seen it as a sign of weakness. Would Sophia have? I wondered. There had been a housekeeper, I mused, another sign that the financial situation had been less desperate when she was alive. Had she considered herself the stronger one in the marriage and he had come to think so too? Perhaps he had merely been trying to shield me from the inevitable sadness involvement with him would bring. But, as I went about my tasks mechanically in the gatehouse, doing everything in the end, because I could not bear to be idle – changing beds, finding more pillows to give Jack's shoulder more support, moving his, Marcia's and Bob's stuff down to the guardroom and Emery's as well as my own up to the middle bedroom where we would have to share a bed again – I could not avoid self recrimination. I felt that I had bungled and given offence, to a man whom fate had already given more than his share of misfortune, and it gnawed at me.

Now, when I could have done with Francis's sweet plainchant in that attic as consolation, there was none. Why would there be? I asked myself. Why would a sixteenth century priest know that a thoughtless, self obsessed accountant from the twenty-first century needed comfort? Why would he give it? He, too, would probably have judged me had he known my case.

But the work I had thrown myself into helped, as work always does. By the time I had made numerous trips from the bottom of the gatehouse to the top and down again, via that perilous circular staircase, I was hot and tired and my legs ached. My strapped up ankle was protesting despite the painkillers I downed like sweets. If any spirit other than Francis had put in an appearance I would have chased it away and even Francis would have had to sing for his supper.

Marcia arrived in a taxi with Jack after five. He was still in pyjamas and dressing gown, pale, but I could see he was trying to be lively.

'I've told him he needs to rest,' Marcia said, eyeing him sternly. 'You heard what the doctor said, didn't you?'

Jack nodded. He looked round the guardroom, a huge space compared to the attic and unlike the attic it had its own bathroom. He would of course share it with his parents for the remainder of the holiday and I had prepared Emery's single bed while his parents would have my double.

'Try the pillows,' I suggested to him. 'You'll need to be comfortable.'

'I don't want to go to bed now,' he said. 'I've been in bed all day...'

Marcia gave him one of her looks.

'Oh, all right...' He sat down on the single bed when she drew back the covers and allowed her to lower him slowly down to the pillows. It hurt, but he just gulped that back and smiled up at me. He was no help at all finding the best arrangement for the pillows, insisting that they were all fine. As we fussed, trying this way and that, I reflected on how fond of him I had become in a few days and how upset I would have been had he been lost to us last night. How much greater Nicholas's pain must be, with the loss of his own daughter. It was unimaginable.

'What do you want to eat?' Marcia asked Jack.

'Beans on toast,' he said promptly.

'I'll make it.' I went up to the little turret kitchen, set the tray and put the beans on. I felt, not happy, but at least more useful than I had felt a couple of hours ago. There had been no telephone call from Nicholas yet, of course, and in a way that was a relief, partly because I was afraid of saying the wrong thing again and partly because although Father Draycott's arrival might be a long term solution, I did not want to be the one to tell Marcia about it. It seemed a job best left to emollient, genial Alistair, who as headmaster of a private school must have plenty of experience in dealing with formidable mothers.

The hot day was melting into another balmy evening. We had been lucky with the weather at least. From the kitchen window I saw Nicholas on the lawn with Madogany, throwing a yellow ball for him. Madogany trundled around, as if trying to console his master, the threadbare ball dangling from his great, hanging jaws, while Nicholas seemed calm. Or was it simply numbness? He's better off without me, I thought, mortified all over again. He has too much to contend with as it is. Oh God, he'll miss Madogany when he loses him too. It won't be long now…

And suddenly I was weeping myself.

'What's up, Gen?'

I turned round. Emery had come into the kitchen, in blue and white striped shirt and pale trousers, a ridiculous straw boater on his head which he had presumably bought on the Isle of Wight. Had his infidelity been my trouble it would have been a crass thing to say. That's Emery for you.

'It's none of your business.' I found a paper towel, blew my nose and washed my hands. Now that I thought about it, I should have realised the other three were back; I could hear Elizabeth's high pitched voice below.

'Want me to make Jack's toast?' Emery asked.

'Of course not.' I was savage.

'Those beans are going to stick to the pan.' He peered at them, poked them with the wooden spoon.

I wrenched the spoon from him and stirred, rescuing them just in time, then dropped the bread slices into the toaster. Emery drifted out the kitchen again. Bob meanwhile brought in some shopping. He saw my face.

'Poor Imogen, you've been doing all the work while we've been gallivanting around…'

'It's not that.' I smiled at him. 'I'm fine, really.'

He looked embarrassed now. I suppose he assumed I minded about Emery. The telephone rang in the drawing room. He escaped to it. I heard him answering questions about Jack, then he put his head round the door.

'It's for you. Nicholas.'

I suppressed turmoil. The toast popped up. 'Tell him I'll be half a minute.'

'I'll take the toast down…'

But I shook my head and carried the tray carefully down to the guardroom, where Marcia had been joined by Emery and Elizabeth around Jack's bed. Illness can become a spectator sport.

'Yay!' Emery said. 'Champion toast!'

Jack, who never needed patronising to eat, gave him a look which was surprisingly like Marcia's.

'I've a telephone call,' I said, putting the tray into her hands. It served the double purpose of deflecting her curiosity. I went upstairs slowly to find Bob fretting at my delay. He shot downstairs when I took the phone lest he be in the way.

'Imogen?' Nicholas sounded cheerful enough, if slightly wary.

'Yes.'

'Father Draycott and Father Coll have arrived. Come round and meet them.'

'Will do. See you in a minute.' I spoke normally too; the last thing I wanted to do was become a problem for him in my own right.

First, though, I put away the shopping. Then I went up to the middle bedroom with the fabulous Jacobean fireplace which was once more Emery's and mine. I washed and changed my old t-shirt for a new yellow silk top. Before I left, I put my head into the guardroom and told Bob I was just nipping round to the manor house for half an hour. He nodded cheerfully, too kind to ask questions.

I walked out into the dreamy summer evening, which would have soothed less jangling nerves than mine. Yet again the difference in temperature between gatehouse and the air outside struck me forcibly. Would the exorcism change that? Of course an old stone building would always be chilly, but all the same…

The taller child with the dirty white scarf on her head was in front of me, carrying a wooden pail in each hand. She was still barefoot as all the children had been, and her little feet squelched in the mud. She walked slowly. No doubt the pails were heavy. Beneath her old brown shift her dirty legs were thin. Either she was half starved or she was growing fast, or both.

The taller child with the dirty white scarf on her head was in front of me. I was back in the sixteenth century, with no more warning than before.

Only an instinct for survival prevented my frightened scream. I looked round frenziedly, saw people – serving men and women by their drab clothes – suddenly all around me. I raised my arms to ward them off. But none of them seemed to see me. They were going about their business unperturbed, carrying chickens, furniture, baskets of eggs and loaves and fish. I glanced up at the sun, which was almost overhead. So it was earlier in the day than it had been in my own time. The door to the Hall stood open. Perhaps there was a feast in prospect, the same feast they had been preparing for when Freya glimpsed them on the day of the accident.

I moved cagily to the manor house wall and stood with my back to it, cowering, still convinced at first that someone would see me. But gradually it dawned on me that, though I could feel the warm stone behind me, I was, in effect, a ghost. And very few people in my own time had the ability to see ghosts. Perhaps it was the same in reverse and there had been no need for my panic the last time I had been in this world. With this growing certainty, my terror began to recede and my curiosity increased.

This time I went into the Hall, which rang with the moving of benches and the hanging of colourful painted cloths, the grunting of people at work. It was hot, filled with the sweat of many bodies. I saw Anna Mervyn again, as though she had only just walked in after speaking angrily to Bilson on the gatehouse threshold. This was quite likely the case. I laughed suddenly; these people might have been sixteenth century puppets kept for my amusement with no life when I was not here.

The funny people.

Anna Mervyn was speaking sharply to a small, jowly man in dark clothing which looked newer, and better, than that worn by the servants. I reckoned he was the household steward. I wondered whether Anna always spoke sharply, or whether Bilson's refusal to let her see Francis had put her in an uncharacteristically bad mood. Something about her mouth, which turned down at the corners, told me she was frequently sharp.

Another woman entered the Hall, from an internal door in a different position than I remembered in my brief sojourn there. From her gown of fine grey wool I saw she was a gentlewoman like Anna, but younger. Was this Isabella Raymond, Dominic's wife, or a guest? Fair curls strayed from her lacy coif. She had delicate features which would have been appealing had they not been marred by a wine coloured birthmark on her left cheek and nose. She moved gracefully towards Anna, who turned to her too matter of factly, it seemed to me, for her to be a guest. The two gentlewomen left by the same internal door the younger had come through.

Deciding to follow, to see what the rest of the manor house looked like before the classical alterations, I moved quickly to the same door. Would the funny people see the door open and close? I didn't care. Intoxicated with the power of being invisible, I skipped away from two serving men rotating a long bench and dodged laughing around women carrying piles of linen. I reached for the door handle.

What stopped me? Sixth sense? The hair rising on the back of my head? I think most people know when they are being watched. For wretched seconds, I dreaded to look round. Not Clement. Please, not Clement. Would he be able to touch me, seize me as he had his brother? Surely, no one would believe him if he claimed to see me. They would think him bewitched…

This gave me enough courage to turn round slowly. I scanned the busy, toiling mass of people in the Hall – it should have been a cheerful scene, but somehow it was not – and saw no one looking at me. Clement was not in the Hall and never had been. It had been my imagination, nothing more.

Then movement near the door caught my eye. The tall child with the dirty white scarf must have come into the Hall because she was now leaving it. She must have put down her pails down because she was leaving quickly. Running, in fact, as if something had frightened her. I saw two men exchange glances and shrug, tolerantly enough, as if to say, what can you expect of a backward child...

I had frightened her. She was a funny person who could see ghosts.

'Hey!' I ran after her. I don't know what I thought I was going to do if I caught her up. 'Stop! It's all right! Stop!'

You don't interfere if you go back in time – that's obvious – but there I was, haring after this dirty, skinny child, hampered in my sandals by mud which her bare feet now skimmed. She had had a good start and she was going away from me, towards the gatehouse. Leave it, I thought, you'll just frighten her more, she'll forget she's seen you, and your jeans and your watch...

I didn't stop. She went on running. Then, a few yards beyond the gatehouse door where Anna Mervyn had argued with Bilson, she stumbled with exhaustion, falling on her face. Her little white scarf came askew, revealing tufted chestnut hair with bald patches. Oh God, I thought, the poor mite's got alopecia, that's why they think she's backward. I reached down to lift her and she shrieked, trying to struggle free.

'It's all right.' I knelt, mud forgotten, put my hands on her bony little shoulders and tried to quieten her. 'It's all right, I'll not harm you…'

She stopped struggling and turned on her side so that I saw her profile. She had brown eyes in a thin, tearstained face. Her grubby fingers crept towards my knees. Denim, of course, which she had never seen before.

'Jeans,' I said, as if she were a toddler learning to speak, as if I would ever be able to help her from a distance of five centuries. I regretted it instantly. If she came out with an unfamiliar word she would be thought even more backward.

A toddler would have repeated the word, but this child did not. I felt relief at first. That perhaps I had not interfered with the course of history after all. Her fingers reached my knees, touched the denim. She pulled away as if the material had stung her and began to cry.

'Hey, it won't harm you,' I said.

Then I looked at her more closely.

The hair rose on the back of my neck again. Abruptly, I knew. What I should have realised all along. Why there had never been any trace of her. I snatched her up and turned her to face me fully. She looked at me with her father's haunted eyes.

'Freya,' I said.

CHAPTER TWENTY

I WAS overcome. For Nicholas. For myself. I simply put my arms round the sobbing child and held her, sobbing with relief myself, blessing that sixth sense which had made me follow her.

No wonder she had run away from me. The sight of me, a woman in twenty-first century dress – jeans – must have been too painful, a half-remembered dream from her own time which must have seemed like a nightmare. What name had they given her, if they had given her one at all?

How had she gone back in time? How had it happened? Had Artus collided with soldiers from the sixteenth century that evening? With the rider on the black horse, as I had almost done in reverse? But witnesses had seen her still clutching Artus's neck long after Sophia had fallen. Or had she still been visible in our own time for a while when already in the past? Then why had Artus not gone back in time also?

It didn't matter now, I only needed to know why she had never returned to her own time. It was fourteen months, for Christ's sake. Beneath my relief, fear gnawed at me that having encountered her I might now be stuck also, that Nicholas would never know what happened to her. If I got Freya back, would she adjust? Fourteen months was a long time in a child who had been six and was still only eight. How could her absence be explained? I didn't care, so long as I could get her back.

If only I had recognised her the first time I had seen her, so much taller than the sixteenth century children! I had returned to our present then, avoiding that red car by inches, Alistair running towards me. If he had seen Freya with me, he might have died of shock…

'Freya,' I said, almost laughing, 'Do you remember Uncle Alistair? He's so good and kind…' Inspiration. 'Madogany? Do you remember Madogany?'

It struck me that if we didn't get back, I was only making it worse for her. But it was too late. She was nodding her head and crying harder, wanting that big, furry, chocolate friend to cuddle, not me, a stranger. I stroked what hair she still had, so luxuriant in that photograph, its filthy scantiness the physical manifestation of the stress she must have been through, finding herself in the harsh, alien land of the funny people after witnessing her mother's death.

'I'll get you back, Freya,' I said.

So there I was, committed to a promise. I felt instantly that I had made a mistake. And she didn't even know my name yet.

'I'm Imogen,' I said. 'I know your…'

Daddy. He still loves you. His heart is broken without you. I couldn't say it. I dreaded her reaction too much. If I couldn't get her back to him, it would only increase the cruelty of her life in this fearful time.

'I'm Imogen,' I repeated. 'Come on, hush now. I'm going to help you...'

A shadow edged into my consciousness. Francis's stooped, old gaoler Bilson was approaching the gatehouse door, a bundle of staves in his hand. It made me realise that all this time there had been people nearby, going about their business for the feast as before. They could not see me, but not one of them had come to find out what the matter was with the child crying on the ground. Didn't they care? Had they never wondered where she had appeared from so suddenly? Were they simply accustomed to her, a little simpleton tolerated so long as she carried out her menial tasks? For the sixteenth century, I suppose, it was a form of kindness. They could have sold her to a travelling fair as a freak.

Bilson didn't see me either. He could hardly have missed Freya, but he ignored her and turned for the gatehouse. Freya, though, had seen him. He must have frightened her at some point in the last fourteen months, for she jumped up suddenly, taking me by surprise, and bolted.

'Freya!'

I ran after her, but my blasted ankle had taken enough and was now hampering me. Oh God, I couldn't lose her. Not now. Suppose I went back to my own time alone, having seen her? The guilt would be unendurable.

'Freya! I'm here to help you!'

She was taking me towards the woods where I had first glimpsed her. I knew I would lose her there. 'Freya, please! *Daddy wants you back!*'

She stopped, turned. I saw the anguish in her little face, then she was off again in a storm of weeping. Soon she had gone altogether. I searched and searched for her, calling her, but hobbling as I was I stood no chance. Eventually, I sank down to my knees, my face in my hands, bitterly conscious that I had made everything worse for her. She might never come back to Deverell. Even if she tried to, she might be lost in those woods. She might starve or be taken by that travelling fair.

Presently, I tightened the strapping on my ankle, stood up drearily. Go back, I told myself. If you get back to Deverell in the twenty-first century you can at least tell Nicholas his daughter is alive…

I had another unwelcome thought. Was Freya meant to be alive? Should she have died like her mother, falling from the big, galloping horse in her own time? If I brought her back, would she survive? Oh God, what was worse? Suffering in the sixteenth century or oblivion in the twenty-first? It was a horrible dilemma.

I went back slowly, listening to the birds sing in that godforsaken, lovely wood, seeing smoke from the manor house rising above the trees in the intense heat. I was still in the past, then, with no idea when – if – I would return to my own time…

The gatehouse door stood open.

Perhaps Bilson had deposited his bundle of staves and gone off for more. Perhaps this was before Francis had been captured; I was too ignorant of the sequence of events leading to his capture to make an estimate and nothing about these cracks in time seemed to be chronological. But I took my chance anyway, looking around me at the busy, oblivious people before hobbling up the step and into the dark gatehouse, my eyes adjusting slowly.

I peered into the guardroom, which looked as it had on my last visit, dirty and laden with weaponry. No food basket stood on the table this time, instead an old breastplate, the metal rusty and dented. I went on upstairs. There was no handrail to lean on, not even a rope. I kept my weight on my good ankle and managed somehow. As before, the doors to what were now the drawing room and middle bedroom were shut. My heart beat faster with exertion and anticipation as I went up beyond them. There was a rope here at least, where the windows stopped. It felt greasily unreliable, but I clutched at it.

Jack's door was open.

I took the final steps slowly, trying to quiet my breathing, and walked into Francis Deverell's vile, stinking prison at last.

He was beneath the window as I had expected. Only his head, back and shoulders were free to move. They were keeping him in a sitting position, in crudely made but heavy stocks. Perhaps these stocks were always here, a symbol of Clement's authority; chances were he was a local magistrate – in the sixteenth century the gentry often were – and that this place served as a lock-up. Francis's legs splayed out in torn and filthy breeches. I had expected a cassock, but quickly realised that he would of course have been in hiding. He wore a ragged, bloodstained shirt and sleeveless brown jerkin, He was dozing. His dark, silver streaked, bearded head had fallen on the upper stock holding his wrists. Urine glistened on the floorboards between his legs. An empty tin bowl lay upturned and stained nearby. I saw no sign of a drinking vessel.

Tears in my eyes, I came as close as I could.

'Father Deverell,' I said softly. 'Father Francis.'

Did I expect him, of all people, to be aware of me? He had heard Jack praying with him, after all. But he didn't raise his head. Don't wake him, I thought, ashamed, he has found a moment's rest. I drew back, fighting disappointment, and examined the rest of the room. It was bare, the sloping rafters crawling with woodlice. I recoiled, turned back to Francis and managed to kneel.

'They're going to bring you peace,' I said. 'There are two priests here, Father Draycott and Father Coll. Your faith never died out. It's all over the world. It's still in England. Father Draycott and Father Coll are going to bring you peace.'

I was speaking for my own comfort, of course, since it seemed I could bring him none. He stirred, shivering. For a hopeful moment I thought it was on account of me. But when he raised his head he looked past me. Young Jack had unwittingly been right. Frighteningly, Francis's thin, melancholy and feverish face would have reminded me of Nicholas had it not been swollen and bloody about the lips and bruised over the left eye. I don't know what he looked at – I glanced over my shoulder and saw nothing – but he half smiled. I suppose his fever had made him delirious. If he saw something to comfort him, I was glad of it.

I examined the stocks which held him prisoner. I hadn't the remotest clue how such things worked, only that he must have been in agony. If I could have got him out of them I would have – and to hell with history. I even began yanking at the top one, but it was heavy and seemed to be fixed, presumably hammered into slots I could not see. Francis started. I realised he had felt the wood move as I yanked at it.

'Father Francis,' I said.

I tugged the wood again, harder, determined that he notice me. Why was it they could all see Freya and not me? Because she had been here longer? Was it because they could see her that she had not been able to get back to her own time?

'Father Francis!' Shouting now. He had begun to pray aloud, in Latin, his eyes closed. Had I frightened him, or had he taken it as a sign from God?

Hesitantly, I reached out to touch him. Why did I hesitate? Because he was a priest, unused to women? Or because I was afraid he would not feel my touch?

'Francis.'

A woman's voice, but not mine. I jumped, spun round. His sister-in-law Anna Mervyn stood in the doorway, her sallow features working with emotion. Francis's eyes opened. I saw dread in them, for Anna, not for himself, as I realised by his words.

'Go away, before he sees you…' A wheezing croak, not a voice.

'Do you think I fear Clement's knave? These are his. He can do without, for once.' Anna walked rapidly towards Francis, a horn cup and wooden bowl in her hands. There must have been broth in the bowl; I smelled meat and vegetables. She began to spoon it into him as though he had been a child, too quickly, for he must have been half starved, but she was evidently determined to get it into him even if it choked him. It did choke him and when she had to pause she looked impatiently at him. She reminded me of Marcia suddenly and I laughed in spite of everything.

'Dominic is returned,' she said.

'No, I won't have him risk himself...'

'The mute got to Tychborne.'

Tychborne. A person? A place? I could not tell. But in the neighbourhood almost certainly, or she would not have said that Dominic had returned. And to use a mute, who could not blab or be questioned easily, was clever if heartless.

'He must not risk himself,' Francis said, 'nor must Raymond.'

Anna shook her head scornfully. 'Tom Raymond wrings his hands and weeps and does nothing.'

'I thank God,' Francis said.

I supposed Tom Raymond was the father or brother of Dominic's wife, Isabella, and the ancestor of Grace from the riding stables.

'God will not thank him,' Anna retorted. 'I will not stop Dominic. I could not and I will not.'

The feeding resumed, vigorously, then she held the horn cup for him, which presumably contained beer. No more words were exchanged during the process. I had the impression no more were needed, that these two people knew each other very well. They were of an age. He would have been a young priest when she was a young second wife to his eldest brother, William,

Dominic's father. Though his parish was in Southwark, he must have visited Deverell.

'I'll bring you more,' she said when the bowl was empty.

'No, Anna, no...'

But she took one of the thin hands which dangled from the upper stock and held it between both her own strong fingers.

'God has not forgotten you,' she said.

He did not reply. He looked down at her fingers, then up at her face with bloodshot but steadfast eyes. It was a quiet, affectionate silence in that appalling place. Then, far below, a creak on those treacherous wooden steps. I found myself spinning round faster than Anna did. I ran to the threshold, looked down. At first I saw nothing, hearing only grunts, shortness of breath. Then, more steps starting upstairs. At least two men. I already knew who they were. Bilson and his master, Francis's brother and Anna's brother-in-law, Clement.

CHAPTER TWENTY-ONE

ANNA was on her feet, defiant and angry, standing protectively in front of the stocks. Clement entered the attic first. In spite of myself, I huddled away into the corner where Jack's old brown chest of drawers and cupboard should have been, but he was like the rest; I was unseen.

'So you've found him,' he said to Anna.

I had not been able to distinguish Clement's features by night. In daylight I saw a resemblance to Francis. But there was more weight on him, more redness and choler in his face, more forcefulness in his gestures.

'Yes, Clement, I have found him and seen how you keep him. You bring shame on this family, brother.'

'He is a traitor.'

'He is your brother.'

'Get out of here, woman.'

'I will not,' Anna said.

'This place is forbidden.'

'I am no servant,' she snapped.

'I am master here.'

'I am no servant.'

They eyed each other warily, with open hostility.

This was a confrontation I sensed had been long in coming. I could imagine the tensions which Francis's capture had brought into the open. Clement might have been in legal possession of Deverell since Dominic's treason with Norfolk eleven years before, but it sounded as though he was not yet accepted. And in all likelihood it was Anna who had led the resistance. Had she lived here all that time? There was dower property, but perhaps Clement had not dared send her away...

'You are but a woman, madam, subject to your Queen.' As he turned slightly, I noticed that one side of his face was caved in; he had lost more teeth on that side. He motioned angrily for Bilson to leave the attic. The servant did so, shutting the door, though I reckon the old reptile listened behind it.

'Subject to your Queen, madam,' Clement repeated. What did he suspect? Did he know that Dominic was in the neighbourhood, at or with this Tychborne?

'I am Queen Elizabeth's good subject,' Anna said.

'You are a Papist, madam.'

'I am Queen Elizabeth's good subject, as is this man.' She pointed vigorously to Francis, who had his eyes shut, as if disassociating himself from the quarrel. I saw the priest in him now, his serenity while the other two quarrelled. 'You think, brother, to look well in the Queen's eyes by keeping him in shame like this?'

'He is a traitor, madam.'

'He is your brother!'

'Aye, madam, to my shame!'

Anna drew a hard, difficult breath, the first sign of weakness I had seen in her. There were deep bags beneath her eyes, the sign perhaps of more than sleeplessness, her sallow skin was tinged with yellow and her fine, dark gown hung from her bony frame. I wanted to step forward, put my arm around her, lead her from this ghastly attic. What could she do, a woman in the sixteenth century? Yet the Queen was a woman…

'You bring disgrace on the Deverell name,' she said. 'Do you think your great friends at court will honour you for this? They will take your prisoner and spill his blood for you, but they will not think well of you for it.'

'We are already marked, madam. We have been marked for years because of your stepson. You cherished that boy too much, madam, you encouraged him in treason and rebellion!'

He could only mean Dominic and his involvement with Norfolk's revolt. Anna pursed her lips, shook her head and turned away. It seemed to be an old accusation, one she had tired of.

'Tonight, when they dine in my house,' Clement said, 'you will see how great men honour me. You are but a vexation here, madam.'

'Leave her be, brother,' Francis said.

Clement swung round on him, fist raised. 'I'll take no orders from a traitor!'

Francis did not flinch, but stared him out. Abruptly, Clement swung back to Anna, who still had her back to him. 'You admit it then? You encouraged the boy! You encouraged him!' Pointing furiously towards Francis.

'I admit nothing. I am the Queen's loyal subject.' Her voice was weary, but she must have known how dangerous this conversation was. If Clement could betray his younger brother he could betray his elder brother's wife.

'I will have you out this house, madam,' he said.

She faced him at that. 'You wouldn't dare!' But I saw doubt in her eyes. Perhaps Clement had bided his time until now in a household where the servants might have held to the old ways. Francis's arrest was his chance to purge it.

'I'll dare,' he said. 'Think you I don't know about your idol worship and idolatry behind my back? You keep an evil chamber, madam!'

'Peace, brother,' Francis said. 'Leave her be. She is sick…'

This time Clement's fist hit home, knocking Francis sideways in the stocks. Anna screamed, running towards them, hanging onto Clement's arm to prevent another blow. 'Stop this cruelty, brother!'

Clement flung her off. She stumbled backwards, towards me. I caught her. I know I should have stepped aside and let her fall, but I couldn't help it. She was old for her time and sick and in anguish. I felt her bones beneath the wool of her gown, which smelled of aniseed. Her little yellowing ruff brushed my ear. Seconds later, I had her upright once more and she turned, her worn face illuminated by joy, tears spilling from her eyes. She dropped to her knees, her fingers at her ebony crucifix.

There was only one explanation; in her distress, her desperation, she had mistaken me for an angel, unseen, but definitely on the side of the Catholics.

While she prayed, I practically lost my nerve, realising how stupid I had been. I almost bolted from the attic in my fright, but that would have drawn more attention to myself. I stayed where I was, shaking, shrinking further into the corner, as Clement hurled more invective at Francis.

'Enough.' Anna was on her feet, resolute again, filled with certainty, thanks to my idiocy. She walked over to Clement. 'Enough, brother. You damn your soul more with every word.' Such was the alteration in her voice and face that even Clement ceased his shouting and stared at her. She placed her hand on Francis's shoulder. 'God has just now given me a sign, brother. He will not let us fall.' I was certain now that she had mistaken me for an angel. Her voice hardened as she turned to Clement. 'Francis will be a martyr in heaven. When you come to be judged, God will know what you have done. He will see that you have the foulest heart that ever blackened this family.'

'Your Papist signs mean nothing,' Clement spat, but there was less assurance in his voice, reminding me that he had broken with his childhood faith, exchanging it for another kind of security. How much did it trouble him?

'When you shoved me, brother, He did not let me fall,' Anna answered confidently. It was a threat. Clement grew paler. 'His angels have held me in their arms,' she said gently to Francis. 'It is a sign.'

Did he believe her? I thought not, though I am not sure why, but he smiled at her, obviously glad that she had found peace. I was reminded of Nicholas's smile when Jack showed him his stitches.

'God's blood, woman, you lie!' Clement shouted.

Anna smiled. 'Why, brother Clement, I pity you.' She touched Francis's cheek with her hand and made the sign of the cross over him. 'We shall meet in a better world, brother Francis.' She took her crucifix from her own neck and put it round his. Then she walked quietly from the attic.

'She lies!' Clement roared when she had gone.

'Think you so, brother?' Francis sounded almost detached, as though he were not in ignominy and jeopardy. I suppose he was already preparing to leave this world. He must have helped hundreds to do the same and now his own time approached.

'They come for you tonight.' Clement leaned towards him. 'They will take you to London. There, they will put you to the question. We will see how your Papist angels support you then.'

He wrenched the crucifix from Francis's neck and stormed out, slamming the door. I heard him bellowing down the staircase for Bilson, who would presumably be in trouble because Anna had managed to get into the gatehouse. A considerable amount of trouble, I hoped, since it would cover the sound of my opening the attic door. I did not want to leave Francis, but I must try again to find Freya.

Thinking himself alone, Francis had put his head down on the stocks and resumed his Latin prayer.

'Sing,' I said aloud. 'Please, sing for me…'

Nothing happened, of course. So I walked towards him. I reached out my hand, aching to touch him. If he thought me an unseen angel too, it would comfort him, make him certain that Anna had been right. But I knew nothing about Catholicism and he was a religious while she was not. I did not know what his reasoning might be. I recalled his reaction when I had yanked at the upper stock. Suppose he thought me a demon, sent to tempt him? I could not bear that.

'Father Francis,' I said again. 'Please, sing.'

Of course he did not. But presently he looked up and beyond me, as he had done before, at his own source of comfort, and his face grew radiant again. As before, I saw nothing. Clement's bellowing was increasing downstairs. Time to take my chance. I slipped out, glancing behind. Francis's eyes were still rapt; he had not even noticed my opening the door.

I crept downstairs, heart thudding as I neared the ground floor. There were scuffling yells from the guardroom now as well as shouts, and the sound of blows. It sounded as though Clement was chasing Bilson round the room with one of the staves I had seen stacked up where Emery's bed should have been. Something dark on the stairs caught my eye. It was Anna's crucifix. I snatched it up – interfering unrepentantly with history again – and went on. I ran past the guardroom and out into the mud.

Straight into two servants carrying a trestle table. It winded me, naturally, while they dropped the table in shock.

'Sorry,' I gasped, as if they could hear me. I left them looking all about them, puzzled and scared, while I stumbled on. It hurt. I hoped I hadn't cracked a rib. I grew aware of my ankle again and paused for breath, trying to think. Had Freya come back to the manor house or gone further away?

'Freya!' I shouted in despair. 'Freya!'

The sound of hooves. I shrank against the manor house wall. Every time someone else appeared I ran the risk of being seen. Sooner or later, a newcomer would be able to see me. It was a brown horse, not the larger, black one I had seen on my previous visit to the past, but I knew immediately that this rider in a buff jerkin was important from the way he clattered past me. A dirty youth appeared from the Hall to catch his horse and he dismounted rapidly. He looked to be a soldier, seasoned and weather beaten, and I guessed he brought news for Clement.

'Where's your master?' he called to the youth, who was now leading the horse away. The youth turned, looking frightened.

'I'll have him fetched, sir…'

No need. The gatehouse door slammed behind me, the bar thudding into place. Clement walked rapidly passed me. He must have heard the horseman arrive, so Bilson had a reprieve and Francis was once more isolated.

'Sir Clement…' The horseman bowed and took a thick brown packet from inside his jerkin.

'Aye. Come inside.' Clement snatched the packet, nodded towards the Hall and strode towards it. The horseman followed him.

'You!' Clement stopped suddenly, almost causing the horseman to cannon into him. 'Little lack-a-tongue! Come here!'

For a moment I thought Clement had seen me, but my dismay turned to terror, for it was Freya he was shouting at. She had just emerged from the Hall with a leather bag too large for her little arms. So she had come back, after all. But lacking a tongue? Had the shock of what she had been through made her mute?

'Freya!' I called. 'Over here! Stay with me!'

She looked at me uncertainly with a tear stained face, causing Clement to stare my way but see nothing.

'Come here!' he bellowed at her.

It was my fault. If I had not distracted her, she might have managed to run away from Clement. Every instinct I had told me to run to the frightened, bewildered child and lift her up. But Clement and the servants who had stopped to watch couldn't see me. They would think her possessed, lifted by a demon. So I had to stand helplessly by while Clement went to her, flung down the bag and boxed her ears.

'I'll make you speak!' he shouted.

He lifted her himself, like a demon, tucked her crying under his arm and strode on into the Hall. I stood looking after him, thunderstruck, remembering now what Anna had said to Francis. Then I started running after him.

The mute got to Tychborne.

Anna had used Freya as a messenger, to help a man who would die a traitor, and Clement knew about it.

CHAPTER TWENTY-TWO

THE Hall, which was still filled with servants, grew silent as Clement strode through it with Freya under his arm, the horseman following.

'Back to your work!' Clement roared at them.

He snatched up a lantern, flame inside horn, and flung open one of the internal doors. Following, I found myself in a dark, narrow passage and almost immediately descending stone steps into a narrower one. I kept a mental note of our route somehow as we turned corners, stale air rushing past me as Clement hurried on. Soon I was in a barrel vaulted, earthen floored cellar, its sole illumination the lantern which Clement set on a narrow stone ledge. I guessed we had come down to the level of the original manor house. Now an empty cellar without a door, this might have been part of the original kitchens; a shadowy archway suggested a bigger room beyond it. In other circumstances it would have been fascinating, but I could only look at the sobbing Freya, whom Clement now set down and pinned into a corner with his foot while he tore open the package.

Think, I told myself, distraught. What am I in this time? A spirit? A poltergeist? I had a huge advantage in that Clement couldn't see me, the horseman couldn't see me. Freya could. She was looking at me now, crying in my direction, openly seeking my help. She's recognised my clothes now, I thought, she knows I'm from her world. She can remember her own time…

I felt the burden of responsibility. If I didn't get her back home, it would be even harder for her than if she had never seen me. But first I had to stop Clement questioning her right now and I didn't see how I would manage it. He was perusing the contents of the package, his mouth moving silently with the words.

The lantern. They would see it move, think me a poltergeist. If I didn't get Freya out of here, they would accuse her of devilry as well as spying, but it was my only chance. There was no other object in the cellar.

'I'm going to grab the lamp!' I shouted to Freya. 'If Clement drops his foot run towards me! Okay?' I thought I saw comprehension in her desperate eyes. 'Good girl. Just run towards me. That's all you have to do.'

'It's not enough!' Clement bellowed suddenly. The noise of him in that confined space was appalling. He hurled the packet to the damp earth. The sound echoed and the horseman quailed back over the cellar threshold; I guessed Clement's temper to be well known. 'What do they think I am? How can I stop treason with so little horse and foot? I need more men, now!'

So far as I was aware, the only treason afoot was the rescue of his own brother from the gallows by their nephew. It didn't seem treason to my twenty-first century sensibilities, but whatever the horseman knew, he was too sensible to argue; it was not his job. He moved backwards again, into the passage, leaving Clement to take his rage out on Freya.

'Coward!' I yelled at him.

Worryingly, the messenger seemed to sense my presence. At least, he turned towards me, puzzled, as if he had heard a distant sound. But I had no time to make sense of it, for Clement had dragged poor little Freya out from behind him. He patted her clothing all over, found nothing incriminating on her.

'Well, little lack-a-tongue?' he bellowed. 'Have you taken it already? What have you to tell me, eh?'

He was hurting her, forcing her arm back from her shoulder. She screamed and went on screaming, struggling and ducking her head. I looked round frantically for some means to help her.

He raised his hand. 'Where have you been, eh?'

She let out a wail and closed her eyes.

'Stop it, you bastard!'

I ran forward and seized the lantern, swinging its brightness in his eyes. He cried out in amazement and fright, letting go of Freya.

'Come on, Freya!'

I seized her hand, pulling her with me. The swinging lantern in my other hand threw mad shadows as we barged past the horseman and out into the passage.

With my ankle injury, she was faster than I was. I could have let her run ahead of me, but I dared not let go of her. I wanted to keep her with me until I came back to our own time, so that she would come with me. So I kept up with her as best I could, gritting my teeth through the pain. I glanced back, saw no pursuit yet. Soon, though, Clement would recover and start searching for a witch…

'I'm a friend of your daddy's,' I panted as we stumbled down the dank, narrow passages, more mad shadows on the narrow walls. 'If you stay with me, I'll get you back to him…'

It was a promise. It committed me. One must always keep one's promises to a child. Freya looked across at me and I saw the hope in her eyes. There was still no pursuit. Perhaps Clement and the horseman were too afraid to leave the cellar. It would be pitch dark in there now without the lantern. I hoped savagely that he was wetting himself with fear.

'Take the lantern,' I said, slowing as we approached the internal door to the Hall. 'The funny people won't think it strange if you carry it. If I did it would look as though it was floating. You're the only person who can see me…'

She understood at once, tear stained but nodding her head, and took the lantern from me carefully.

'Walk normally,' I said. Would anyone wonder how she had got away from Clement? Would anyone care?

We pushed the door open together and with my arm round her shoulder she walked through the noise and bustle steadily, threading through the busy servants, none of whom glanced in her direction. Anger grew in me. She had been among them fourteen months and it seemed that none of them, not one, felt any concern or affection for her. Was it because she had become mute?

Or because they knew she was being used as a messenger in treason? They dared not be seen to be with her lest they implicate themselves...

'Good,' I said. 'Outside. Keep walking.'

I had no idea where we would go. I knew only that we had to stay out of Clement's sight until we got back to the twenty-first century. How long would it take? Last time I had been here overnight.

Shouts behind us made me turn. It sounded as though Clement had come to his senses and initiated pursuit.

'Run,' I said. 'Run!'

Freya bolted, of course, running past the gatehouse door. It wasn't surprising; she must now be even more afraid of Clement than she had been before. I couldn't hold her; it would have meant using force and I didn't want her to be afraid of me too. She had to trust me if I was to get her back to our own world. So I hobbled after her.

More shouts, oddly far away. I glanced backwards all the same with an alarming idea that I was visible now. Perhaps the longer I stayed in the sixteenth century the more visible I would become. Perhaps Freya had been invisible at first...

She was getting away from me. She had turned left sharply and bolted into the woods I had been in before, where I had seen her with the other children without recognising her. 'Slow down,' I panted. 'My ankle's hurt...'

I don't think she even heard me. At least, she paid no heed. And of course the wood was more uneven underfoot than the mud. But I had to keep her in sight. Suppose I went back to our own time without her?

Nicholas would never forgive me. As if I would ever forgive myself.

'Freya!' I hissed. 'Stay nearer me!'

But she was already gone. I looked round frantically, saw nothing but trees. They seemed more alive than in my own time; even on the edge of the wood they had a secretive, sheltering air, protecting Freya.

'I'm here to help her,' I said aloud, half afraid, wholly exasperated.

The trees did not answer.

I listened, heard no sounds behind me. We seemed to have shaken Clement off, suspiciously easily, I reckoned, but I could do nothing about that. I could only hope that the shouting we had heard had not been connected to Freya, but it seemed unlikely.

Tychborne, I thought. If it or he was near, she might be making for there or him. Would Clement anticipate this, send men by another route to catch her?

'Freya!' I began wandering about the wood, disorientated once more. I expected to stumble across villagers' cottages any moment, inhabited by the parents of the other children I had seen. They would pay rent to Clement along with God knows what other manorial dues he still exacted. 'Freya!' I whispered.

Cold steel at my neck. I was a twenty-first century woman, but I had no difficulty recognising it and froze in terror.

'Be still,' a man said behind me.

I hadn't planned to be anything else. I even put my hands up, though I didn't know whether the sixteenth century recognised this as a gesture of surrender. My legs nearly dropped me to the ground there and then, and I trembled, because whoever he was he could see me…

'Move…' He seized my arm, thrust me forward in front of him. I stumbled ahead of him, forcing myself to think. He seemed to be on his own. He hadn't called to anyone else. Was it possible he wasn't one of Clement's men? No, don't get your hopes up, Imogen. In any case, why would he be friendly, whoever he was? He was pressing a sharp blade into my neck…

I tripped. He hauled me upright. My neck hurt now. The blade had pricked into it as I tripped. Ankle, ribs and now neck.

'I can't walk far,' I said angrily.

Why say that? How arrogant, how stupid could I be? As if the realities of the sixteenth century did not apply to me. Not surprisingly, my captor's grip on my arm tightened. 'Quiet,' he growled.

I felt my own blood trickle warm down my shoulder as we continued, going deeper into that sinister, strangely silent wood. I glanced at the hand gripping my arm. Youngish, I reckoned, about my own age. Not work worn and with finger nails less dirty than I would have expected. A gentleman then, but that didn't make him any less of a threat. On the contrary, it made it likelier he would take a rapid decision about my immediate future…

Then I saw Freya, peeping out from behind what seemed to be a wall. She didn't look frightened.

'Who is he?' I demanded, as if she could speak. She ignored the question, bobbing back behind the wall. I was almost upon it now. My captor shoved me towards it and I saw a ruin overrun by bramble bushes and ferns. Only the corners and two low side walls still stood. Much of it must have been raided for Clement's renovation of the manor house.

'In.' He pushed me into what once have been a small chamber. Here the bushes had been partially cleared. I saw, not a peasant's earthen floor, but rough flagstones. Worn niches for vessels still stood in the walls. It had been some sort of tiny religious foundation, I guessed, dissolved fifty years or so before by Queen Elizabeth's father, Henry VIII. A hermit's place, maybe, or a chantry established to pray for the souls of the Deverells.

'Is this Tychborne?' I asked Freya.

She looked at me blankly.

Perhaps I was wrong. Or perhaps they had never told her the name of the place she had taken messages to. That seemed the likeliest explanation for where I was. She had run here for shelter. She saw my captor as a protector. But if Clement knew about it, his soldiers would be upon us any moment.

'Let me go,' I said, for my captor was still holding me in front of him. 'You don't understand. You've been found out. They're onto you…'

It was interfering in history with a vengeance. It didn't occur to me at the time; I was too afraid. For answer, he found both my arms and forced them behind my back, hard. 'Tell me your name,' he snarled.

'Imogen Webb.'

The silence of surprise. I had disconcerted my captor. It dawned on me that with my jeans and shoulder length hair he had thought me a boy. Suddenly, he swung me round to face him and I saw his face for the first time.

'Dominic,' I said.

CHAPTER TWENTY-THREE

He was of course seeing my face for the first time since taking me captive. I realised that he remembered me from the Lady Chapel and Bishop White's funeral by night. But so far as he was concerned that had been twenty two years ago and I was unchanged. He simply gaped at me. He must have thought me a witch.

'You've been found out,' I said. 'Clement knows.'

He went on gaping at me. He was so different from the sturdy, round faced boy in the Lady Chapel. I knew that he was now thirty four, but he looked older, his face lined and soured by suffering. He wore leather jerkin and breeches, muddy from riding, and his thick, dark hair was windblown.

'Clement knows!' I shouted at him.

Freya evidently caught my urgency. She took Dominic's hand and shook it. The fearless gesture told me that though he might have used her as a messenger this brooding man had never hurt her. He looked down at her now, with a faint smile, then back at me.

'He sent you, didn't he?' he whispered.

It was somehow obvious to me that Dominic did not mean Clement had sent me. Beyond that, I was clueless and in a dilemma. With the lessening of fear, my sense of history was catching up with me, much too late. Whatever I said might affect my own time, most of all Nicholas's life...And why could Dominic see me? Did it mean everyone would see me now, or just him?

'No one sent me,' I said. 'What is this place called? Is this Tychborne? Is Tychborne a person or a place?'

Suspicion stole back into his face. Had I been on his side I would not have needed to ask this question.

'What are you?' he demanded, suddenly brutal. Brutal and, I realised, disappointed. He seemed to feel in some way betrayed. Had he thought me an angel and now suspected I was a devil? Or had he expected to meet someone else?

'I'm Imogen,' I said. 'I'm from... ' There was nothing I could say. *I'm from your future, my past, where your son inherited from your childless Uncle Clement and your faith survived...* A future which might now alter anyway because I had just gatecrashed history.

'Tell me who you are!' he yelled, pushing me suddenly into an old, ruined corner. His hand groped roughly at my breasts, not in a sexual way, but as if to check I was a real woman, not a youth disguised as one. My breasts were never large, but they were there all right. I realised that my sex was protecting me from further violence for the moment, but that might not last. Sixteenth century men were hardly renowned for tenderness to women.

'Who sent you?' he demanded. 'What do you know about me?'

'Please,' I said. 'I heard your stepmother and your uncle Francis talking. You've been discovered. You have to get away from Deverell.'

He looked at me, or rather past me, as if for the first time considering what I was actually saying. 'Where were they?' he demanded.

'In the attic where Clement's holding Francis,' I said. 'Anna must have got in while Bilson's back was turned.'

'Who sent you?'

'No one. I came by myself. I'm a…traveller.'

He looked down at me, examining my jeans for the first time. He reached out as if to touch the denim, then stopped. 'Where are you travelled from?'

'London,' I said.

His dark, level brows shot up. It made him more suspicious, of course. London was where Queen Elizabeth was and it was the city where Protestantism had taken early root long before she came to the throne.

'Why are you dressed like that?'

'To travel fast,' I said. 'Will you heed my warning or not?' When he half turned away from me, I gave up and put my arms round Freya, who had been following all this intently. She had to be my priority. 'Keep close to me,' I whispered. 'I'll get you back home. You need to be with me.'

But her eyes were on Dominic. It was clear she was attached to him; he had evidently shown her kindness in this harsh world.

'Face the wall, woman, now.' Dominic turned round.

'No,' I said. 'You don't understand. Dominic, please listen to me. Clement was questioning this child about you. He hurt her...'

But he tore me away from Freya, turned me round and seized my arms. I struggled, but his strength was unbelievable. Before I knew it, my face had been scraped against the cold wall and my wrists were tied behind me with what felt like rope. I suppose he had concealed it inside his jerkin.

'Hurry, woman.'

He dragged me round to face him, clapped his hand over my mouth and began hauling me out the ruin. Freya ran alongside. I saw anxiety in her eyes for the first time since she had been in Dominic's presence. He ignored my struggles and her anxiety and started hauling me though the trees.

'Mother of God, woman!'

Between my ankle and my reluctance I was hindering him considerably. So presently he lifted me up and strode through the wood at speed. I ducked into his jerkin to avoid the branches he shouldered aside rebounding on my face. Leather and sweat bumped against my nose in equal measure. And all the time little Freya kept up with him, beginning to cry now.

'Where are you taking me?' I demanded.

He did not answer. Almost at once I heard a whinny. The large black horse I had seen on my previous visit was tethered beneath a great oak.

'That was you!' I exclaimed. 'You nearly galloped into me!'

This had no effect whatsoever. He hoisted me over the saddle, so that I landed ingloriously on my stomach, and reached for Freya. She shrank back. I understood; she had witnessed her mother's death in the saddle, but Dominic did not know that.

'Come here,' he said, exasperated rather than harsh.

She backed away from him, shaking her head.

'Come here!' He half laughed at her, obviously trying to reassure her. I was amazed. I had expected him to lose his temper with her. It seemed a very un-sixteenth century attitude towards a child, never mind one who was hampering his plans.

But it didn't work. She just shook her head, almost apologetically, as if appreciating his efforts, young as she was, and ran away through the trees in heaven knows what direction.

'Mother of God...' He began to run after her, then stopped.

'Now she's lost again,' I muttered. 'Thanks a bundle.'

I don't know whether Dominic replied to this bitter and completely pointless remark, because at that moment I tumbled to a wheat field and the trees disappeared with the black horse. The main road appeared on my right. I was further from the manor house than I had been last time I came back to the twenty-first century. I could not see the turn off into the Deverell estate.

The wheat had broken my fall; it could have been serious otherwise. As it was, I lay there winded. I was as relieved as ever to be back in my own time, but could still have howled my heart out like a child with pain and frustration. I had promised Freya I would bring her home and now I had broken my promise. It had been such a near thing. Suppose I had returned when I had my arms round her? Or would she have slipped from my grasp anyway, destined never to come back? Why was she different?

The thought of Nicholas finally got me upright. With some difficulty, since, like the rosary, the rope tying my arms behind my back had returned with me. Why could things come back with me?

Between rope and my injured ankle it was probably quite a performance, but no one was around to see it. Eventually, I hobbled towards the main road and across it. As the sun began to set, I kept walking down the grassy verge, wildflowers to my left, cars whizzing past to my right.

'Are you all right?'

A maroon car had stopped. The couple inside it looked at me with concern and not a little curiosity.

'Yes, I'm fine.' I tried to pretend that I just happened to have my arms behind my back. I was instinctively protecting modern day Deverell, I suppose; the last thing they needed was scandal. But of course the car had come up behind me. The couple had already seen the ropes and my distress must have been obvious enough. The woman, olive skinned with curling dark hair, got out the passenger seat.

'Have you been kidnapped or something?' She was already reaching for the ropes to untie them. The driver got out, reaching for his mobile phone.

'Don't worry,' he called over the car roof. 'We'll get the police.'

'Please, I'm fine,' I said, flexing my stiff arms and shoulders. 'It's not what it looks like. It was a joke…'

'Some joke!' The woman was indignant. She eyed my yellow silk top, which was dirty where Dominic had checked I was a woman. I could imagine what she was thinking. 'Where do you stay? We'll run you home…'

How could I tell them I had come from Deverell? They seemed level headed people, not the sort to gossip or spread it over social media, but it would get out eventually.

'I'm not from around here. I'm staying at the old almshouse,' I said. 'It's just five minutes away.'

This was plausible enough, since I had noticed that there were a few bedrooms above the restaurant. Now that my arms were free, I could call Nicholas on my mobile from there to come and pick me up. Best of all, it was in the direction the couple had been travelling, so would not inconvenience them.

'Are you sure?' The man studied me, mobile poised. 'Don't you think you should take that ankle to hospital?'

'He's right, you know,' the woman added. 'It needs attention.'

'No, really, my husband can see to it. It's not that bad…'

'If you're sure…'

They got me into the passenger seat and drove me to the almshouse at speed, still trying to persuade me en route to let them take me straight to police or hospital. They were a wonderful pair. I felt guilty for deceiving them, but needs must. How on earth could I have explained anyway?

Smiling gaily, I waved them off from the pavement outside the medieval archway which led into the almshouse courtyard. Then I took my mobile from my back pocket and made my call. Even then, though, I was in two minds about telling Nicholas that Freya was alive. Might it not just give him false hope? If I didn't get Freya back it would be so cruel. I would decide what to do once I was speaking to him...

'Hello? Deverell Manor.'

A man's voice. Not Nicholas. Not Alistair. For a few moments I thought time had played another trick on me and that I was speaking to, say, Nicholas's father, or grandfather. Or even that I had already altered the future and that someone else now owned Deverell Manor...

'It's Imogen,' I faltered. 'Imogen Webb. Is Nicholas there?'

'Imogen. How do you do?' He had a beguiling West Country accent. 'This is Father John Draycott speaking. They've told me everything that's been happening to you. Nicholas has had to go to the hospital. I'm afraid his mother has had a fall in her house. But she's all right,' he added kindly. 'You didn't turn up earlier, so I take it you went back in time again?'

'Yes.' I was floored. I had so wanted to speak to Nicholas. But it wasn't Father Draycott's fault, so I kept talking. 'It's a long story, but I've ended up at the almshouse restaurant. Could someone...?'

'With you in a trice, Imogen,' Father Draycott said and hung up.

I tried Nicholas's mobile number. He answered almost at once. 'Imogen? Thank goodness. Where the hell are you? I wondered what was wrong when you didn't turn up. Did you back in time again? Are you all right?'

'Yes, I went back in time again.' I stepped aside to allow a party of American tourists into the almshouse archway. 'How is your mother? What happened?'

'Oh, she's not too bad,' Nicholas said. 'Another fall, but she's coping. She's doing too much, won't accept she's growing old. Can I come and get you? Where are you this time?'

'At the almshouse. It's okay. Father Draycott's picking me up.'

'That's a long way. How did you get so far? Are you all right?'

'I'm all right. I met Francis…' I hesitated.

'You met Francis? What's he like?'

'Religious and gentle, as I imagined. He couldn't see me. Dominic could see me. I spoke to him.'

'You had a conversation with Dominic?'

'Well, a brisk one. He wasn't in a good mood, not with me anyway.' I remembered Dominic's astonishing tenderness with Freya. 'Nicholas…' Suddenly I was crying. I should have been standing here on this pavement with his little daughter. I imagined her drawing heads because she was so ragged and dirty, bewildered with traffic she had not seen for fourteen months, staring at my mobile phone as I gave it to her to speak to Nicholas.

'Imogen?' he said. 'What's the matter?'

I suppose I ought to have kept it secret until I held him in my arms, but I couldn't. 'It's Freya,' I said. 'She's alive, in the sixteenth century.'

CHAPTER TWENTY-FOUR

FATHER Draycott was as fast as his word, his silver four wheel drive screeching to a halt outside the almshouse. He was a small, dark, wiry and bespectacled man who did everything at twice the rate of everyone else.

'Imogen.' He came towards me, holding out his hand. 'Do you need a drink? This is a splendid old place, you know.'

He didn't give me a choice, just ushered me into the restaurant. I soon found myself sitting in a little private room with modern stencils and medieval stone carved heads high up on the walls and a brandy and a mixed grill on a table in front of me. And he was tactful. He fidgeted, but didn't demand to know what I had been through. He examined with fascination the crucifix Anna had given to Francis and I had found on the stairs.

I was grateful for his forbearance. Nicholas's reaction to my news still filled my thoughts. 'She's alive? In the sixteenth century? You mean, here, at Deverell, but in the past? You can't mean it, Imogen. How do you know it was her?' Then, when he finally accepted it, 'How is she? Is she well? How have they treated her? What does she look like now? Has she grown?'

Considering the state of Freya and how I had seen her treated, by Clement at least, none of my answers could have satisfied me, never mind Nicholas, so I held off on detail until he got here. Meta and Alistair would stay on at the hospital. Meanwhile, urged on by Father Draycott, I tried to eat.

Emery had texted me *Are you still in the manor house?* I considered ignoring it, but had visions of Marcia storming round to see what had become of me and crossing swords with the other priest, Father Coll, who was innocently holding the fort there. I therefore texted back to Emery *Count me out for the rest of the evening*, to which he responded immediately with a nonchalant *Suit yourself.* Actually, I wouldn't have minded seeing him; he was familiar and easy going and the world I had just experienced was neither.

'Oh dear, you can eat more than that, surely,' Father Draycott said. I saw why he got on well with Alistair. He looked sorrowfully at me until I picked up my knife and fork again. I had managed more than half of the mixed grill by the time Nicholas arrived, transformed, euphoric, taking me in his arms and kissing me in front of Father Draycott, who slipped discreetly out into the courtyard.

'Did you get a picture of her?' I realised I hadn't thought of it. 'It doesn't matter,' Nicholas added quickly, seeing my dismayed face. 'Your mobile wouldn't have worked anyway.'

'It might have. The camera doesn't need a signal.'

I could have kicked myself.

'It doesn't matter.' He kissed me softly, held me at arms length to examine me. me. 'Poor Imogen. You've been through the wars.'

I became aware just how scruffy and sore I was. 'I'm fine,' I said lamely.

He didn't believe me, but presently he sat beside me, holding me tight, and I told him everything. I did not dwell on Clement's brutality to Freya, but Nicholas imagined the worst anyway. The trouble with euphoria is that it fades quickly and he grew silent under the reaction. It was not enough that Freya was not dead. The reality was that she might as well have been. For the moment, she was a pawn in a deadly business and he could not help her. Even if she survived Dominic's plans and Clement's brutality, there was no guarantee she could ever come back.

'I'll get there again,' I said. 'I'm bound to.' I doubted that I would have any more success the next time, but did not say so to Nicholas.

'No exorcism.' He was numb, speaking slowly, trying to come to terms with the return of his heartache. 'We guessed what had happened to you and decided not to start until you were back. Now we can't do it at all in case…'

In case it worked and sealed Freya's fate and cut her off forever.

Darkness down, we returned to the manor house.

Father Coll was young for a priest, perhaps under thirty, and not yet assigned to a parish, but helping out at a retreat near Father Draycott's. He had a slight speech impediment and I reckoned the Catholic Church had judged him too timid for even a country parish. He was of medium build, reddish haired, with poor skin and a jaw too large for the rest of his face. Only his large, blue eyes were attractive in a tranquil, unworldly sort of way. I was glad I had texted Emery back; Marcia would have eaten him alive. It had been something of a wild goose chase for the two priests so far, who agreed that exorcism was now too risky, but they had already arranged to stay the night anyway.

Father Draycott fetched a tablet from his four wheel drive and went onto the internet to research medieval crucifixes, zipping about the information highway like nobody's business. He told us that he knew a couple of experts in the field, but where would he say he had obtained Anna's crucifix?

My ankle strapped up again, my ribs bruised but not broken, I decided I had to get back to the gatehouse, to maximise my chances of a quick return to the sixteenth century. Nicholas hunted out a capacious brown leather satchel which had belonged to Sophia and which Freya might recognise. Into this we put a torch, rope, elastic bands, pieces of wire, spare mobile phone, compass, bottled water, first aid kit and chocolate bars. I slung it across my body at once, resolved to keep it there even in bed (I didn't care what Emery made of that) so as not to be taken by surprise. Meantime, I tried to suppress my qualms at the prospect. The more I saw of the sixteenth century, the less I wanted to be there.

Father Coll asked to come to the gatehouse with me. He wanted to see Francis's attic. He wanted, in fact, to pray there. He was young and earnest. I was at a loss. I couldn't face a scene with Marcia when I had managed to avert one earlier.

'You don't know Marcia, Father,' I said feebly. 'She doesn't even know what's going on yet. We were going to let Alistair tell her.'

This argument might have held water had Alistair himself not arrived home at that moment. Meta had insisted he come back, since her mother would be in hospital overnight anyway.

'Of course I'll ask Marcia if he can pray there,' he said airily. Well, I suppose he was used to dragon mothers. 'If she wants to know more, I'll tell her the whole thing. Time someone did.' He turned to Father Coll. 'I'll be back soon, Father, then you can go round.'

Nicholas gave me a great hug as I left the manor house and sent Madogany with Alistair and me, as a furry ice breaker.

Bob opened the gatehouse door. He looked like the proverbial startled rabbit, but Alistair was suavity itself. 'Alistair Sievewright, Nicholas's brother-in-law. How do you do? I must apologise for arriving so late, but I wondered whether I might have a word with your good lady and yourself?'

'Of course, of course, come in...'

Bob fell over his feet, pulling back the heavy oak door. We went on up to the drawing room, where Marcia was prevailing on Emery to finish drawing Elizabeth so that she could be sent to bed. Jack was already asleep down in the guardroom. Madogany was an ice breaker all right. And he broke more than ice. After his exertions climbing the spiral staircase, he plumped himself down in the middle of the drawing room with a whistling sigh and a fart, making everyone laugh.

'Bed, Elizabeth, now,' Marcia said. She must have sensed that Alistair was not here for a social call.

'I want to cuddle the dog...'

'One minute to cuddle the dog then.'

Rather stagily, I thought, knowing all eyes were upon her, Elizabeth got down on the floor and flung her arms round Madogany. Considering that she was merely trying to delay bedtime, he put up with this very well, bestowing a lackadaisical lick on her before settling his big head down on the carpet once more.

'Bed, Elizabeth,' Marcia warned.

Elizabeth disappeared at last.

It felt strange to be back in the domesticity of the elegant drawing room with its comfortable furnishings and standard lamps lit against the darkness, a room I had appreciated before I knew of Dominic and Francis and Anna Mervyn. Alistair, who had asked about Jack's health and politely refused tea, had seated himself in one of the armchairs, apparently at ease.

'I'm not sure how to begin,' he said. 'I don't know how much you know of the history of this gatehouse, but it has a rather terrible story.'

I saw Bob glance triumphantly at Marcia, who ignored him. Had he been trying to tell her, after all, heroic in his own way?

'I suppose most old buildings do,' Marcia said graciously to Alistair. 'It's part of their fascination.'

'Indeed.' He had captivating crow's feet at the corner of his eyes when he smiled and his plummy voice was warm. Marcia was leaning towards him in her chair, melting under his charm already. 'This story relates to

Elizabeth's reign. A Catholic priest was held prisoner in one of the attic rooms before being sent for torture and execution in London.'

'He sang!' Bob burst out. 'Plainsong!'

'Quite possibly,' Alistair said gravely. 'He seems to have been very religious to the end. No doubt it helped him.'

Marcia had shot Bob a narrow look. 'Which attic?' she asked Alistair.

'The one occupied by your son, I believe.'

Marcia's mouth opened, just a little. Then she closed it again. 'I see.'

Alistair was pleasant, bland, apparently unaware of her discomfort. 'It so happens that we have a young Catholic priest, Father Coll, staying at the manor house, who has expressed a wish to pray in that attic room. I understand that your son now sleeps downstairs, so it's empty. Would you allow Father Coll in there tonight for a few moments?'

Such was his courtesy that nobody could have refused without seeming churlish. Certainly not Marcia, who nodded almost immediately.

'Why not?' she said. 'I can go upstairs and stay with Elizabeth so that she doesn't disturb him.'

'Thank you.' Alistair inclined his head. 'Thank you very much. He will be very grateful to you.'

Bob gave Emery and me a look of appeal, evidently wanting to ask more questions, but not liking to bring the subject up without our support. Emery, who had perched himself on the sofa, pretended not to notice. I smiled encouragingly at Bob, who ventured, 'It's all been very strange. This holiday, I mean.'

'Has it?' Alistair was kindness itself. 'You mentioned plainchant?'

'Yes.' Bob was eager. 'I've heard it. And Imogen has too.'

I couldn't let him down. 'More than that,' I said.

Marcia stirred uneasily in her chair. 'Bob sings in a choir,' she said. 'Music's in his head all the time. Isn't it, Bob?' Pretending she had not heard my statement, she smiled at Alistair. 'Such beautiful music. I'm not surprised he can't forget it.'

Alistair and I exchanged glances. Obviously Marcia wasn't ready to be told the whole story. Alistair murmured something about Tallis and Byrd, then let it go. I would have told her everything whether she wanted to hear it or not – Jack had been injured, after all – but she was capable of making the connection for herself if she wished. Alistair was a genial man and I suppose he was thinking of Deverell. It was not in the estate's interests to antagonise or alarm the holiday makers who stayed in the gatehouse. They brought desperately needed income, after all. So he stood up and held out his hand to her once more.

'Excellent. I'll ask Father Coll to come round now then, shall I?'

CHAPTER TWENTY-FIVE

'WHAT was all that about?' Emery asked, still perched on the sofa as Marcia accompanied Alistair and Madogany down to the front door. Bob had already retreated into the kitchen. I heard him surreptitiously opening the biscuit tin.

'It's about an idealistic young priest wanting to pray in the attic,' I said. 'He considers the executed priest to be a martyr for his faith.'

Emery dropped his sketchpad onto the sofa and laughed. 'Do me a favour, Imogen. I can work that out. I'm not stupid. What's going on?'

'Depends what you mean.'

He pretended to sigh. 'All right, let's start with Nicholas.' He looked very hard at the dirty mark on my yellow top.

Suddenly it was all too much for me. I turned on him. 'You told me his daughter was dead. She's missing, not dead! I could have put my foot in it!'

'Ah.' He raised his eyes to the fine ceiling.

I stared at him. Had he known the truth all along? Had he misled me on purpose so that I would put my foot in it? I couldn't believe he would be so malicious.

'Trust me to get it wrong,' he said. 'I suppose the poor kid's unlikely to be alive. They just haven't found her yet.'

'No, they haven't found her yet.'

I turned away from him, unsure of him, disgusted with myself for marrying a man whom I could even suspect of such a ploy. I heard him hop off the sofa behind me, felt him catch at Sophia's satchel. 'What's with this then?'

'You wouldn't believe me,' I said wearily.

'Try me.'

'No.'

'What's Nicholas up to?'

'It's none of your business, Emery.'

'I'm married to you.'

'Not for much longer.'

'Okay, I give in.' I could imagine him raising his hands playfully. 'Marcia might not want to know, but I do. There have been strange things happening in this gatehouse, haven't there?'

Genuine interest, or merely an attempt to win me over? I realised that I did not know my own husband well enough to tell. I kept my back turned to him.

'Father Coll, he's here to exorcise the place, isn't he?'

'He intends to pray in the attic, that's all.'

Then Marcia came back into the drawing room. She shut the door forcefully without actually slamming it. 'May I assume, Imogen, that you've been taking me for a fool here? What's actually going on?'

I turned round. 'You could have asked Alistair,' I said coolly.

'I don't think he wanted to tell me.'

I was in no mood for her. 'You mean, you're less embarrassed asking me. Alistair would have told you had you shown any interest.'

'Ladies, ladies,' Emery murmured, delighted.

'I didn't want to embarrass Alistair,' Marcia hissed. 'Your Nicholas is his brother-in-law.'

'What's that got to do with anything?' I demanded.

'Don't pretend you don't know what Nicholas is angling for,' she said.

Then I realised. I was utterly dumbfounded. 'You think Nicholas has been playing tricks on us all? To make sure Emery and I aren't reconciled? How do you imagine he would contrive that? Why would he even try? Marcia, have you any idea what he's been through in the last fourteen months? And the last thing he would do is hurt a child!'

'Hurt a child...?' She looked bewildered.

'You've never asked Jack why he fell, have you?'

Now she looked affronted. 'Of course I have! He ran downstairs! He told me so. He's done it all holiday! He does it at home except the stairs aren't as steep!'

'Well, it wasn't Nicholas's doing then, was it?'

Jack had confided in me and I was on the verge of telling her what he probably still wanted to be kept secret from her. I didn't even care. I was too angry about her slandering Nicholas, even if she was clutching at straws in her refusal to believe that anything odder was happening in the gatehouse. But Father Coll knocked on the downstairs door just then. Bob dropped the biscuit tin and shot out the kitchen past us, taking the chance to escape his quarrelsome womenfolk.

'All right, what did you mean about Nicholas?' I hissed at Marcia.

She looked annoyed. I suppose she was already regretting her insinuations and expected me to have the tact to forget about them.

'Oh, never mind,' she muttered.

'Don't start making accusations about him to Father Coll,' I warned her. I had no intentions of backing down. I had already had to pay out enough tact on this holiday to last me a lifetime and the sixteenth century had not improved my temper. 'What goes around, comes around.'

Marcia stared at me, this new, ferocious Imogen, then turned to Emery, who had perched himself on the sofa again. 'Well, it looks like she'll be asking for a divorce. Get yourself a good solicitor.'

At which point Father Coll entered the drawing room.

He must have sensed the atmosphere and been surprised, since Alistair would have reported that all had gone smoothly. He looked round hesitantly, and turned to me. I suppose I was the only familiar face.

'Can I pray now?'

His speech was hard to make out, between shy mumbling and that oversized jaw. Even his accent seemed strange. I was glad Elizabeth was not there to giggle.

'I'll show you upstairs, Father,' I said.

Marcia followed us, went into Elizabeth's room and shut the door. I took the young priest into what had been Jack's room and explained that Francis had been kept in stocks beneath the window. Father Coll looked round, fascinated.

'Did you see him?' he asked.

'That last time, yes.'

'How was he?'

'Gentle. He had the martyr temperament, I'd say.'

I imagine Father Draycott would have laughed and said that most martyrs were actually rather a nuisance for those who had to deal with them, but this young priest remained serious. 'It is the will of God,' he said.

'It was, yes, of course.' I worried I had given offence.

He looked at me, evidently perplexed. I suppose he thought me glib.

'How does it happen?' he asked. 'How do you go back?'

'The world changes around me and I realise it eventually, unless I drop from the back of a vanishing horse, in which case it's more sudden and painful …'

'I want to come with you…'

'Believe me, the sixteenth century's overrated.'

He looked at me curiously. 'What do you mean?'

'I mean that I've always loved history, but having experienced it, I find the reality of it frightening. And England in 1582 wouldn't be very safe for you, Father, so I don't think you'd enjoy it there.'

But still he looked wistful. I began to wish he could accompany me. It might cure him of his romantic notions. But better not; it might also cure him of his head, not to mention other bits of him. I remained to be convinced of his survival skills.

'Oh well,' he said, resignedly. He looked down suddenly, took a piece of paper from inside his prayer book. 'Nicholas asked me to give you this.'

It was a copy of Ranald's latest email from the British Library, concerning Francis's interrogation by Elizabeth's interrogator, Richard Topcliffe. I thanked Father Coll, left him kneeling in the attic and went down one floor to the bedroom with the magnificent Jacobean fireplace, the room I now shared with Emery.

Ranald's email left me enlightened, but depressed. The political aspect dominated; for most of the sixteenth century politics had meant religion. And of course they had tortured poor Francis. Even by the ghastly standards of his time, Topcliffe had been what the modern world would call sadistic. He had been convinced that Francis must be part of a wider Catholic plot to dethrone the Protestant Queen Elizabeth. Which entitled him to put his prisoner, already weakened by hunger and pneumonia, to the manacles, the hot iron and the rack.

It was clear from the interrogation notes that the Deverell family had been under suspicion since Dominic's involvement in the Duke of Norfolk's plot twelve years earlier, which went some way to explaining if not excusing Clement's paranoia. Francis was repeatedly questioned by Topcliffe about Dominic's current whereabouts, but could give no answers. And the questioning went further back than Norfolk's rebellion, all the way to the Catholic Bishop John White, whom Dominic as a page boy had mourned in the Lady Chapel of Winchester Cathedral where White was buried. In those days, Francis had been a young priest in Southwark, part of White's bishopric, and would have mourned him too.

Under interrogation, Francis did not attempt to deny that he blamed Elizabeth for White's ill health and premature death when he went to the Tower and lost his bishopric after opposing the new Protestant Queen's plans for the Church. 'I have scraped Deverell's conscience today and will do so again tomorrow,' Topcliffe had written to Elizabeth's spymaster Walsingham on the subject of White.

Sure enough, the next day, Francis had not denied that he had known White's adopted son, a handsome and virtuous young Catholic named Jan, who was rumoured to have Plantagenet blood. Although nothing had been proved at the time, Elizabeth had suspected White and his fellow Catholic bishops of plotting to supplant her with this young man, and she was a monarch with a long memory. And so, since Francis would not or, more likely, could not, lead them to Dominic, the events of more than twenty years before were used to justify his execution as a traitor at Tyburn. In effect, he had died for his devotion to a long dead Catholic bishop.

Nicholas had scribbled a note to me on the email.

Dearest Imogen

This makes me afraid to let you go back there. As Freya's father, I should be the one to do it. Please, please, be careful, darling. Don't take any stupid risks.

All my love,

Nicholas

PS – Not a word about what became of Dominic. Looks as if Topcliffe thought he was still alive. If Clement killed him, would he not have told Walsingham as proof of his loyalty to Elizabeth?

My eyes filled as I read the note again. What constituted a stupid risk? If it came to my life or Freya's, what would Nicholas want me to do? It was the sort of question better not asked, and I didn't intend to.

I was frightened. Oh God, I was frightened. Only by leaving Deverell could I hope to avoid a return to the darkness of the past. It could take me now. Any moment. I had never seen this room in the sixteenth century. What had been here instead of this charming bedroom with its soft bed and white counterpane?

Below, someone knocked on the front door. For a distraction from fear, I jumped up and ran downstairs. Bob popped his head round the stairwell, then retreated when he saw me do it. It was Nicholas.

'I can't leave you to go alone,' he said. 'I've got to try to go with you.'

CHAPTER TWENTY-SIX

I WENT outside with him, closing over the oak door. He took my hand, drew me nearer to him.

'Don't let go of me,' he said. 'We need to be touching when it happens. That might do the trick. I can't just wait for you again. I'm Freya's father, for Christ's sake. You've done so much and all I've done is sit here, time after time, and waited for you. You've taken too many risks already and perhaps if I can get back there too I can bring her home…'

Or be trapped yourself, I thought. Like Freya, he was a Deverell. It was illogical, I know, but the only reason I could think of for her never returning. I was too scared by the possibility of losing Nicholas to voice my dread of it. Perhaps he sensed it. He held me closer still as we strolled in the direction of the manor house, past the entrance to the lawns where Madogany waited, crouching, ball in mouth.

'No, not him too,' I said. 'Were Labradors around in 1582? Surely there weren't any chocolate ones…'

'Not Madogany,' Nicholas confirmed. 'No touching Madogany.'

So we threw the ball for him, but sidestepped him. Which, since he was a dog who loved to be fussed, was just another sadness in that difficult, moonlit night. Eventually, we got Alistair to call him back into the manor house. Nicholas and I walked a little more, then sat on a bench at the edge of the furthest lawn. I rested my head on his shoulder.

'I've spoken to Lionel Freese, the Anglican priest I was with when I met you at the cathedral,' he said. 'I know him quite well. He's okay to trust, so I told him everything. He met Father Draycott in Bristol a couple of years ago and wants to help too. I think he'll probably arrive in the morning.'

'What on earth did he think?'

'Same reaction as Father Draycott. Nothing fazes these religious types. They see a lot of life, I suppose.'

'Father Coll seems desperate to meet Francis.'

Nicholas smiled. 'Well, nothing fazes the older ones…'

A sound from the undergrowth behind us. A fox, I supposed, but I looked round anyway. 'What is it?' Nicholas asked.

'Didn't you hear anything?'

'No.' He clutched me harder. 'What was it?'

'Don't know.' I glanced round. 'Still in our own time.'

We stood up cautiously, arms round each other, and walked crab-like to the bushes. My heart hammered.

'Nothing there,' Nicholas said. Still holding onto me, he made a couple of sweeps with his hand. 'No, nothing. It's all right.'

I nodded, but a sixth sense made me look round again. This time I saw a figure stealing across the lawn a few feet away from us. He must have passed us while we were checking the bushes. He was heading for the gatehouse. I pointed silently, trying to stay calm.

'What it is?' Nicholas whispered.

'Over there? Can't you see him?'

Nicholas was frantic. 'No. Where?'

'There. I think it's Dominic.'

Nicholas started running where I had pointed, pulling me with him. 'I can't see him.' He was almost sobbing with frustration. His inability to see Dominic in our own time suggested that he would not be able to journey into the past with me. But I could no longer see Dominic myself.

'He's gone,' I whispered. 'I saw him when he'd been hiding in the guardroom fireplace, remember. If it was night for him just now in 1582, he might have arrived this way before hiding. Just before the soldiers banged on the unused guardroom door.'

'Jack,' Nicholas said. 'If he reaches the guardroom Jack might see him. Or at least hear him. He might hear the soldiers bang on the door. He'll be afraid…'

I was torn. I felt I ought to go to Jack, but suppose, having glimpsed Dominic, I was meant to go back into the sixteenth century here and now? Suppose I missed my opportunity to bring Freya back?

I turned to Nicholas. 'Oh God, what do I do?'

'Go to the guardroom. We know Dominic went there. It'll help reassure Jack too if he hears anything.'

He was right. Why hadn't I realised it? My brain was frazzled. I nodded, set off again, then stopped, hearing voices nearer the house. Dominic's voice and a woman's, not Anna Mervyn's.

'It must be his wife Isabella,' I whispered.

Nicholas stared at me. 'I can't hear her. I can't hear anything…' His hand in mine clenched into a fist.

'They're arguing.' I could hear the voices more strongly now, coming nearer us again. Was Isabella, whose father Anna considered a coward, trying to warn Dominic not to try to rescue Francis? Had she become aware of Clement's plans to bring in the soldiers tonight? 'I think she's telling him it's too dangerous,' I whispered. 'She must be. What else would she be saying?'

Nicholas did not answer and the night grew lighter. I looked round, puzzled, and saw the last strands of sunset. The day had grown less old. I was back in the sixteenth century and alone. Holding Nicholas's hand had made no difference; he had not been able to come with me. I wondered what he had experienced. Had I simply vanished in front of his eyes? It was bad news anyway, suggesting that my merely being in contact with Freya would not be able to bring her home.

I made out the white of Isabella's coif twenty yards or so in front of me. She and Dominic were still arguing. I crept closer. From further off I heard the sounds of many voices. The feast must be in progress now. But as I grew nearer to Dominic and Isabella, I could hear them distinctly and see them faintly. He was angry. She was distressed.

'Be quiet, woman. Leave me.'

'My babies are taken from me, now my husband…'

I realised that I had never seen any of their three sons, the eldest of whom could not be older than nine. Even by the standards of their time, the youngest at least should still have been at home.

'You've said enough, woman. Go back to the Hall.'

'I can't let you, my love…'

He reacted brutally to the endearment, seizing her wrist, I think, for she gave a little gasp of pain. 'Betray me, would you?'

She squirmed, her breath coming hard. 'Husband, no. No, I would not!'

'Then get back to the Hall. They will miss you. You will lead them to me!'

He pushed her away from him. She stumbled towards him again, weeping, and he seized her. 'Why, what would you have me do, wife?'

His voice had changed. There was still anger in it, but excitement now too. Before she could answer, he had shoved her up against the wall, lifting and pushing her stiff, dark skirts above her waist. It was a swift, thrusting coupling. He kept his hand over her mouth, whether to stifle protests or pleasure I couldn't tell, but she made no struggle and her body heaved with his. Regardless of her feelings, I was stunned enough for two. That he could stop for this in the face of such danger beggared belief.

When he finished, he let go of her. She smoothed down her skirts, her stiff farthingale askew. She was matter of fact and practical. I heard no weeping or distress now. What he had done had been welcome all right.

'Back to the Hall, now,' he said. 'Do you hear me, woman?'

She nodded.

'Swear an oath!'

'I swear it, husband.'

'You'll not betray me?'

'No, husband.' She sounded calm now, resigned. I realised now what the purpose of that vigorous coupling had been. In their world a wife was tied to her husband whether she liked it or not. Isabella was fortunate in her marriage. Dominic might seem rough compared to Nicholas, but she knew no better, they were in a perilous situation and he was attractive, potent and reckless. By satisfying her, he had reinforced the bond between them.

'Leave me.' He pushed her away and this time she went, through an archway in the manor house wall no longer there in the twenty-first century. Dominic headed towards the gatehouse.

I was in a quandary, unsure which of them to follow. Neither, perhaps. My mission was to find Freya and with luck her part in this sorry story was over. She was likely still hiding out in the woods. First, though, out of curiosity, I followed Isabella, who was walking into light.

The splendour of the newly built manor house by night took my breath away. I was seeing a sight twenty-first century eyes could only try to imagine. Everything was new and sharp. A dozen torches on wall brackets in the courtyard picked out in gold the rows of mullioned windows and the high battlements. The number of torches was presumably an extravagance, reserved for occasions like this feast. Clement evidently meant to impress an important guest.

To my left I glimpsed in darkness the smaller courtyard where the kitchen windows threw out electric light in my own time. Isabella walked on ahead of me, expertly keeping her gown out the mud. I saw by the increased light that the gown was dark blue velvet, edged with lace. Her ruff, too, was delicately worked. Her hair was concealed under the coif I had seen earlier with another smaller coif pinned on top. She was obviously got in up her finery for an important guest.

A servant stood respectfully outside a grand entrance I did not recognise. Latin words were crisply carved into the stone above the oak door, which stood open. This, in a part of the house demolished in the eighteenth century, was presumably another entrance to the Hall, on the opposite side of it to the door I had followed Anna Mervyn through, the entrance which still stood today. The sound of many voices within grew louder as Isabella and I approached the door. Someone was playing a lute.

'Is the earl still within?' Isabella asked the servant. She sounded in control of herself. The encounter with her husband might never have happened.

'He is, madam.' The servant bowed slightly.

An earl being feasted at Deverell? I was filled with curiosity. No wonder Clement had crowed to Anna. He must be planning to hand Francis over to this great man at court, to curry favour with the Queen and prove his religious loyalty. It would atone for Dominic's disloyalty in the matter of Norfolk's revolt.

Isabella stepped over the Hall threshold. The servant looked at me. I looked back at him, unconcerned at first, until I realised that he was not simply looking in my direction. He could actually see me.

'Who are you?' he demanded. 'What do you want?'

I backed away fearfully. 'Sorry,' I said. 'Wrong house.' The most useless three words ever uttered. A youngish man with a bent nose and a beard, he frowned at me, then beckoned me forward.

Could everyone see me now, or just him? I had no intention of finding out. I limped away from him as fast as I could, hoping that since he was posted at the door, he could not follow me far. But he called into the Hall and another servant emerged. To my horror, he could see me too.

'Sorry,' I said again, raising my hands. 'I'm just leaving.'

I should have known it would not work. Strangers were less common in the sixteenth century, especially in the country. Whether or not these men knew Francis was being kept prisoner in the gatehouse, they must be aware of tensions within the family they served. They would know that a messenger had arrived for Clement on urgent business. They would know something was up…

'Please,' I said. 'It really doesn't matter.'

But the second servant had run forward and grabbed my arm. I fought him, reckoning that a young, fit, well nourished twenty-first century woman would have a chance against a bow legged sixteenth century serving man. But he simply knocked me flying to the mud.

I couldn't believe it. Nobody had ever hit me in my life before. While I lay there, stupefied, they lifted me up between them and dragged me over to a smaller door on the other side of the courtyard. They opened it and threw me into darkness, then slammed and locked the door on me.

For a few minutes, my sore face and my terror got the better of me. Worst of all, it was my own stupidity, my over-confidence, which had got me in such danger. What was it Nicholas had written? *Don't take any stupid risks.* I ought to have realised that if Freya had become visible to the sixteenth century, so might I. I should have stayed away from the light. I should have gone to the woods, looking for Freya. That was what I had meant to do. They would send for Clement, who would suspect me of involvement in Dominic's plans. Did my now being visible to everyone mean that, like Freya, I was here to stay?

Horror of that, and of what might Clement might do to me, the need to get out of here, eventually started me exploring. My new prison had a cold earth floor and smelled of damp and leather. I prodded around for walls, felt nothing for a while then grazed my knuckles off freezing stone. I stood up, lifted my arms and felt a damp, barrel vaulted roof. The place seemed to be just a disused storeroom, presumably where they locked up drunken servants or troublesome strangers like myself until the master decided what to do with them.

I was too frightened to call for help; it would only draw unwanted attention to myself. At some point I recovered my wits sufficiently to remember that I still had Sophia's satchel round me. I got it open with trembling fingers and scrabbled for the torch. It worked. Its strong, comforting beam showed me the barrel vaulted storeroom with a strong door I had surmised. When it also showed me fungus and spiders I switched it off.

Since the torch had worked, I tried my mobile phone. It was of course useless, even, oddly, the camera, which ran on battery like the torch. At least it meant I could not have taken a picture of Freya for Nicholas if I had thought of it. All the same, I flung mobile and torch back into the satchel, annoyed and frightened.

The door was muffling the sound of the feast. I heard nothing. I stood a few more minutes, shivering, then realised my knuckle was still bleeding. For something to do, I groped in the satchel for the mini first aid kit. My fingers encountered the pieces of wire which Nicholas had added at the last minute. 'In case you need to pick any locks,' he had said with his gentle, worried smile.

The memory of that smile was enough to give me hope.

'I'll get back to you, Nicholas Deverell,' I said aloud. 'And I'll bring your daughter with me.'

I ate one of my chocolate bars for strength, found the biggest piece of wire and set to work.

Imogen Webb, lock-picker extraordinaire. I was proud of my handiwork, and supposed that all I had to do was cautiously push the door open.

Unfortunately, there turned out to be an external bar across it too. I hadn't heard it crash into place. It was possible I had briefly lost consciousness as they threw me into my prison, thanks to that blow on the face. But it meant I was still captive. I sat back, arms aching after picking the lock, and cried with disappointment and terror.

CHAPTER TWENTY-SEVEN

I TRIED to think of a cover story, but it was hopeless. If I was a stranger, I was suspicious. If I was not a stranger, I would have been known locally. As to my sex, if I was a woman I might receive less brutal treatment, but that was debatable; there might be other unpleasant and particular consequences to my being found to be female, and in any case they would wonder why I was dressed as a man. Not that men dressed in jeans and cotton tops in the sixteenth century anyway. They'd certainly wonder about the style and material. Then there was Sophia's satchel, filled with twenty-first century equipment. They would think me a witch.

Since my watch had again failed and all outside sound was muffled, I had no idea how long they kept me in my prison. It was still night when the bar was heaved up. One of the serving men who had thrown me in dragged me out into a semi-circle of men waiting for me to be brought out. The feast must be over; the courtyard was darkened, only one torch flaming in a corner, and two of the men held horn lamps of the type I had swung at Clement.

My captor held me fast by the arms as the semi-circle inspected me. To my unspeakable relief, the group of men did not include Clement, who was presumably still entertaining his guest the earl, but it did include the small, jowly man I had seen previously in the Hall and thought might be the household steward. It seemed I had been right; he was first to speak.

'What is your name, varlet?'

'Imogen, sir,' I said, glad that it was a name sixteenth century people knew. And there was no point in lying. My life was at stake and I calculated they would be less likely to suspect a woman of treason.

They all looked at each other in astonishment. It was clear that like Dominic they had thought me a young man.

'Imogen,' the steward repeated slowly.

'Imogen Webb, sir,' I said. The truth is easier to remember. My heart was pounding so much with terror that it was all I could do to speak.

He slapped me suddenly across the face so hard I would have fallen but for the servant holding me. It stung so much my eyes filled. I began to cry and made no attempt to stop myself, it being a womanly thing to do.

Not that it worked.

'Search him,' the steward ordered.

One of them dragged Sophia's satchel over my head. They got it open, held a lamp to it and gawped at the contents. One of them picked up the mobile, holding it gingerly in two fingers. Another lifted the torch, which still worked. Thank God he didn't work out how to switch it on.

'What is it?' the steward demanded, pointing to the mobile.

'It's a...a lamp, sir. But it's broken. It's all broken,' I added desperately, seeing one of them pick up a chocolate bar in mystification. Damn, I should have eaten them all while I had the chance.

'Where are you from, boy?' the steward demanded.

'London, sir, and I'm not a boy.' Wait till daylight, I thought, you'll see my face. I'm in my thirties, for heaven's sake. The lamplight was evidently giving me an unwelcome youthful glow. When the disbelieving steward slapped me a second time, I had a feeling I didn't have till daylight.

'Take his clothes off him,' he ordered.

I should have had puffed breeches with points, of course. They gaped at the slim line of my jeans. The zip defeated them. After a moment's incredulity, the man holding me let go of my arms and hauled off my cotton top. So now they saw a bra for the first time too. But beneath it, breasts, which have not altered since the sixteenth century. I could see from their faces that they were flabbergasted.

The steward rubbed his chin in consternation. 'Give her the shirt,' he snapped at the man holding my top, who obeyed. I put it on, triumph mixing with fear. 'Where are you from, wench? What do you here?'

'I'm from London, sir.' I slipped into my best imitation Cockney. 'I ran away because my mistress misliked me, sir.'

'Ha! What about the master?'

I said nothing, allowing the insinuation to stand and the men to leer knowingly at me. I was mortified, frightened now for a different reason, but better to be thought a trollop than a traitor.

'We'll find you a shift, jade,' the steward said. 'This is a decent house.' He nodded to one of the men, who set off for the house. 'Get in,' he added to me, pointing to the prison they had dragged me from. When I hesitated, he hit me a third time, as hard as before. So much for my sex. 'Do as you're bid, wench!'

I stumbled back into the barrel vaulted room. They stood outside, guarding me, until the man he had sent for a shift fetched an old linen affair which stank of urine and sweat. The steward brought it into the dark little room, a lamp in his hand. 'Make haste, wench, or it will be the worse for you.'

In silence I put the vile thing on, unzipped my jeans – he heard the unfamiliar sound with unconcealed curiosity, his eyes following my hands – and took them off. He jerked his head in the direction of the servants, who obediently closed the door. I realised why quickly enough.

'No,' I said. 'No, not that…'

The price of being a trollop instead of a traitor. The steward was already unpicking his codpiece, his tongue stealing from his mouth.

'This is a decent house, you said!'

I ducked away as he tried to grab me and kicked him hard between the legs. He let out a howl and fell to his knees, clutching himself. I tried to bolt for it, but one of the servants outside shoved me back inside and came in himself. It was the man with the bent nose who had first sent me flying.

'Bind her,' the steward panted from the ground.

'No! Stop it! No!'

But I was powerless to stop them. Another servant entered and the two of them tied my wrists painfully behind my back with the rope from Sophia's satchel. I don't know where they took the rest of the satchel's contents.

'I'll have her…' The steward dragged himself to his feet, leaned against the wall. 'I'll have her first.' Then he vomited.

So, until he recovered sufficiently to have me, they tied my feet as well and left me alone in the darkness again.

The ground was shaking. I had relieved myself like an animal. Then I must have dozed despite my cold and dread and pain, because the shaking woke me up. It was still dark. I realised when I heard a prolonged, thudding that the shaking was the approach of many hooves.

Jack's soldiers. Coming for Francis in the night.

Dominic would be hiding in the guardroom fireplace now, to cross the guardroom once the soldiers had gone upstairs, follow them and lose his life in a futile, heroic attempt to stop them taking Francis. I wept quietly. I had been so afraid for myself in the last few hours, but others were suffering too and I had done nothing to help them. I did not even know where little Freya was.

~

There was a pale blue bath to my right. I blinked at it. I turned my head, saw a matching washing hand basin and W.C.. The walls were papered, pale blue with tiny white roses. There was lilac linoleum and a thick white rug beneath me. Above me was white plaster in a circular pattern.

I was back in my own time. Where the barrel vaulted storeroom had been there was now a little bathroom. It was quaint, its décor dating from the 1970s, and evidently unused; it smelled musty and I saw no toilet roll, shampoo or bath gel. A little spare bathroom, then, in a part of the house no one went to now, on the opposite side of the courtyard from the living quarters of the Deverell family today. It was the most welcome little bathroom imaginable, because it was not part of the sixteenth century. I looked round it with fond, grateful eyes, unutterably glad to be back in my own time. It was even morning, judging by the quality of the light coming through the little frosted window.

I was however still tied up with twenty-first century rope and sixteenth century knots. I was both stiff and sore. My filthy shift stank to high heaven. Presently, I found strength to wriggle about and try to loosen the knots behind my back. At first I did not call out. I hoped to free myself and sneak back to the gatehouse for a bath and fresh clothes before encountering Nicholas.

The knots proved too tight for me. They did things thoroughly in the sixteenth century. I began to lose hope that I could free myself. When I finally got myself to my feet and edged to the door my fingers straining behind my back found it locked. Meanwhile, I heard sounds of cars coming and going outside, their doors banging, of Madogany barking with excitement. No doubt the elderly, twinkling eyed Anglican Father Freese would be expected to throw his ball for him. I pictured it, forlornly. Soon after that I swallowed my pride and began to call out for rescue. But no one came. Why would it enter anyone's head that I might be here? The window might not face the courtyard at all; I could not tell since the glass was frosted. I wished I were Elizabeth Weightman. Her childish shrillness might have brought everyone running even at this distance. But I was already hoarse from calling Freya and my voice was not naturally high. It was beginning to give out.

I was cold again, shivering with the start of a fever. Dispirited and exhausted, I knew now what would happen. It was only a matter of time before the little blue bathroom changed back into the barrel vaulted storeroom. To be ready, I had to stay on my feet somehow.

There was great activity beyond the storeroom door, which was now tantalisingly ajar. It was daylight again and I was back to the same moment as always, with the servants bustling about, preparing for the feast. My sense of dread at my enforced return was tempered only by the fact that I was at least upright.

If I met the same servants again or the steward, would they remember me? How could they, since in their time, if this was the same day, they had still to meet me? Had their meeting me last night altered anything in history? What might have happened to my own clothes and Sophia's satchel with its twenty-first century gadgets which they had taken from me yesterday? Would Freya remember me?

Whatever, I could no longer expect to be invisible and would have to hop, tied hands and feet, through the sixteenth century, but perhaps the funny people would all be too busy to pay me any attention.

'Freya,' I said aloud. She was the reason I must keep going. I must make for the ruined religious foundation where she had met Dominic and which might or might not be known as Tychborne. It was out of the common view and chances were she would meet him there again.

I hopped to the door, peered out. A cart was passing, the dirty youth who had taken the messenger's horse driving it slowly out the courtyard. It held sacks and canvas, obviously emptied of its load. With my painful ankle and bound arms I had no means of jumping onto it so, regretfully, I let it pass.

Then I glimpsed Freya, struggling under the weight of a large bundle of wood. I suppose they needed additional fuel for the ovens today because of the feast. She passed within four feet of the door.

'Freya!' I hissed.

She turned round. There was no distress this time. It was obvious at once that she remembered me. It made no sense that she did, but I had no leisure to try to understand. Perhaps I never would.

'I'm tied up!' I hissed.

She glanced round. I held the door open wider with my shoulder. She nipped into the storeroom, dropped her bundle and set about untying me with nimble little fingers. Meanwhile, glancing behind me, I bombarded her with questions.

'Can you remember my name? When did you last see me? Was it yesterday? Do you remember what Clement did to you? What's the name of the ruin where you meet Dominic? Is it Tychborne?'

She nodded to the first question. The rest seemed to leave her as bewildered as I was. I recalled too late that she was only eight years old. That height of hers was so misleading. And her situation was so forlorn. She suddenly seemed on the verge of tears. And still not a word of speech.

'Hey, it's all right.' The ropes off, I dropped to my haunches and held out my stiff, sore arms to her. 'It doesn't matter. Listen, Freya, you have to stay with me. Do you understand? That's how you'll get back home.'

She nodded, but she glanced anxiously at her bundle of wood. It struck me that she was more of a realist than I was. Hope was too painful for her. She didn't believe that she would actually get back to her own time. If she did not, she still had wood to deliver to someone in the kitchen or face the consequences.

'Can you take me to where you meet Dominic?' I asked. I was afraid to go with her to the kitchen. Suppose I encountered steward or servants from last night and they did remember me? But Freya shook her head, glancing at her bundle of wood once more. 'Okay, it doesn't matter.' I could not risk upsetting her. 'Take your wood first then. I'll come with you. Understand?'

She nodded.

'Come on then. I'll help you carry it.'

At that she frowned. I thought I understood. To have both of us carrying less wood than we could have gathered together would have looked like laziness. So I helped her pick up the sticks, loaded them onto her and followed her cautiously out the storeroom.

'Remember, stay with me. I'll follow you.'

At least I wore my stinking old shift now. But of course a shift only constituted underclothing. Between that and the odd length of my uncovered hair, I must have looked like a crazed woman. The servants' clothes in general were old and plain wool, but neat and nearly clean, their linen pale and starched. They obviously took more pride in their appearance than the twenty-first century gave them credit for.

I followed Freya. She walked straight across the main courtyard and laid the bundle of wood down in the little courtyard where the modern day kitchen was. She stood back, as if checking it, then set the two topmost branches at distinctive angles to each other.

'It's a signal?' I said, surprised.

She nodded.

'Who for? Anna Mervyn?'

But Freya was already walking quickly out the little courtyard, through the archway and round the corner, heading for the gatehouse. A thin, old serving woman carrying chickens intercepted her and gave her a sharp order I could not make out, then glanced at me and crossed herself.

'I won't harm you,' I said quickly.

The old woman peered at me, the struggling, clucking chickens still dangling from her emaciated hands. Her worn, toothless face had moles about the mouth and her sunken, cloudy eyes were suspicious.

Because she was old and had crossed herself, it seemed likely that she was still Catholic. I wondered whether she was Anna's agent, come to read the signal on the bundle of wood.

'I won't harm you,' I said again.

Freya meanwhile set off again at speed, heading for the gatehouse. I followed her hastily. I glimpsed Bilson further off. He was talking to another man, who now sat atop the cart in place of the dirty youth. Bilson and the cart driver seemed to be old friends. The gatehouse door stood open. Was this the moment Anna Mervyn had seized her chance to go inside and feed Francis?

To my amazement, Freya ran into the gatehouse.

'Come back!' I called. 'Clement will be here in a moment!'

Or perhaps not. Perhaps it was earlier in the day. The sun seemed higher in the sky and Bilson had not been talking to a cart driver before. There had been no cart there. Anyway, I could not let Freya out my sight again.

She had gone straight upstairs to the attic. I followed, only now realising what it meant. I would see Francis again and this time he would be able to see me.

CHAPTER TWENTY-EIGHT

'CHILD, I bid you stay away from here...'

Francis was talking to Freya as I approached. The words were chiding, but the tone was gentle. She took no notice of the mild reproof, just stood looking at him as though he were a fabled creature, drinking him in. I had no idea how long he had been here, perhaps only a day or so, but this told me that rumour was already rife among the servants. Anna might be using her as a messenger, but she was unlikely to have told her the story behind it or allowed her in to see the captive.

Then Francis saw me, my crazy state of undress and odd hair. I nearly laughed, because his lack of reaction reminded me of those older priests Nicholas and I had been talking about. *Nothing fazes these religious types. They see a lot of life, I suppose.* He simply smiled at me and said, 'Daughter, the child is bid to stay from me and will not. There is danger here.'

I knelt, forgetting how difficult it was to do it, filled as I was with awe and grief. Though his features were eerily close to Nicholas's, he had the beauty of serenity where Nicholas was tormented. I could not bear to think how he would die, though he himself clearly regarded it as martyrdom. Hence the serenity. Did he never waver, even momentarily? I couldn't ask. I did, though, feel a tremendous urge to ask him to sing his plainchant.

'Yes, Father,' I said, 'there is danger here.'

I had envisaged finding out from him what was happening to us in the gatehouse, but now that I was in his presence I was groping for words, filled by doubts about making the attempt. To destroy his tranquillity would have been unforgivable. To say nothing of trying to explain that I was from his future. Even if he believed me, suppose it affected his interrogation by Topcliffe in London?

'Keep the child safe, daughter,' he said. 'You must leave me.'

How can I keep the child safe? I am a madwoman from the twenty-first century who can't get her back to her own time... I said nothing.

'You are troubled, daughter,' Francis observed.

I burst into tears.

There was nothing he could do. I felt his concern and despised myself for adding to his burden, but everything had become too much. I had cried more this week than the rest of my life put together. To my amazement, little Freya flung her arms around me, trying to comfort me. I clung to her.

'Are you of the true faith, daughter?' Francis asked.

The truth would give only more grief to this sick, filthy, doomed prisoner, but how could I lie? He had been a priest for years and would be able to tell. The best I could do was shake my head and answer, 'There are many who are of your faith, Father Deverell. Your faith is still strong…'

How could he know that I was not referring to his own time? He nodded, evidently agreeing with me anyway.

'See to your soul, daughter,' he said, 'before it is too late.'

How could I tell him that I saw no one's God in either of our worlds? I could not bear to grieve him further. I said, 'I will see to it, Father.'

I was calmer now. Freya was still looking at me anxiously so I smiled at her. It might have been a moment to leave. I could see Francis urging me to go with those marvellous, tranquil eyes.

Instead, I asked, 'Is Tychborne a person or a place?'

He regarded me with surprise. He might be religious, but it must have occurred to him that I was a spy and a very incompetent one at that. Like Dominic, he assumed I should have known what was evidently a local name.

'Both, daughter,' he said austerely. So far as he knew it might have been an admission of guilt, but presumably he saw no point in denying it. There might be other evidence against him I was unaware of.

'Forgive me,' I said, before I could stop myself, as if I had betrayed him.

'God will judge us all,' he said, more gently.

'Though I'm not of your faith, I have done nothing to harm you, Father.' I could not bear him to think me in alliance with the brutal Clement.

He almost shrugged. 'I go to God, my daughter.'

The implication was there. And you do not. He was kind, gentle and patient, but I was a heretic in his eyes.

'Father Deverell, I have been no part of your suffering. Please believe me.' I reached out and touched his long, grimy fingers. He looked down at my hand, then up again, his eyes compassionate.

'Where are you from, child? What do they call you?'

'Imogen, Father. I am from...' Dominic had considered London a treacherous place and Francis probably would too. 'Cornwall,' I finished, justifying my lie by the fact of my parents' retirement there.

Francis half smiled. 'I hear it not in your voice, child.'

I flushed, mortified. Another blunder. Now he thought me untrustworthy for certain. Having longed to meet him face to face, I had not bargained for such awkwardness.

'I have lived too long in London,' I said. 'I would never harm you, Father Deverell. Please try to understand.'

He barely acknowledged this. I could see his mind wandering with fever or exhaustion. It was time to leave him. I stood up as best I could, bitterly aware that because of my own idiocy I had not eased his suffering as I had meant to. Jack had done it, but I had made matters worse. I would never forgive myself.

We walked to the door, Freya and I. She looked up at me, wondering at my distress. Francis began talking to himself in Latin. I don't think it was a prayer. I nearly ran back to him and spilled everything I had bottled up.

I am from your future. In the future your faith is strong and they know of your martyrdom. Your brother's descendant Nicholas who looks like you will put it in the gatehouse guidebook...

How much would he have understood?

While I agonised like a fool, Freya shook my arm in warning. I came back to the immediate situation, hearing Bilson's toiling, grunting footsteps on the stairs. Instantly I knew why Clement had discovered Freya was involved in Dominic and Anna's plans. It was because of this moment. Bilson had found her here with Francis.

History was written. There was nothing I could do. I had nowhere to go. I put Freya behind me nevertheless. Bilson swayed into the room, an old wooden bucket in his hand. I remember noticing that the bucket had cracks in its side. He blinked at me with lizard like eyes.

'Who be you, wench? What do you here?'

'I'm leaving,' I said, but he was blocking the doorway. He was old, beery and breathless. My chances of shoving him aside were good, but he would still glimpse Freya unless I knocked him unconscious.

'Who be you?' he yelled suddenly.

'No one,' I said. 'I'm not from here.'

He stepped forward suddenly, swung the bucket at me. It was empty, so it swung fast and hard. It hit me on the arm. I cried out with pain and shock. Freya screamed and he became aware of her presence. He swung the pail at her. She screamed again, ducked under his arm and bolted down the stairs.

'I hope you're proud of yourself!' I exploded at him. 'This man of God's sick to death and she's only a child! Let her alone!' I grabbed his jerkin as he made to follow Freya. My hands slipped on the greasy material. He struck out at me, his elbow catching me in the face. That brought me down.

When I looked up, he had gone, stumping downstairs after Freya. I could only pray she had got away, fast runner that she was, but of course the damage was already done. Now Clement would know about her. And I had lost her yet again.

'Christ!' I said aloud, pounding the floor in frustration, forgetting I was in the presence of a sixteenth century Catholic priest. 'Christ!'

'They will lock the door on you, child,' Francis said. I spun round to look at him. There was a wonder and a tenderness in his face which told me he knew now I was no traitor. I ached to go to him, kneel in front of him and receive whatever blessing he would give a woman he thought a heretic, but he was right. It was too late. I had to go. I could not risk being locked in.

I started to rise, whimpering through the pain in my ankle, then slipped back as what was beneath me turned from wooden board to carpet. I looked round wildly, saw the furniture of my own time and Father Coll looking at me in amazement from his kneeling position beneath the window.

I believe I swore in front of him too.

It was still daylight. 'What time is it?' I demanded.

He looked confusedly out the window, then glanced at his watch. He seemed to take a long time to read it. 'Half past ten,' he said. 'Morning,' he added, unnecessarily given that we could both see it was daylight.

I crouched on the floor for a minute or so, getting my bearings, catching my breath, worrying whether Freya had managed to escape Bilson and what my intervention would mean for her. What would Clement do to her now? In spite of my distress, Father Coll said nothing.

'What happened?' I asked eventually. 'Did you see what happened? Did I just materialise out of thin air?'

He seemed confused again, running his hand through his coppery thatch. Then he nodded.

'What's happening?' I demanded. 'Where's Nicholas? Where are the Weightmans this morning? Have they gone away for the day? How's Jack?'

Too many questions. Father Coll looked agitated. I regretted my impatience. How would he know? He had probably been up here praying for hours...

'It doesn't matter,' I said. 'Don't worry about it. I'll find out.'

'Did you see Sir Francis?' he asked, his face changing to eagerness.

For a moment all I could think of was Sir Francis Drake, then I remembered that in the sixteenth century priests were addressed as Sir. 'Yes,' I said.

'How is he?'

I considered. What would a young, unworldly Catholic priest most want to know about Francis?

'I think he held fast to his faith,' I answered. 'He might have been glad to die. He was sick anyway.'

Father Coll looked reassured.

Slightly unnerved by him, though unsure why, I got to my feet properly this time and hobbled to the door. Opposite, Elizabeth's door stood ajar. I went a few steps down the turret staircase and listened. Deverell Gatehouse had the silence of emptiness. The Weightmans would be away by now, driving to the old heritage railway line they had intended to ride on today. Jack's shoulder must be doing well. Well, he was young. He would heal quickly.

I must find Nicholas, but my mobile was still in the sixteenth century. I had gone beyond worrying what they would make of it. I was more concerned to get to Nicholas. Despite my dire and dirty state, I decided to make my way round to the manor house immediately, before I was swept into the past again.

The gatehouse was indeed empty. On the table in the middle bedroom Emery had scrawled a note to me.

Gen,

Gone to the Watercress Railway. Have fun yourself. Back tonight.
E.

I wondered where he thought I had spent the night.

Outside in the warm, morning air, an unfamiliar four by four stood beside Father Draycott's. It presumably belonged to the Anglican Father Freese. I smiled, imagining the two older men of religion swapping stories of strange happenings in old buildings and of idealistic youngsters like Father Coll.

Nicholas was pacing up and down between gatehouse and manor house. When he saw me, he held out his arms.

'No.' I backed away. 'You don't want to touch me or this shift thing.'

'I don't bloody care. I've been worried about you. Did they take your clothes off you? Imogen, your face. Did someone hit you?'

'Yes, but it doesn't matter…'

'Of course it matters.' He took me in his arms. 'You've done enough. You've been hurt enough. You need to leave, right now.'

'What did you see when I went back last night?'

'You just weren't there any more. Because it was dark I couldn't see the actual moment. I called and called for ages…'

His embrace was so comforting I could have held onto him for ever, but I had to put him in the picture. 'I saw Freya again. She's a plucky little thing. I tried to keep her with me. But I lost her. You've got a little blue bathroom on the other side of the courtyard, haven't you? No one uses it. I was in there, tied up, I don't know how long, before I went back again…'

'What? In the old bathroom? Who…?'

'Clement's serving men. It was a cellar in those days.'

He looked surprised for a moment, then anxiety took over again. 'Never mind all that. You can tell me later, darling. You've got to get into the car and I'll drive you away from here. Right now. You can stay the night at a hotel. The almshouse will do. Come on, before I lose you again.'

'Nicholas, I can't go to a hotel like this! I need to clean up. Look at me!'

He merely kissed me. 'You're still beautiful in my eyes. All right, we'll go to my mother's first. Meta can bring you clothes. Come on, my car keys are in my pocket. We can text Meta on the way.'

CHAPTER TWENTY-NINE

NICHOLAS'S mother's red brick Georgian home, set at the end of a lane a little distance along the road from the almshouse, reminded me poignantly of Jane Austen's cottage at Chawton. So much had happened in the short time since I had been there. My mind and outlook were altered. I was now accepting as normal what I would laughed off as absurdity then.

I felt inexpressibly relieved to be away from Deverell. I also felt guilty. The old lady was in hospital and I was using her shower to scrape off sixteenth century dirt.

'It doesn't matter,' Nicholas said. 'She'll like you.'

There was a photograph of her with the toddler Freya in the drawing room. Fine boned and elegant like Meta, she did not look in the least frail. Perhaps the loss and uncertainty of what had happened to Freya had taken its toll on her health. It was another reason to get the little girl back to those who loved her.

While I had been showering, Meta herself had arrived in my car with a new mobile and some of my clean clothes from the gatehouse. She had brought Madogany with her. He wagged his tail hopefully as

Nicholas made cheese toasties in the pretty, pale green kitchen overlooking a rose garden.

'Are you sure this is far enough away?' she asked Nicholas.

'I'd have thought so. There's never been anything here,' he said. He glanced at me, worried now. 'What do you think? You could always go back to London if...'

'No way,' I said. 'I want to see this out.'

I sounded braver than I felt. Meta smiled at me. 'Don't think we're not grateful to you already, Imogen. It's been horrible for you...'

'I still want to see it out.'

Meta came over to me and put her arms round me. Over her shoulder Nicholas raised his eyebrows and grinned. It seemed I had won over his reserved sister.

Waiting.

Nicholas and Meta had left. Madogany remained with me for company. I threw his ball for him in the garden until he flopped panting at my feet and rolled over to have his tummy tickled. It was a sweet afternoon, balm to my frightened soul, but for the first time I was out of the loop, away from the action, and it felt strange.

Back at the manor house, Nicholas and the priests had to decide whether to risk exorcism. It might bring Freya back or it might close the door on her forever. I imagined them debating, the priests earnest and concerned, Nicholas anguished. Father Coll probably wasn't there at all. He was probably still praying in the attic. Well, I thought, it takes all sorts. Many people swore by the power of prayer and we needed all the help we could get.

In the end, unable to relax, feeling like a spare part, I left Nicholas's mother's house and drove to the cathedral. For solace or for something to do? I wasn't sure.

The vast, ancient building was busy again. An Italian tour bus had just disgorged its passengers and their colourful, chattering groups slowed my progress to the Lady Chapel. To my disappointment – I had hoped for that candlelit winter darkness – it was still daylight there. Cameras flashing around me, I went to stand above Bishop White's modest grave.

'Please,' I said, almost aloud, 'I need to know how it started…'

Daylight remained. I felt exasperated and idiotic. Why would a sixteenth century bishop heed me? I had done more internet research on John White by now and discovered that in the reign of the Catholic Queen Mary he had condemned to the stake those he considered heretics, among them two of the most famous of the Protestant martyrs, Hugh Latimer and Nicholas Ridley. He must have been a harsh man by modern standards, though Dominic had mourned him. God knows what he would have made of the agnostic standing above his grave. I laughed, bitterly, and turned away.

At the bottom of the Lady Chapel steps I came face to face with Father Coll. He was trembling, looking around him in bewilderment at the tourists thronging the aisles. A camera flashed near his ear and he started in fright. Someone bumped into him and apologised, in English, but even the apology seemed so confusing to him it might have been in another language.

'Father,' I said. 'Father Coll?'

He didn't appear to recognise me.

'Father Coll?' I repeated. 'It's Imogen Webb, from the gatehouse. I'll get you out of here, Father. It's too busy for you. Come on, follow me...'

I reckoned the other priests must be here somewhere. I could not imagine Father Coll being able to drive. Nicholas, too, might be here. I decided there and then to return to the gatehouse with them, no matter what objections Nicholas made. I needed to be there. But I had to get this young priest out the cathedral first. It seemed obvious to me now that he was not simply unworldly and deeply religious. He had suffered some sort of breakdown recently. That was why he was at the retreat. What had Father Draycott been thinking of, bringing him to Deverell?

'Come on, Father.'

I tried to take his arm. He shrank from me. He seemed to flee, into the quiet, eerie shadows beyond the Lady Chapel. I gasped, turned round. It was winter night again, incense filled my nostrils and in the candlelight the boy Dominic was standing crying where I had been moments earlier.

I stood rigid, afraid to breathe in case the scene before me vanished. I took in the fine velvet of the black cloth on the altar below the candles. It gleamed as I had never seen velvet gleam before. Beneath Dominic's feet the tomb was newly laid, but without its modern inscription. Don't move, I told myself. You walked towards Dominic last time and he disappeared. You stood on Emery's foot...

I glanced over my shoulder. The great cathedral was in darkness, throbbing with mystery. I realised now how its power was dissipated in my own time and was sorry. I turned back to Dominic. Someone passed me, stepping into the Lady Chapel, a young, dark haired priest, and Dominic ran towards him.

So it hadn't been me he had run to, after all. I had just happened to be standing beside the priest, Francis Deverell, twenty-two years younger than when I had last seen him. He took the boy in his arms, gave him a hug and a gentle shake.

'Quickly, child, there's no time now.'

He was ushering the sobbing boy down the steps as he spoke. They passed me, turning to shadows in the darkness beyond. As my eyes grew accustomed to the dimness I glimpsed more men further down the aisle, manning the doors, keeping watch for Elizabeth's officials. Some were priests, but at least one had a sword. It gleamed in the unearthly light cast down from the cathedral windows.

I could not tell whether this was the burial itself or just a memorial service. What had they done? Bribed the officials? Or did they have sympathisers among the cathedral clergymen? Just over a year into Elizabeth's reign, there might not have been a complete transfer of power or loyalty.

Someone seized my arm, hard. In my curiosity, my need to watch, I had forgotten that I might be watched myself. 'Who are you?' His sword tip was just below my collar bone, light but threatening. I swallowed, trying to tell myself it was bravado, that he wouldn't kill me in a sacred place.

'I'm a friend,' I got out.

'Who are you?' He had a West Country accent, his words clear, his tone decisive, as though he were used to giving orders. A young gentlemen then, perhaps a knight. He was dark haired, tall even for my own time, with features which were sharply handsome in the elusive light.

'Imogen,' I answered, almost defiantly.

He stared at me, set me backwards for a better look at me. I saw confusion and dismay in his face.

'Who are you? Where are you from? Why are you here?'

But someone came up and touched his arm. The others were leaving. So he hauled me with him. The darkness thickened behind us as someone put out the candles in the Lady Chapel. We were almost running now, as though discovery were imminent, shadows all around us hurrying too. I saw a lamp, a side door held open by a frightened old priest. My captor flung me through it ahead of him and suddenly I was outside in sixteenth century Winchester. I gasped with the cold, my feet slipping on icy ground. Below an intensely starry night, the great Gothic cathedral loomed above us. Horses waited nearby, their breath freezing on the air.

'Scatter,' my captor hissed.

Obeying him, men sought their mounts. I glimpsed Dominic. He was staring at me. So that was how he had remembered me, not from the Lady Chapel, but afterwards. Then Francis pulled him away towards his pony.

'Where's Tychborne?' Another gentleman's voice, coming from one of the men already mounted nearby.

'He was here, your grace,' my captor answered. 'He should be here still.'

Your grace? There was a *duke* at this funeral? Was it Norfolk, twelve years before he lost his head? I was intrigued, but could not see the face closely enough to match him to any portraits I knew.

'No one has seen him come out,' he hissed. Duke or not, he sounded afraid. 'He may have been discovered.'

Beneath my fear, my brain was working. Was the Tychborne they spoke of the father of the Tychborne connected to Dominic's plan to rescue Francis from the gatehouse twenty-two years in the future? Or was he the same man at a younger age, as Francis was?

'I will search for him,' my captor said.

A pause. 'Would that you were in my service, Sir Ralph.'

'I will be in no man's service, your grace.'

My captor, the young knight, Ralph, spoke with a firmness that bordered on scorn, as though ducal rank meant nothing to him. He turned back to me. Then he was gone and I was blinking in twenty-first century sunlight.

CHAPTER THIRTY

SHAKEN but fascinated, I rang Nicholas immediately on my mobile. At first he was too horrified to listen.

'Darling, what were you thinking of? You should have stayed in my mother's house. You've done enough. Anything could have happened to you.'

'I'm fine. Nothing happened I couldn't handle, if you'd let me tell you...'

In the end, curiosity got the better of him. I told him about my brief experience, sitting on a bench round the side of the cathedral in the warm, dreamy summer sunshine, so different to that tension filled, icy night long ago. The small arched door held open by the frightened old priest was still there.

'The duke certainly could have been Norfolk,' Nicholas said. 'According to Ranald's emails, Bishop White was one of his tutors in Queen Mary's reign. And Dominic was in Norfolk's household by the time of White's funeral. Norfolk could hardly have got into serious trouble for mourning White, at least not so early on in Elizabeth's reign, but I suppose he didn't want the new Queen to find out.'

'I don't think Sir Ralph thought much of him,' I observed. 'I wonder whether they found Tychborne. Isn't it odd that the name Tychborne crops up in 1560 as well as 1582? Though I suppose Francis crops up twice too…'

'It is odd,' Nicholas said. 'I can't help feeling this never to be seen Tychborne is a key to everything that's happened to you this week.'

'What do you mean?' I asked.

'I don't know. It's just a feeling, a hunch…'

'Work on your hunch then. I want to know more.' I stood up, began walking to my car and dropped my bombshell. 'Nicholas, I'm coming back to the gatehouse.'

'You're what? No, Imogen, no way…'

'You can't stop me. I've paid to be there.'

'Imogen, don't be flippant. Think how you felt this morning. You'd had enough. You're hurt, for Christ's sake…'

He was right, of course, and I dreaded more danger, but it was as though I were pulling at a scab. Against my own better judgement, I knew I couldn't drop out now. I would never be able to live with myself if I didn't get Freya home.

'I'm coming back,' I told Nicholas. 'I'd better round up Father Coll. He can't cope with the tourists here…'

'Father Coll? He's still praying in the gatehouse.'

'No, he isn't. I met him in the Lady Chapel, just before I went back to 1560.'

'You what? Hold on a minute. I'll check…'

I heard him speak to Father Draycott and the priest's exclamation of surprise in the background. Presently, Nicholas reverted to me. 'No, he would have told Father Draycott if he meant to go to the cathedral and he can't drive. He's afraid of cars, apparently, and Father Draycott says he has no money on him for a taxi.'

'But I saw him. Nicholas, I saw him. He was here. I'll look for him now, okay? I'll call you back.'

'Fine. I'll go round, check the gatehouse and get back to you.'

I hurried round the side of the cathedral, seeking Father Coll in the heat of an August day, just as my young knight Ralph must have sought Tychborne all those years ago in the icy stillness of a January night. I practically had to push through the tourists. The cathedral seemed to be getting busier. It occurred to me I hadn't a hope of finding him. My best chance was to enlist one of the guides. But before I could do this Nicholas rang back. Father Coll was still in the attic of the gatehouse.

I was shaken. I had seen Father Coll in the cathedral in the present day. The sixteenth century was difficult enough to fathom without the twenty-first turning into a puzzle also.

'Did you ask him whether he came here?' I demanded.

'Of course not. It was obvious he hadn't moved from the spot. Apart from anything else, how could he have got back so quickly?'

'Nothing's obvious,' I pointed out. 'Ask him. See what he says.'

'Imogen, Father Draycott says he's mentally fragile.'

'I gathered that.' I was relentless. 'Is he actually an ordained priest? If he is, why is he at the retreat? Why did Father Draycott bring him? Ask, Nicholas, even if they are your guests. Something's wrong.'

'He's Tychborne,' Nicholas said abruptly. 'Father Coll is Tychborne.'

'*What?*'

I stood rooted to the spot, a German woman bumping into me. She didn't apologise and neither did I.

'Tychborne?' I whispered. 'Tychborne?'

'He was in the cathedral, mourning Bishop White with the others in the Lady Chapel,' Nicholas continued rapidly, 'but then he was thought to be missing. Suppose your knight Ralph never found him? Suppose, as Freya was sent backwards in time, he was sent forward, to our present and his future?'

I could hardly get my breath. It fitted. The young priest's extreme shyness, especially of women, his fear of cars, his slowness in telling the time from his watch, the impression he gave of general unfitness for the modern world....

'Suppose he's trying to get back to the cathedral,' Nicholas said. 'He's up in the gatehouse attic, praying to Francis for it. He almost made it just now, when you saw him, but he was still in our time.'

'He referred to Francis as Sir Francis,' I said. 'It's not what priests are usually called now. I thought he meant Francis Drake at first.' It was all coming back to me now, what I had might have thought strange at the time had I not been tired. 'When I told him I had seen

Francis he asked how he is, not how he was, as though he knew Francis personally...' Something else occurred to me. 'Nicholas, if Tychborne's gone missing in 1560, will that affect events in 1582?'

'It might. If he's the same Tychborne as Dominic's plotter. There might be implications. He must think so, if he's trying to get back. But how would he know his own future ? Which year is he trying to get back to? ' Nicholas sounded excited, then his voice changed. 'Oh, Christ...'

'What is it? Nicholas?'

'I was in the Lady Chapel at the moment Freya and Sophia's accident happened. Tychborne was there in the sixteenth century. Perhaps that's no co-incidence.'

Father Draycott, wiry and intense, listened curiously to what we had to say. Then he answered our questions to the best of his knowledge.

There were six of us around the big kitchen table, the two older priests, Catholic and Anglican, Alistair and Meta and Nicholas and me, with Madogany snoring just beyond the French windows which were open to the sunshine. Meta served iced lemon water in blue tumblers. On the ledge above us, the photograph, as if Freya's face didn't haunt me enough already.

'I can't be exact right now – I can check the date for you – but it's certainly around fourteen months since he turned up,' Father Draycott said. 'He was reported to the police by members of the public, wandering around near the cathedral. He was a strange and rather smelly individual, no doubt about it. He didn't seem to know where he was. Well, that wouldn't be surprising if your theory's right.'

'And he immediately showed an inclination for the Catholic faith, I take it?' Alistair asked.

'Yes, the only way of calming him appeared to be having priests visit him. So he was moved to the retreat in my parish in Somerset quite early on. And of course he was found dressed in something resembling our modern day cassock, which was a clue.'

'What did you think of him?' Meta asked.

Father Draycott smiled wryly. 'I can't say it crossed my mind that he was from the past, if that's what you mean. I assumed he was an idealistic young priest who had had a nervous breakdown and lost his memory of who he was. I assumed that his identity would come back to him after a period of tranquillity and contemplation. They've become fond of him in the retreat and he helps out quite a bit now, though I gather the electricity and the cooker and dishwasher gave him terrible frights at first. Now we know why.'

'And his name?' Meta asked.

'Well, one of the nuns at the retreat was on holiday to the Scottish island of Coll. A postcard from her reached the retreat on the same day he did.'

'Why bring him to Deverell?' I asked.

Father Draycott spread his hands. 'I happened to be at the retreat when Alistair here telephoned me. He overheard and asked to come with me. I assumed he was just interested and that it might be a good outing into the world for him, under controlled conditions as it were. He's accompanied me on the odd parish visit before. We were trying to normalise him as far as we could. Apart from anything else, it might jog his memory as to his identity.'

'It looks as though you were unwittingly led to do the right thing,' Father Freese remarked. 'It may be Freya's only means of rescue, if we could work out how.'

There was a little silence. We could discuss every angle as long as we liked, but there was a decision to be made which discussion merely postponed. Inevitably, everyone turned to Nicholas, who had taken little part in it. It was Father Freese who spoke the actual words.

'I'm afraid it's your decision, Nicholas,' he said gently, 'and we simply don't know what we're dealing with here. If we carry out an exorcism, will it have any effect? Will it send Tychborne back and restore Freya, or will it lock them both out of their own centuries for good?'

Nicholas was colourless, his hands clenched together on the table. I yearned to touch him, but the moment seemed too vital for a distraction like my love. Outside, a meandering bee bumbled above Madogany's sleeping head. I remembered how Freya had wanted that large, furry friend to cuddle. *We have to try*, I thought. But I didn't say it. Father Freese was right. It was Nicholas's lonely decision. Even Alistair stayed silent, his eyes dropping to the table.

'If it goes wrong,' Nicholas said at last, 'I can't live with that. I can't bear the thought of her stuck there for ever.'

We have to try, I thought again, but it wasn't my decision. There was another silence around the table.

'What about speaking to Tychborne?' Meta murmured. 'Would he be able to tell us something that might help us decide?'

It was an intelligent suggestion, one no one else had thought of. Father Draycott scratched his head. 'I don't know,' he said. 'I simply don't know.'

'Might it not relieve him to talk about it?' Alistair asked. 'He's been keeping it inside himself for fourteen months.'

'If it doesn't relieve him, it might shatter him,' Father Freese said. 'It might be the end of him.'

'We have to risk that,' Meta said. 'I want Freya back.'

'We should consider, though,' Father Freese pointed out. 'We don't know how history could be affected if Tychborne doesn't return to his own time.'

'Or if Freya stays there,' Father Draycott acknowledged. 'What does she do? She's only a poor little waif at present, but suppose she survived the disease and the dirt, as she has until now, and someone subsequently cared enough to take an interest in her? Speech might return and she's bright. Some intellectuals believed in the education of women in the sixteenth century, more than in any other time until our own. With even a child's knowledge of the twenty-first century, Freya could initiate changes in the course of history in so many ways we couldn't begin to count them.'

'It's not likely, though, is it?' Meta said. 'And would history not have changed already? How do we know?'

'We don't,' Father Freese said. 'It is not given to us to know.'

'There is something else,' Father Draycott said. 'I can't be sure, but I am beginning to wonder…'

We all looked at him curiously. More discussion. Deferring the moment of decision.

'The Catholic Church has its own historical records,' he continued. 'I've been in touch with the archivist at my old seminary. The sixteenth century is his area of particular expertise. Priests were often executed in batches and it seems that Francis didn't die at Tyburn alone. The priest who shared the scaffold with him was a Father Giles Tychborne.'

CHAPTER THIRTY-ONE

W̱ᴇ ᴀʟʟ looked at each other. I think we had all decided immediately that Father Draycott's hunch was correct.

Alistair spoke first. 'So if Tychborne gets back to the sixteenth century, to 1560 where the knight Ralph was looking for him, a horrible death awaits him twenty-two years later, presumably as a result of Dominic's plan to rescue Francis. He was very likely captured that same night.'

'We can't save him?' I shuddered. It was so horrible. He was in the twenty-first century, where he should have been safe. I had spoken to him.

'Not if he doesn't want to be saved.' Alistair sighed. 'That would be meddling. We might not be able to do anything anyway. We don't seem able to prevent you from going back in time. And for all we know, he sought martyrdom for his faith. They did in those days, on both sides of the religious divide.'

'He was taking risks in 1582 certainly,' Father Draycott said. 'Just like Dominic was. It's curious that there's no record of Dominic's death. Take the seminary. Even though he wasn't a priest, the Church might have kept some records because of the connection to Tychborne, but there's nothing.'

'There's nothing in the British Museum either,' Nicholas said. 'Ranald's been trying to find out, but so many records haven't survived...'

Outside, Madogany raised his big head and growled.

'Not again,' Nicholas muttered. I guessed he meant Vaganov. It was all we needed. Madogany got to his four feet, his growls increasing.

'I've had enough of this.' Nicholas stood up.

'I'll come with you,' Alistair said. Both he and Meta stood up.

'No, I'm all right.' Nicholas stepped angrily through the French windows, Madogany padding alongside without being told to, still growling.

'I can't just stay here and do nothing,' Meta said.

Alistair put a soothing hand on her arm. 'Nicholas can handle himself.'

Meta shook him off impatiently. 'I grew up here too. And he might need a witness.' She left quickly, disappearing around the sunny corner.

'Mobsters trying to buy Nicholas out,' Alistair explained to the priests.

Father Freese nodded sadly; Nicholas had evidently told him already. Father Draycott tutted, shook his head indignantly.

'Meta still thinks of Nicholas as her little brother,' Alistair added ruefully. 'I suppose she always will. Twelve years is a gap.'

We waited tensely around the table, hearing nothing. No sounds of the four by four doors slamming. No sounds of their engines. Had Nicholas headed them off before they reached the gatehouse?

Ten minutes or so later, Nicholas and Meta returned, Madogany following placidly. He lay down in his usual spot and went to sleep.

'Nothing doing,' Nicholas said, puzzled. 'It's not like the old boy to get it wrong. I suppose he is getting old...'

Madogany obligingly farted in his sleep to prove his point. We all laughed with the release of tension.

'Dogs never lose their protective instincts,' Father Draycott said. 'It must have been something, surely.'

'Yes, he's got a special growl for that lot,' Alistair said. 'They were here all right. If they'd dropped off a stooge he'd still be growling.'

It was another little mystery, but it had served to break up our discussion around the kitchen table. Nicholas decided to speak to Father Coll. We had to try to confirm whether he was Giles Tychborne. Father Draycott went to fetch him from the gatehouse attic. The Weightmans would soon be back anyway. The hot afternoon was turning to warm evening.

'I wouldn't be surprised if the attic's empty,' Meta remarked. 'He's probably gone back to his own time already. Perhaps that's why Madogany growled. Perhaps he can sense alterations in time.'

'It was his Vaganov growl,' Nicholas reminded her. 'And Tychborne's had fourteen months to get back. Why would he manage it now?'

Meta persisted. 'Because he's here now, where Francis was held. Where we assume he was arrested or captured.'

'But why not the cathedral? That's where the switch happened.'

'Freya wasn't at the cathedral, remember,' Meta said. 'She was here. The switch happened in two different places miles apart. And why twenty-two years apart in the sixteenth century? It's so odd...'

'Well, if Tychborne's gone back, where's Freya? She's not here, is she?'

Meta bit her lip, said nothing else. Nicholas came over to me, took me out to the garden. The strain in him was obvious without him saying so. I sat him down on a bench and massaged his shoulders.

'It'll be all right,' I said. 'Tychborne being here must be a good thing. It must have been meant somehow. That's what Father Freese says too.'

Nicholas smiled bitterly. 'Someone up there's pulling strings? We're being made mad before the Gods destroy us?'

'Father Freese is a good man. They're both good men.'

'I know, I know.' Nicholas rested the side of his face on my hand. 'Oh, Imogen, what would I do without you? You were sent to get me through this.'

'Don't be idiotic.'

'Well, what have I done to help matters? Nothing. Everyone else is doing it for me. I feel so useless.'

'That's not true. You're the one who'll have to decide what to do.'

Father Draycott appeared with Father Coll.

It was the strangest feeling looking at this naïve, almost shambling figure. He would have been unprepossessing even in the sixteenth century, where there was no attempt to alter nature's, or rather God's, handiwork. In the twenty-first century, they would have tried to help his stammer and overhanging jaw. As Father Draycott brought him over to us, he seemed to wince in fear.

'Don't worry now,' Father Draycott said to him. 'Nicholas just wants a quiet talk with you.'

Father Coll sat down beside us uneasily. He was trembling. Nicholas looked appalled. I suppose he instinctively dreaded comparison with the brutal interrogators this frightened man would eventually face in his own time.

'This isn't anything important, Father,' he said. 'I merely wondered whether the name Giles Tychborne meant anything to you.'

Father Coll drew a terrible, whooping breath. Sweat appeared on his pocked face. His eyes veered between the three of us. 'Steady now,' Father Draycott murmured to him. 'Is your name Giles Tychborne?'

A quick nod.

'Father Giles Tychborne?'

Another nod. He stared down at his trembling hands. We looked at each other, half relieved, but utterly perplexed. How did we tell a bewildered man he had journeyed more than four hundred years into his future? How much had he guessed already in the fourteen months he had been here? What if he asked about his own fate? It was a dilemma I had not needed to face with Freya. Suddenly the past seemed simple.

'There now,' Father Draycott said. 'That wasn't so bad.'

There was no reply.

'I bid you welcome to Deverell Manor, Sir Giles,' Nicholas said eventually. It was a kind of beginning again, as though the young priest had turned up at the manor seeking shelter for the night in the sixteenth century. Giles responded to it, looking up, a hint of reassurance in his face.

'Would you like supper, Sir Giles?' I asked, following Nicholas's lead, playing the role Giles would have expected in a sixteenth century woman.

He nodded. 'I thank you.'

I stood up and dropped a curtsey – yes, in jeans – and made my way back to the manor house. Alistair, Meta and Father Freese were waiting anxiously.

'He's Tychborne,' I said.

They stared at me, absorbing the implications.

'Tychborne from 1560?' Meta asked eventually.

'Probably. Maybe not. He could be a relative who was young in 1582…' I broke off uncertainly. 'We'll have to try asking what year he thinks it is.' The potential for distressing him again was obvious.

'Well, we know the 1560 Tychborne got lost at Bishop White's funeral, however briefly,' Alistair said sensibly. 'We can ask him if he was at the funeral. If this is a younger relative from 1582 he would have been too young to be there.'

I looked at him gratefully. 'My brain's fried.'

'You're exhausted, my dear.'

Father Freese was peering out into the garden. 'Do you realise,' he mused, 'I could ask Tychborne what Bishop White was actually like. White nearly derailed the Elizabethan religious settlement. They had to send him and Bishop Watson to the Tower so that they couldn't vote against it in the Lords. And he burned Latimer and Ridley at the stake in Oxford…'

'You can't ask that,' Meta said. But I saw the fascination in her own eyes. 'Do you think Tychborne ever met Queen Elizabeth?'

We were all getting slightly hysterical. It's not every day you meet someone from the sixteenth century. Even Alistair had a dreamy look, but I didn't get the chance to inquire whom he wanted to ask Giles about, for at that moment Nicholas and Father Draycott brought our strange visitor into the kitchen.

CHAPTER THIRTY-TWO

IT WAS the oddest meal I had ever known. We sat round the table as though our chairs had turned to eggshells.

Though his unfortunate jaw was something of a hindrance, the nuns at the retreat had obviously taught Giles twenty-first century table manners. That was his concession to his surroundings, as it were. Our concession was silence from Meta and me (I've often doubted whether sixteenth century women were actually as subservient as all that, but we took no risks) with Nicholas, our host, taking the lead in conversation.

'You have been praying in the gatehouse, Sir Giles?'

Giles nodded eagerly. 'I would go back, sir.'

Back in time, or back to the gatehouse? The double edged statement nearly made me choke on my chicken salad. I caught Alistair's eye. He winked at me – he could never be grave for long – and I nearly burst out laughing. Exhaustion was making me light headed.

'You shall go back, Sir Giles,' Nicholas assured our visitor. I could not decide whether he was answering in both meanings, but held my peace. I think Meta had kicked Alistair under the table. 'However,' Nicholas continued, this formality suiting him strangely, 'we do have guests staying there at present.'

Giles looked disappointed.

Madogany edged nearer the table, nearer Alistair to be precise, and drew his jaws together as though he were starved. Alistair slipped him some chicken. He gobbled it noisily, thus giving himself away.

'An old but handsome dog, sir,' Father Draycott observed to Nicholas, surreptitiously tossing down some chicken himself. More noisy chomping beneath the table. Father Freese followed suit. Madogany sighed in contentment.

'You knew Bishop White, Sir Giles?' Father Freese asked.

Everybody else tensed, but Giles merely nodded, his eyes filling. 'I have come from his funeral, sir. He was the saintliest of men.'

This was one question answered at least. We had the 1560 Giles Tychborne with us. It seemed certain now that he was the man who would die with Francis twenty-two years into his own time, provided we got him back, of course. It seemed also that Giles's last memory of 1560 was fresh in his mind, fourteen months later. He must have dwelt on it, brooding, throughout his exile in our mad century.

'Indeed,' Father Draycott said. 'Bishop White was God's servant first.'

Giles evidently recognised the neat paraphrasing of More's words on the scaffold, spoken twenty-five years before 1560. His eyes lit up and he nodded.

'God's servant above all, sir,' he said.

I thought of those White had condemned to burn alive, of the fate awaiting Giles himself, and shuddered. But I said nothing. I remained the very image of a subservient female throughout the meal. Between us we were doing well, relaxing Giles into a certain graciousness at odds with his clumsy appearance.

'His Grace of Norfolk showed Bishop White much honour at the funeral,' Father Freese ventured.

'Greatly. I am glad of it,' Giles answered.

Meaning, probably, that he hoped Norfolk would cast aside his Protestant veneer and revert to the old faith. I wondered whether he had taken anything to do with Norfolk's subsequent rebellion.

Alistair said cautiously, 'Sir Giles, regarding the Southwark priest named Francis Deverell…'

Giles actually smiled. 'He is like a brother to me, sir.'

Madogany sat up and barked, half heartedly, tail wagging. He subsided almost at once and presently I heard screeching far off. It was Elizabeth; the Weightmans must be back at the gatehouse. I supposed I ought to go round and see them at some point, though I no longer felt much connection with them. I could not believe I was married to Emery. It seemed an absurdity.

'Francis Deverell was at the bishop's funeral?' Father Freese asked.

Giles nodded. 'He could not absent himself from that, sir.' He looked at Nicholas. He must have seen that similarity which had made me so uneasy. 'You are of Francis's family, sir?'

This was awkward. How much did he realise of his plight, hundreds of years away from his own world? He had been told about Francis's death in 1582; that was why he had sought prayer in the attic. He must know now, if he had not realised before, that he had been in his own future for fourteen months. But if he was from 1560 he would not know that he would be executed alongside Francis. We had not known ourselves until so recently.

Nicholas handled the awkward moment well. 'I am honoured to be of his family, Sir Giles.' He gestured towards Meta. 'As is my sister.'

Meta gave Giles a dignified nod. He bowed his head to her. 'Madam.'

Madogany sat up and barked, not half heartedly this time. He padded to the French windows and stayed there, head back, his deep barking growing louder and more agitated. The noise was tremendous.

'Not Vaganov,' Nicholas said, shouting to be heard. 'Different bark.' He stood up, as did every one else, and went to the window, putting his hand on the old dog's collar. 'Hey, shush, boy, shush!' But Madogany was not to be silenced. Peering out, I glimpsed a man in a buff coat and breastplate carrying a sword.

'It's a soldier,' I said. But he was already gone. Everyone stared at me. Giles seemed to shrink against the kitchen worktops.

'If it's a soldier, he's from 1582,' Alistair said, 'but Giles is here. We have to get him back to 1560 first, haven't we?'

Nobody answered because nobody knew. We were all at a loss. Madogany went on barking.

Giles crossed himself. 'What mean you, sir?' he asked Alistair.

An invisible object hit the window hard. Nicholas stepped back. Madogany went wild, jumping up and straining to be let loose.

'Something's happening,' Father Draycott said. 'We're all aware of it this time, not just Imogen.'

'We're under attack,' Alistair said. 'Perhaps somebody hid here that night.'

Without warning, Giles pushed past Nicholas and ran from the kitchen, heading round the corner towards the gatehouse. I think we were all too surprised to follow at first. Then another invisible missile hit the window, cracking it. Nicholas jumped back sharply. Madogany got free and shot away, barking madly.

'He'll be killed,' Meta exclaimed and started to run after him. Nicholas grabbed her, hauling her back. 'I'll go after him. You stay here.'

But Meta had had enough womanly subservience for one night. She shook him off indignantly. So we all went out into the garden, anticipating mayhem. But nothing else happened. Shaken, we looked at each other. The whole incident had lasted less than a minute. There was no sign of Giles, but eventually even Madogany came padding back and greeted us like long lost friends.

'You're going on a lead,' Nicholas told him.

We stood there, in that beautiful garden, trying to understand what had just happened. 'Time blurred?' Father Freese suggested at last. 'Everything's speeded up since Father Tychborne got here.'

'Do you think he's got back?' Alistair asked quickly.

I saw the hope in Nicholas's face. If Giles had gone back to his own time, it might mean Freya was here. Surely she would make for the house. She might be here any moment. His eyes scanned the grounds rapidly and of course saw nothing. I slipped my hand into his. He held it tight.

'If he has got back,' Father Freese said, 'let's hope it's to 1560 and not 1582.'

A childish scream. From the gatehouse. Nicholas let go my hand and whirled round. 'No,' he said, 'that's not Freya.'

'Elizabeth, again,' I said. In my mind's eye I saw Jack lying on the gatehouse steps. It had been dark then and it was suddenly dark now. Frightened, I clutched at Nicholas's arm, heard Meta give a little cry behind me. That was when I realised it had gone dark for all of us. No friendly light came from French windows. And Elizabeth was still screaming.

'Dear God,' Father Freese muttered behind me. To my right Father Draycott had begun to pray.

'Link hands,' Alistair ordered. 'There should be six of us. I want everyone to say his or her name out loud.'

We obeyed. It calmed us somewhat. I even began to feel relief that this time I was not alone. But Madogany was half barking, half whining.

'I need to find Freya,' Nicholas said. 'I have to get to those woods…'

'I wouldn't.' Alistair was firm. 'You won't find her in the dark and six of us can help her more than one. Take the gatehouse first. The Weightmans must be terrified. Anything could be happening in there. They have children too, Nicholas.'

Nicholas drew a sharp, angry breath, but he stayed with the rest of us. We made our way slowly round the corner. Everything was in darkness. I felt like a veteran with everyone else slipping about in the mud.

'Wait,' I said. 'It's all wrong. The courtyard should have been lit up like a Christmas tree. They were giving a feast for an earl…'

'Is it later at night?' Father Draycott suggested. He glanced up to the star strewn sky, but of course their positioning told him nothing; he was in a different time.

'Perhaps they carried out the arrests much later in the night, to catch Francis and Dominic off guard,' Alistair said. 'And Clement wouldn't want to disturb the feast while he was entertaining this earl. If the earl was staying overnight, he could show him the prisoners next morning.'

No sooner had he spoken than the past slipped away. Daylight returned. The six of us were revealed to each other, muddy footed and ashen faced, beside one very muddy, whining Labrador whose tail was beneath his legs.

'Thank God,' Meta whispered. 'Thank God…'

Alistair put his arm round her. 'The Weightmans,' he said. 'We'll have to tell them now. I should have done it before, shouldn't I? It would have been less of a shock for them now.'

'Marcia didn't want to know,' I said.

Nicholas was still angry. 'I'll tell them now.' He went forward to the gatehouse door, but it opened before he got there.

Emery stood on the threshold. He had his ridiculous boater on his head, but his face was frightened and bewildered.

'Nice timing, Nicholas,' he said, his voice growing more hostile with every word. 'We're leaving. We're not staying here another night.'

CHAPTER THIRTY-THREE

'A MAN came out the guardroom chimney,' Elizabeth sobbed. She was curled up in Marcia's arms on the drawing room sofa. 'It went dark and then a man came out the chimney. He was a scary man...'

I didn't doubt it. Dominic, of course. I had seen him emerge from the chimney myself. It seemed a long time ago now.

'Did he say anything?' Meta asked. She was sitting beside Marcia and Elizabeth on the sofa.

Elizabeth shook her head and buried her face in Marcia's shoulder. Marcia patted her automatically, while looking up and glaring at Nicholas.

'You should have told us,' she said. 'We would never have come here.'

'The disturbances only began this week,' Nicholas said with more patience than I thought Marcia deserved. Considering how angry and distraught he had been earlier, I could only admire his dignity. 'You'll get your money back, of course.'

'That's good of you,' Bob said.

Marcia looked over to Father Draycott, who was standing near the window. 'Are you going to exorcise the place?'

'We don't know,' Nicholas said, but he kept his torment out of his face.

'Why don't you know?'

Nicholas did not answer immediately. He obviously saw no point in telling the Weightmans about Freya and Giles. I think he was right. The Weightmans would never believe it. By comparison with time travel, ghostly activity was mundane. 'It might be dangerous,' he said at last.

'Well, you'll lose business if you don't,' Marcia hissed. It was a threat; she was going to broadcast her family's experiences to the world. Since he had no right to try to stop her, Nicholas did not rise to the bait.

'What do you mean, dangerous?' Emery demanded, more observant than his sister. He was perched on the window seat, his tone still hostile to Nicholas. I had never seen him like this before. I suppose, from his point of view, Nicholas had gone off with his wife and frightened his niece. It made my blood boil that he didn't appear to take into account his own infidelity or Nicholas's powerlessness in the grip of darker forces, but I bit back my fury. This was no time for recriminations and Emery and I were finished. After tonight I need never see him again.

'I'd have thought that was obvious,' Father Freese said.

Nicholas shook his head slightly at the well meaning intervention.

'Well, pardon my ignorance,' Emery retorted.

'It's for Nicholas to decide,' Father Draycott said. 'Nobody's denying that the supernatural has been at work here. How the problem is resolved need not concern you and your family.'

'I want to know,' Jack said. 'I want to stay.'

He was sitting in one of the armchairs, his injured shoulder propped up on cushions, his face eager and curious.

'For goodness sake, Jack,' Marcia snapped. 'We're going to start packing in a minute. We're staying the night in a hotel.'

Jack looked mutinous. 'I want to stay. I want to see the singing priest.'

'Singing priest?' Marcia said. She swung round to Alistair. 'The one you said was held prisoner in this gatehouse?'

Alistair nodded. 'In 1582, yes. We think the man who tried to rescue him hid in the gatehouse chimney. Your daughter glimpsed him tonight. He was the singing priest's nephew.'

Marcia digested this, then brought her guns to bear again. 'You should have told us. Elizabeth's been frightened for nothing.' She looked accusingly at me. 'You were in on the secret, I suppose?'

'No,' Nicholas said. 'Imogen knew no more than we did. We've only found out this week ourselves. We've had researchers on the job.'

'Research,' Marcia sneered. 'That hasn't helped us, has it?'

'You'll have a full refund,' Nicholas pointed out, again.

'I don't want a refund,' Jack said. 'I want to stay.'

'You're not staying and that's that,' Marcia said.

Nicholas's mobile bleeped. 'Excuse me.' He turned away, checked the message. I heard him draw breath sharply. Father Freese was also checking his mobile. Nicholas took me aside quietly. 'It's from Lydia Freese, Lionel's wife,' he said. 'She's a cathedral guide. She must be there at the moment.'

'Has Giles turned up there again?'

'No.' He showed me the message.

Vaganov's cars burned in the cathedral close. All dead.

I was aghast. It was a shocking and horrible end. The cathedral close was the last place I would have expected such an occurrence. I would not have sought that fate even for Vaganov. But I was relieved that one pressure on Nicholas had lifted. My love for a gentle man was making me savage.

'It's connected,' Nicholas said to me as Father Freese showed his message to the Sievewrights and Father Draycott. 'It's got to be. Madogany thought Vaganov was here, then suddenly he wasn't.'

'Hang on, Nicholas.' It wasn't the first time he had been ahead of me. 'Are you saying you think Vaganov and his goons went back in time? That they came here to put more pressure on you, that somehow their cars were set alight here in the sixteenth century, but ended up in Winchester Cathedral close in the twenty-first? Winchester's miles from here.'

'It must have been the moment Giles disappeared,' Nicholas said. 'How else could Vaganov get to the cathedral from here so quickly? And who would set fire to cars in the close in our own time? Perhaps there was a fire here in 1582.'

'If you're right, time's getting crazier,' I said. And more dangerous, I might have added. Not to say ironic, since burning alive had been the fate of Bishop White's religious opponents in the sixteenth century. Don't be idiotic, I told myself. What would Vaganov's death have to do with Bishop White? And yet it had all seemed to begin fourteen months ago in the Lady Chapel…

'Are you okay?' Nicholas asked me.

'I'm just getting crazier as time gets crazier,' I said, smiling and trying to make light of it. But I knew it was one of those notions that never quite go away.

'What's going on?' Emery demanded. 'Why are you all whispering?'

'Nothing that need concern you,' Alistair said. 'I take it you'll be packing now, Mrs Weightman? Nicholas will have your refund ready when you are.'

Marcia looked taken aback. 'Of course,' she said.

'Has Jack's fall anything to do with this?' Emery asked suddenly. My heart sank. He was not the ambulance chasing type, but this would be the perfect way to get back at Nicholas.

'Well, Jack?' he asked.

Jack, with wisdom beyond his years, said nothing, but the tension seemed to rise in the drawing room. Meta was sitting bolt upright now.

'You told us you saw soldiers,' Elizabeth almost sang at Jack.

Emery's face lit up. 'Ghostly soldiers?'

'You weren't here,' Jack retorted.

'Don't be cheeky,' Marcia snapped.

'But I was here.' Elizabeth bounced on the sofa in her glee. 'You said you saw soldiers. You said you saw soldiers.'

I could have clapped my hand over her mouth, but it was too late. Emery was off the window seat now, pointing at Nicholas. 'You weren't going to tell us, were you? You were going to let us leave without knowing. No wonder Jack fell downstairs. He must have had such a fright.'

'I tripped,' Jack said. 'It was nothing to do with the soldiers.'

'Oh, really?'

'You went to a party in London!' Jack shouted. 'You left Imogen alone!'

'Jack!' Marcia exclaimed. 'Apologise, now!'

'No,' Jack said.

The lights left us. Elizabeth shrieked. Someone was shouting in the bedroom next door. I recognised Clement's voice. Madogany whined, his tail between his legs. The shouting next door grew louder.

'Everyone stand up,' I warned, 'or you'll fall,'

Meta shot to her feet, followed by a startled Jack.

'What's happening?' Marcia demanded. Then she and Elizabeth tumbled to the floor as the sofa disappeared. I was malicious enough to wish Emery had still been on the window seat. Elizabeth burst into terrified wails.

No wonder. The softly lit drawing room had become a moonlit chamber with rough stone walls, everything bare except the odd pallet on the ground on stinking floor rushes. When I turned to look out the window, I saw utter darkness on one side and the flickering glow of torches from the courtyard on the other. It wasn't just me. We were all in the sixteenth century.

CHAPTER THIRTY-FOUR

MADOGANY sprang like a younger dog at the shadows on the wall, barking frenziedly and incessantly.

'Stay calm, everyone,' Alistair called out. 'Don't move until your eyes adjust to the darkness. I think we might be in the sixteenth century.'

He was calm himself. His authority just about held things together for the moment. Emery and the Weightmans initially seemed less stunned than they would have been had they known nothing about the week's supernatural activity. Only Elizabeth panicked, howling and huddling into Marcia.

The sixteenth century?' Marcia said. 'Are you out of your mind?'

'I'm afraid not,' Alistair said. 'The good news from your point of view is that the locals may not be able to see any of us except Imogen.'

'The locals?' Marcia was bemused. 'There's no one…'

But Clement's shouting was louder now. No one could doubt now that we were no longer alone in the gatehouse.

'What do you mean, they can see Imogen?' Emery whispered.

'It's happened to me before,' I said. 'You become visible eventually.'

'We're invisible first though?' Jack said. 'Wicked!'

'Sh!' Marcia ordered. She turned on Nicholas. 'Is this some sort of joke? Are you trying to frighten us?'

'It's not a joke,' Meta said coldly.

Emery swore, fear in his voice. Father Freese had fallen to his knees. Madogany began scrabbling at the door.

'That's Clement next door,' I said. 'Someone to avoid.'

'Who's Clement?' Jack demanded.

'The priest's brother, who captured him.'

Emery laughed shakily. 'That's enough now,' he said to no one in particular. He held up his hands as if surrendering. 'I admit it, you've made your point.'

'We have no point to make. It's not a joke,' Meta repeated.

'You're kidding me! You have to be! You're going to do ghost tours here, and you're trying them out on us!'

Meta did not deign to reply.

Silence fell as reality began to sink in. Emery had the presence of mind to take out his mobile and try it. He swore again; the mobile was dead, as mine had always been. Seeing this, Elizabeth wailed louder. Marcia tried to soothe her, fighting fear, looking accusingly at Bob, who made no sound, but I saw the terror in his face. Father Freese stood up, went over to him. They stood together quietly, Father Freese praying again. Presently, Bob began praying too. Jack edged over to me. Nicholas and Father Draycott dragged Madogany away from the door.

'Shush, boy, good boy! Be quiet! Good dog!'

But nothing would shut Madogany up. Tension rose in that shadowy room.

'Knock the mutt out!' Emery yelled.

Alistair gave him a look that showed he wanted to knock Emery out. 'No need to worry,' he said. 'Time will right itself. It always has with Imogen up until now.'

'Imogen's really gone back in time before?' Emery stared at me, suddenly comprehending the reason for my odd behaviour this week. Then he panicked. 'We've gone back in time?' he yelled at Alistair. 'Think about what you're saying! Suppose it's different now? Suppose we can't get back?'

'If they can hear any of us, it will be you,' Alistair pointed out. 'Look at Jack over there. Not a word out of him and you're three times his age.'

Emery glanced round sheepishly. Even Elizabeth's wails were lessening, though her face was still buried in Marcia's waist.

'All right,' he said, 'but you'd better have a plan to get us out of this.'

'The plan is to stay quiet and wait,' Alistair said. 'It's obvious they don't use this room.'

Emery pointed to the thin pallets. 'They sleep here, don't they?'

'Unlikely,' Father Draycott said. 'Only the priest and his gaoler have been sleeping in the gatehouse.'

'And suppose that changes tonight?' Emery muttered, but he stepped backwards towards the window and didn't continue his argument.

'Can anyone make Clement out?' Father Draycott asked. 'I thought I heard the name Tychborne.'

'Who's Tychborne?' Marcia demanded. She turned to Alistair. 'Who's Tychborne? Another nephew of the singing priest?'

I saw my own indecision mirrored in Alistair's eyes. Was there any point in telling her that Tychborne was the man she had known as Father Coll? There was too much to tell and we barely understood it ourselves…

'A second priest, who tried to rescue the singing priest,' Alistair said. 'He and the singing priest's nephew were acting together.'

'What happened to him?' Jack asked.

'He was executed at Tyburn alongside the singing priest.'

'What happened to the nephew?'

'No one knows.'

Jack nodded, then said, 'I'll listen at the door.' He put his young ear to the wall, stayed there for perhaps a minute. It seemed longer. He shook his head reluctantly. 'It's all muffled and angry, so I can't hear any names. I'll open the door.' He set off fearlessly for it.

'Oh no, you don't…' Meta, who was nearest, grabbed him back and marched him over to Bob.

'Perhaps Father Draycott heard the name Tychborne clearly because he's a priest too,' Emery said.

The implication – that Father Draycott might die with his sixteenth century counterparts – was clever and gratuitous. Everyone remained silent for a few minutes. Even Madogany was growing less agitated in the arms of Nicholas, who crouched on the floor. But no one could make out anything of the bellowing next door.

'I hear music,' Jack whispered presently.

'They're holding a feast,' I said. 'Clement must have left his earl at the feast to come round to the gatehouse.'

'He's captured someone,' Father Freese said. 'Tychborne, do you think?'

It seemed all too likely. It was appalling to think of.

'Don't interfere,' Emery said. 'We can't interfere. We can't change history.'

'Unless we're part of history already,' Father Draycott said.

Emery groaned. 'I knew you'd say that. That's all we need. A Catholic priest with a death wish…'

I thought, *why did I marry that man?*

I started to speak, angrily, but Father Freese got there before I did, equally angry. 'If you were prepared to give it a moment's consideration, sir, you would realise that Father Draycott may be right.'

Emery sulked in the shadows, but said no more. There was silence again, broken soon afterwards by a child's cry down below our windows. Madogany whined. Nicholas was already on his feet, running to the window.

'Freya!'

Five of us ran to the window, saw nothing; she must have been directly below the gatehouse. Nicholas fought with the window catch, but it was jammed.

'I've got to find her.' He ran to the door, wrenched it open. Torchlight from the stair flooded the room. He was illuminated less than a second. He was gone, his feet frantic and uneven on the wooden steps. Madogany followed him, bounding madly like a dog half his age, sending Meta flying in her efforts to stop him. Alistair lifted her to her feet, turned to me.

'I think you should stay here, Imogen. They can see you.'

Then he was gone too.

'I don't care if they can see me,' I burst out to Meta. It was frustrating. I had done everything until now. But I realised that Alistair had been right. If I didn't stay hidden, I might endanger Freya when she was so close to rescue, so close to seeing Nicholas again...

'I'm sorry,' Meta said, and took my hand.

'Who's Freya?' Marcia asked softly.

'My niece,' Meta answered. I don't know whether I had expected her to evade the question.

'But Nicholas's daughter is missing,' Emery said.

'Think about it,' Meta answered and left him to work it out.

I ran back to the window, but saw and heard nothing at first. Then, movement below, the flash of a dropped torch and shouting. It was Nicholas, like a berserker. And Madogany biting, barking and growling. The terrified yells of men set upon by two invisible men and an invisible dog. As the goons turned and ran, they stumbled into view, four grotesque shadows in the torchlight. They whirled, flailing uselessly, and went down beneath Alistair's finely judged blows, Nicholas's fury, Madogany's teeth. How long it was after that I have no idea, but suddenly I saw Nicholas and Alistair sprinting back towards the gatehouse. Nicholas was carrying a ragged bundle, hugging it to him, while Madogany gambolled alongside them like a puppy.

'Oh God, they've got her...'

Tears spilled out of me. I turned, found everyone else behind me. The nearest shoulder was Father Draycott's. He comforted me as though I were a child, turning me gently to face the door so that I saw Nicholas run in with Freya in his arms.

Father and daughter were both weeping, Freya clinging to Nicholas, Madogany dancing round her dirty, bare feet. Meta ran to Alistair and embraced him, then turned to Freya and hugged her, but did not try to detach her from Nicholas.

'You've done God's work today...' Father Freese was weeping.

The Weightmans stood back, allowing Freya's family privacy, but Jack was cheering under his breath and Elizabeth was peering over at Freya with intense curiosity. 'She smells a bit, doesn't she, mummy?'

'One more remark like that and I'll leave you in the sixteenth century,' Marcia shot back.

Nicholas sat down on the floor, still cradling Freya. Madogany licked her face voraciously. She put out a skinny arm to cuddle him and he flung himself against her in delight, nearly crushing her.

Emery was at my shoulder. 'You might have told me 'missing' meant she was stuck in the past,' he murmured.

'You'd have believed me, would you?' I tried to move away from him. He followed me.

'Gen, suppose we don't get back? Suppose the kid wasn't meant to be with us? She might have landed us all here for good.'

'You'd better not let Nicholas or Alistair hear you say that.' I turned my back and walked away from him. This time he didn't follow. What he had said was a possibility, of course. We simply didn't know, but I was determined not to think about it for now. I had learned not to think too much this week.

Alistair came over to me, smiling wryly.

'What happened down there?' I asked.

'We met a group of Clement's men,' he said, 'bringing Freya here, for questioning probably. We got there just in time, I think.'

'You took them all on?'

He smiled. 'Nicholas too. And Madogany. It was a pleasure. I always wanted to be invisible to the enemy.'

I laughed. Now that Freya was re-united with Nicholas, the rough, moonlit chamber was a different place.

'The front door was unlocked and the guardroom empty,' Alistair said. 'Bilson must be next door with Clement. Oh, and Nicholas wants to speak to you.'

'I should wait a bit. I'm not family…'

'Think you might be now.' And Alistair took my arm and brought me over to Nicholas, who lifted Freya up so that she could see me better.

'Look, sweetheart,' he said. 'Do you remember Imogen?'

She nodded on a crying jag. I knelt down. Madogany, expert ice breaker, head butted my kidneys and I landed on top of father and daughter. Freya actually giggled with us as Alistair pulled me up to my knees. Nicholas caught my hand.

'Don't distance yourself,' he whispered.

'Freya needs all of you for a while,' I said.

'And I need all of you. Here.'

His words amazed and delighted me. I didn't know how to reply.

'Give it thought,' Nicholas whispered and put his head back down to Freya. I had hesitated too long. He was diffident and must have thought me reluctant.

'I don't need to think about it,' I said.

He looked up, eyes soft in the moonlight.

Then the screaming began next door.

CHAPTER THIRTY-FIVE

Freya whimpered, burying her face in Nicholas's shoulder again. Marcia automatically put her hands over Elizabeth's ears. Everyone else froze.

They were a man's screams, repeated, helpless, agonised.

'It's Giles,' Meta whispered. 'It must be, unless they've brought Francis down from the attic.'

We all listened, appalled. The screams did not stop. I thought I heard the word *Miserere*, drawn out into a shriek.

Emery was first to speak. 'You can't interfere. It's history. It's already happened.'

'Easier said than done,' Father Freese replied. 'And how do we know we haven't brought it about?'

'Who's Giles?' Bob asked.

'Tychborne,' Meta said. 'Father Giles Tychborne.'

'So they tortured him before they hanged him at Tyburn?'

Meta nodded. Bob shut his eyes, pressed his hand to his forehead. Still the screaming continued. Silence. Marcia winced and shook her head, as if trying to make herself deaf. Freya went on whimpering despite Nicholas's attempts to comfort her. Madogany whined.

'We've got to do something,' Father Freese said. 'We're here now, and it's happening next door. Most of us are still invisible, so it's not a great risk.' He looked at Alistair. 'What do you think?'

'You can't,' Emery put in. 'You just can't. It might backfire on us ...'

'I for one can't listen and do nothing,' Alistair said.

I think everyone except Emery felt better after that.

'I can't stand by either,' Father Draycott said. 'It's history, it's the stuff of my reading in Seminary, but I can't stand by...'

'Nor me.' And Bob put his hand up like a timid but determined schoolboy in class. Marcia didn't object.

I was moved. Less than a week ago, none of us would have believed what was happening to us could be possible. Now, frightened though we all were, we were finding the courage not just to face the sixteenth century, but to engage it.

Nicholas broke the silence. 'You know I'd help in any other circumstances, but...' He looked down at Freya, who still whimpered in his arms. I was glad he had put her first. The lover in me was glad, too, that he would not be risking himself.

'You certainly can't leave her, Nicholas. Four's enough.' Alistair was decisive in the moonlight, disposing his troops.

'I'll go,' Emery said, 'against my better judgement, mind.'

Alistair nodded approvingly. 'No need. You can keep an eye on this room. Remember, Freya and Imogen are visible.'

'Hey,' Meta hissed. 'Marcia and I aren't useless females, you know.'

'I should think not.' Marcia advanced on Alistair.

'Now, ladies, you know I'd never think that.' He stepped back adroitly, opened the door softly. Our brief, almost desperate levity evaporated as the agonised sound from next door grew clearer with the opening of the door. The screams were turning to moans; the prisoner was losing strength.

'Bloody hell,' Emery muttered. 'What are they doing to him?'

'We'll stop it,' Alistair said resolutely.

At that moment the screams ceased. Most likely the prisoner had lost consciousness.

'Better that way,' Alistair remarked. 'We'll make sure it doesn't start again, shall we? Let's go…'

He made to leave the room, but stepped back in surprise as the door swung towards him. A middle aged, magnificently dressed man entered, looking about him curiously, a dirty horn lamp in his hand.

Dread filled us. Most of us gasped, jumped back. Father Draycott crossed himself. Elizabeth shrieked and went on shrieking.

'Fuck me,' Emery said, trembling all over. 'Is he from the sixteenth century? Oh, fuck, who is he?'

Marcia put a hand over Elizabeth's mouth and gave her a little shake. 'Stop it, he's harmless, nothing's going to happen to you…'

But she was staring at the newcomer as she said it.

We were all staring at him, because he was staring back at us. We were no longer invisible. We had lost our protection much quicker than we had anticipated. It changed everything.

Nicholas stood up, still holding the whimpering Freya, and edged backwards with her. Bob and Father Freese both moved nearer them to hide her from the newcomer.

He was still trying to make sense of his surrounding, obviously taken aback by so many oddly dressed strangers. He was white haired and paunchy. Veins stood out on his plump cheeks. No doubt he thought, as did the ageing queen and the rest of her courtiers, that gaudy finery made up for the loss of youth. I could not distinguish accurately the colour of his doublet and breeches in the lamplight, but the satin gleamed. The lace on his ruff and sleeves must have cost more than an ordinary man could hope to earn in a lifetime.

'Robert Dudley,' Meta whispered, evidently recognising him from his portrait as an ageing man before I did. 'The Earl of Leicester. Queen Elizabeth's lover.'

Journeying into the past was mind boggling enough, I was only just getting accustomed to it, but to encounter a well known figure in sixteenth century English history, someone I had read about in numerous books, whose portrait as an athletic but conceited young man I had also seen, who had rebelled against Queen Mary and almost married Queen Elizabeth... I was struck dumb.

What a coup, though, for Clement. Dudley was well known for his hard line attitude to Catholics. Having him as a guest was an impressive way of demonstrating that the Deverell family had joined the winning side.

'What means this?' Dudley demanded, recovering his wits. I saw the unthinking arrogance of a man who was powerful at the court of a powerful Queen. 'Who are you varlets?' He caught sight of the two priests. 'Ha! Papists!'

There were twelve of us, so discretion got the better part of valour. He turned round, evidently intending to summon Clement and reinforcements.

Alistair stepped forward. 'I don't think so, old chap...'

He snatched the lamp, thrust it at me and seized Dudley. He swung him round vigorously to face the wall, put his hand over his mouth and dragged his arms behind his back.

'Someone's trouser belt would be handy,' he remarked. 'Next time I travel to the sixteenth century, I'd really prefer to meet Roger Ascham...'

'Will this do?' Father Freese took off his belt.

'Just the job.' Alistair smiled grimly. 'I'll hold. You tie. Hard, mind. We don't want him getting free...'

While he held the struggling Dudley's arms together, Father Freese looped the belt round his wrists, ruining the fine lace. Without being prompted, Marcia produced a handkerchief to gag Dudley with. She did this herself, efficiently, before returning to the still crying Elizabeth.

'I suppose you decided to explore your host's house when the prisoner lost consciousness and the fun stopped?' Alistair manhandled the furious, struggling Dudley into the far corner and thrust him squatting into it. 'There's an interesting staircase in this gatehouse. What a pity you didn't happen to fall down it...'

Dudley spluttered indignantly, eyes popping above the gag.

'He's trying to say something,' Jack said.

'He wanted to marry Queen Elizabeth, but he was already married,' Meta explained. 'His wife broke her neck and died falling downstairs. So the Queen couldn't marry him because of the scandal.'

'Never!' Jack was at his most wide eyed. 'Did he push her?'

'People thought his servants did,' Meta said. 'We could ask him...'

'Listen to yourselves!' Emery exploded. 'They're going to find us! They'll be the ones asking the questions, not us! And we know how they ask them!'

'Be quiet!' Meta hissed.

Panic stricken though he was, Emery was right. The sang-froid we had managed to catch from Alistair could not hide the danger we were in. Invisibility no longer protected us and someone would come looking for Dudley soon. Such an important guest would not be left to his own devices. I wondered gloomily what the penalty was for imprisoning a Tudor queen's favourite. At her uncle's outburst, Elizabeth began wailing again.

'There was no option,' Alistair reminded Emery. 'He was about to call for Clement, who wants to question Freya.'

'We need to jettison him, now,' Emery said. 'Tie his feet too, take him downstairs and leave him outside in the darkness. They won't find him there for a while. They'll find him here quicker.'

'Quite,' Alistair said, 'though I was going to suggest we should all try to get out, if the front door's unlocked.'

'I'll go and see,' Jack said.

'No.' Alistair shook his head.

'I'll go,' Bob said. 'I'm small and light footed.'

'Bob!' Marcia was aghast.

But Alistair nodded and Bob slipped out without further ado. We heard no sound as we waited anxiously, the two priests standing guard over the apoplectic Dudley. The screaming began again next door. I put my face in my hands. If we got outside, we were abandoning Giles and Francis to the cruelty of history. But what else could we do? We were no longer invisible and our priority had to be the children, especially poor Freya, who had suffered enough.

'The front door's locked now,' Bob said, slipping disconsolately back into the room. 'No sign of a key. Clement must have it.'

This was bitter news, and Bob was only just back in time too. Footsteps pounded upstairs. 'They've found the men you attacked!' Emery hissed at Nicholas.

'You think I care about them?' Nicholas threw back at him.

'Look!' Jack was pointing to the other window, the one which gave a view of the drive. 'Look, it's a fire!'

CHAPTER THIRTY-SIX

EVERYONE except Nicholas and Freya rushed to the window. The vivid orange flames were leaping against the night sky.

'It might be Dominic, trying to create a distraction,' Meta said. 'Of course! We should have realised! That's what Vaganov must have driven into today!'

More pounding on the stairs, down to the ground floor this time, several pairs of feet. Clement and his goons must be leaving to tackle the fire. The front door below crashed shut and locked, hard. In the crisis and semi darkness they must have assumed that Dudley was with them.

Alistair came over to the window and whistled in relief. 'A diversion. Clever. It must be Dominic. We can try and unpick the front door. It's a hell of a muckle thing to deal with, but we'll give it a go.'

'I can do it.' Jack stepped forward.

Marcia glared at him. 'You can do *what*?'

'Good man. Good man.' Alistair clapped Jack on his uninjured shoulder and sent him downstairs.

'So who's the prisoner?' Nicholas asked.

'Ah well, that's the thing.' Alistair looked sombre again. 'It's Giles all right, but our Giles. Giles from 1560, not 1582. He's in his own future.'

It was our worst fear realised. It almost reduced me to despair. 'Time is so skewed, how do we get it back?'

'What do you mean, this Giles is in his own future?' Marcia asked. 'What's this about 1560? You said the singing priest was a prisoner in the attic in 1582.'

Oh heavens, how to explain…

'It's complicated, Marcia.' I took a deep breath. 'The singing priest called Francis Deverell was a prisoner in the attic in 1582. The priest called Giles Tychborne seems to have been propelled forward in time from 1560 to 1582. So here in 1582 he looks twenty-two years younger than he should. We don't know how or why it's happened to him.'

Marcia tried to absorb this, frowning. She didn't ask anything else. I could hardly blame her. She took refuge in action, telling Elizabeth to keep an eye on the fire outside while she herself helped Emery to tie Dudley's feet with his trouser belt.

'I'm going to see Giles,' I said to Alistair.

He caught my arm. 'Maybe not, Imogen. He's in a bad way.'

Dear, chivalrous Alistair. 'I'll be fine,' I said. 'Honestly.'

I wasn't fine, of course. A torch blazed on the wall next door, so I saw everything. I wanted to be sick.

There was no magnificent fireplace in the middle bedroom in 1582, but there was a brazier. They had stretched poor, bruised, bleeding Giles over a couple of benches, heated irons and applied them to his feet. Even if he had wanted to give them information to stop the agony, he could not have done so, because, having come from 1560, he did not yet have the knowledge of Dominic's plans which he would have acquired in 1582.

Father Draycott, kneeling beside him, looked up and shook his head. 'If there's any water anywhere...' he said.

They must have kept water somewhere in the gatehouse. I had seen Bilson cooking in the guardroom. I hobbled down there and found Bob already engaged in a similar fruitless search. We concluded wearily that Clement, Bilson and his informant had snatched up any pails on their way out to tackle the fiery diversion. Poor Giles would have to go without help.

I went back upstairs. Meta, Alistair and Father Freese had joined Father Draycott beside Giles while Marcia kept Elizabeth away. I don't think Giles was aware of us. He was moaning, twisting on the bench. We got him down to the floor as gently as we could. Father Draycott murmured to him in Latin and it seemed to quieten him.

'Does he die now, instead of at Tyburn?' Alistair mused. 'Have we actually altered history? Who does Clement think Giles is? He's too young to be the Giles they know. Or perhaps Clement never met him until 1582.'

I couldn't bear to look at Giles any more. So I went upstairs, to the attic, to see the other prisoner we had all but forgotten. And as I drew nearer, Francis began to sing his sweet plainchant. It occurred to me that he might have been singing all the time, to help Giles, only none of us had heard it.

Like the last time we had met, when Freya had run into the gatehouse, he did not appear surprised to see me, though I was an exhausted, dispirited being with shoulder length hair and wearing strangely straight breeches. Did he remember me from the last time we had met, when he had spoken to me? Nothing fazes these religious types. He seemed to nod at me and went on singing, his bony hands clasped above the wood which kept him prisoner. Well, that was one thing we might be able to do. Suddenly, I was a dynamo of energy. We could surely get him free between all of us.

'I'll be back,' I promised.

I ran downstairs despite my ankle and recruited Alistair, Bob and Emery. They came at once, realising the implications. If we had altered Giles's death, we could give Francis longer life. He could escape, for Jack nearly had the front door open, Dudley was tied up and Clement was still putting out the fire.

'It's all right,' I told Francis. 'We'll try to get you out of the stocks.'

I don't think he cared. He went on singing, a smile playing about his mouth, while the curious beings around him heaved and sweated and swore.

'Door's unlocked and barred inside!' Jack whooped, his voice echoing. I smiled to myself, imagining Marcia torn between pride and mortification. Elizabeth called up a warning that the fire was being put out. And still Francis went on singing.

'Someone shut him up,' Emery grunted.

'Shut up yourself,' Bob muttered.

'He's a fruit loop,' Emery retorted.

'It's called ill treatment and delirium,' I snapped.

'Or faith,' Alistair said.

But moments later the upper bar of the stocks thudded to the attic floor.

'He won't be able to stand on his own,' Alistair said. 'I'll take one arm. Emery, you take the other.' A tactful way of not saying that Bob was too small.

They got Francis upright. He was tall for his time, much taller than Giles. It must have hurt him, but he was still singing as they walked him slowly round the attic a couple of times to test his legs, then over to the door.

'Right,' Alistair said, 'gently does it...'

It was terribly difficult getting that frail, weakened man down to the middle floor in the stair torchlight. It took a long time. I went ahead, afraid all three of them would come down on top of me. Bob followed anxiously.

'Someone's trying the door,' Jack called up to me. 'It's a woman. F-flip, she's got a key.'

'Anna, maybe?' I said. 'Do we let her in or not?'

Nicholas came to the drawing room door, still holding Freya, who was now asleep in his arms. 'No,' he said. He came downstairs. 'It might be Isabella. She's frightened of Clement, so it could be a trick he's put her up to.'

'Let me listen.' I came down to the front door too and put my ear to the door. I heard Anna's voice, calling Francis's name, banging on the door now, having found it unlocked but barred on the inside. 'It's Anna. It's all right.'

So Jack swung open the door. Beyond, shouts and smoke as the erstwhile banqueters fought the blaze on the drive. On the threshold, Anna and, behind her, Dominic, sword in hand. They both looked stunned to see me.

'It's all right,' I said. 'I'm a friend. We all are.'

I stood back to let them in. Anna moved with the slowness of fear and bafflement, staring at my unfamiliar clothes, her fingers clutching a silver crucifix at her throat, but of course Dominic recognised me. He had last seen me tied up on the back of a horse. Suddenly, his sword was on my throat.

'What do you here, woman?'

'I'm here to help your uncle Francis,' I said.

'Dominic?' Nicholas had come down to the ground floor and now stepped forward. 'Don't hurt Imogen. 'She is a friend. We are all friends.'

Dominic's sword went from me to Nicholas, who instinctively shielded Freya from the blade. She stirred in his arms. As if ashamed of threatening a child, Dominic lowered the sword, staring at Nicholas.

'I am her father. I have come to take her home.' Nicholas could have reproached Dominic for putting Freya in danger with his plans to rescue Francis, but he spoke gently. 'Thank you for your kindness to her.'

Dominic nodded, still distrustful. 'What is your business in the gatehouse? The child has not been kept here.'

'We are all here to help your uncle Francis,' Nicholas replied.

'Then help him,' Anna said from the shadows. 'Help him. They will take him and kill him.'

Dominic looked back at her, spoke with more respect than he had shown to the rest of us. 'They are strangers, madam. We know nought of them.'

'We are all friends,' Nicholas repeated. 'I am your kinsman. My name is Nicholas Deverell.'

Dominic scrutinised his face in the flickering torchlight, must have seen his strange resemblance to Francis. But it was not enough. 'I know you not.' He sounded bewildered, then grew angry. Suddenly he had lost control of himself, the blade back at Nicholas's throat despite Freya.

'You think even kinsmen are to be trusted in days like these?' he demanded.

CHAPTER THIRTY-SEVEN

Nicholas held his nerve at sword point. 'Dominic, may I give my daughter to Imogen? She's only a child.'

I was already holding out my arms. Dominic made no objection, so I took the little girl's weight and stepped back. She stirred again and moaned. Nicholas moved in front of us both.

'Dominic, I know what your kinsman Clement has done, but I am of the old faith. I am no heretic and no traitor to your line.'

It was partly a lie, brave, almost reckless, but he knew Dominic had no time to ask more questions and must make a snap judgement and he stood impassive under scrutiny a second time. Abruptly, Dominic nodded, lowered his sword, then pushed past us and sprinted up towards the attics. Nicholas looked wryly at me as he took Freya in his arms once more.

I followed Dominic, who braced himself against the wall as he met the little group of Alistair, Emery and Francis making its way so slowly downstairs.

'Jesu,' he whispered.

He reached forward and in one swift movement took Francis from Alistair and Emery, lifting the tall man up into his arms easily. He made his way down to the tiny middle landing. At which point he became aware of Giles lying in agony on the bedroom floor with Father Draycott, Father Freese and Meta beside him.

He caught his breath.

'You must go, Dominic,' I said. 'You can only save Francis. You can't save them both. We'll stay with Father Tychborne. He won't die alone.'

Then Francis saw Giles. His singing ceased. He raised his hands and twisted his body, struggling feebly against Dominic's strong grip.

'Francis isn't going to let himself be rescued,' Alistair said from above. 'I don't think we're going to alter history, after all…'

'Just take Francis downstairs!' I shouted at Dominic. 'You're stronger than he is! He won't be able to stop you! You're running out of time!' But the young man, so forceful before, looked crippled by indecision. I tugged hopelessly at his arm.

'It's no use, Imogen,' Meta said. 'Francis is a martyr.'

'He can't be!' Jack protested. 'Not after everything we've done!'

In the drawing room Elizabeth began to cry. I ran downstairs, found Anna praying on her knees outside the guardroom. I tried to speak to her, even shook her, but she ignored me. Eventually, I ran back upstairs, just as Dominic took his decision and carried Francis into the bedroom.

'Bloody fool!' Emery yelled at him.

'He was Bishop White's page,' Nicholas said dully. 'He was trained to obey churchmen.'

Dominic set Francis down beside Giles. I was watching his face when he saw Giles. He was blank with shock at first. I could not tell whether it was because Giles was twenty-two years younger than he had been the last time he saw him in 1582, or because Giles had been missing since Bishop White's funeral in 1560 and had now turned up looking no older. As for Francis, I don't think he noticed anything amiss except Giles's suffering.

Father Draycott drew back. Francis knelt painfully beside Giles. He looked at him with gentleness and pity, touching his face and feet.

'He suffers, but he will live,' he said.

I wondered what ghastly knowledge lay behind such certainty. How many others had Francis seen who had been tortured for their faith and not lived? How much more brutally did a man have to be treated in order to die?

'If he's going to live, then in the name of God, get him out of here,' Father Freese pleaded. 'Get away, both of you. I'm an Anglican priest and you're not going to Tyburn for me. Not in my name…'

Father Draycott stood up, red eyed, gave Francis his rosary back, made the sign of the cross over him and Giles, then helped Father Freese to his feet. 'Come on, now, Lionel. It's for them to decide. Perhaps it was meant to happen like this, after all.'

Then the banging began on the guardroom's external door, just as I had heard it in the night. It was too late to rescue either Giles or Francis. Downstairs Anna began screaming. That too I had heard, knowing nothing…

Hearing the soldiers below, Dominic swung round sharply, left the middle bedroom. I knew where he was going. He would hide in the guardroom chimney and try to kill Clement. And he would die, his death covered up by his own uncle, the man he had tried to kill.

'It's the soldiers!' Jack called up. 'There's loads of them! They're breaking down the door!'

The banging on the guardroom door had become thudding, the soldiers using some heavy implement as a battering ram. Nicholas held Freya closer to him, looked at me with horrified eyes.

'They won't know we're here,' I said desperately. 'They won't get Freya. They won't notice us. Not if we stay in the drawing room. Dudley can't call out.'

'Come here then,' Nicholas hissed.

'Jack! Come back up here!' Marcia ordered.

Jack scrabbled up to the middle landing. But instead of going into the drawing room, he peered into the middle bedroom, staring at Francis, whom he had heard but never seen until now.

'It's me,' he said. 'I prayed with you, remember? You changed to English for me. You were saying Our Father. Do you remember?'

Francis's eyes were closed. He was praying. But, hearing Jack's voice, he opened his eyes. How could he have remembered, with his delirium and fear? But he nodded, and Jack smiled, stepped towards him.

'Jack!' Marcia shouted.

'Don't you understand?' he shouted back. 'It's the soldiers I saw! That's why I fell downstairs!'

'Jack, you can't stop them now either,' I said.

He still did not move, so I shoved him towards Marcia. She hauled him into the drawing room. Everyone else from my time was there now, Father Freese weeping in Father Draycott's arms. I stood on the middle landing looking at Francis and Giles in the bedroom. They were praying together in Latin, quietly and calmly, as I knew they would on the scaffold.

'Get in here! Now!' Nicholas yelled at me. He couldn't pull me in with Freya in his arms. Madogany barked madly.

The guardroom door crashed in. Hob nailed boots resounded on the floor. But Francis and Giles continued praying. I couldn't move. I had seen more of their world than anyone else; no matter the consequences, I simply couldn't leave them there, alone and defenceless. But Alistair leaned forward and dragged me into the drawing room. He slammed the door.

Weeping, unable to fight him or look at anyone else, I bent to the key hole, so that I glimpsed the first of the soldiers to reach the landing, a small, sweating man in a filthy padded jacket, with a dirty, scarred face and bloodshot eyes. Madogany went into a frenzy, jumping and scrabbling at the keyhole, barking desperately.

We heard everything, the blows, the bawling of orders, the sheer chaos of too many undisciplined men carrying out a shameful mission. Then, with Dominic's arrival, resistance at last, and the clash of weapons. Anna's screams grew nearer, then turned into the howls of grief.

Moments later, the electricity came on. We had returned to our own time.

It was a shock in itself. We felt relief, of course, at first.

'We're back in the present!' Elizabeth screeched. She jumped up and down, bouncing on the suddenly luxurious soft furnishings, trying to make Marcia join in with her. 'We're back in the present!

Dudley had gone. And Freya was with us. Unused to electric light, she woke up, rubbed her eyes, saw Nicholas and smiled.

'We're all here, even my little girl's here...' Nicholas all but collapsed on the sofa with her in his arms. Madogany put two huge, chocolate paws up and began licking her face ecstatically. Nicholas held out his hand to me blindly. I took it, but I knew that if I sat down beside him I would never stand up.

Jack was trying to hold back tears. 'The singing priest recognised me.' He turned to Alistair. 'Will it happen again?'

Now that the danger was over, Alistair was shattered. Only his schoolmaster's instinct enabled him to answer the boy's question.

'Not to you, young man,' he said. 'Somehow, I don't think it'll happen to anyone again. That felt like an ending.'

He was right. I could feel it myself, but I was too exhausted, too distraught, to try to work out why.

'Thought you were a goner there, Gen,' Emery said at my elbow.

I had no energy and less inclination to reply. And I don't think even Emery expected it. Already, the relief was no longer enough, for any of us. We were all drained, overwhelmed, heartbroken by our inability to help Giles and Francis and Dominic. History had defeated us in the end. Marcia said something about hot baths and food, but it seemed an impossibility, an irrelevance. Even Elizabeth was crying again after that moment of jubilation.

'I need to pray and say Mass,' Father Draycott said. 'Anyone who wants to join me is very welcome.'

'I'll join you.' Father Freese straightened up.

'I must get Freya out of this... these... things...' Nicholas was done in.

Meta came forward and gently took the little girl from him. Freya turned, saw her aunt and put her arms wearily round her neck. They left the drawing room, with Madogany frisking after them like a puppy, his tail wagging incessantly.

'Something's happened to that dog,' Alistair said, puzzled.

Bob went to the door. 'How about the bedroom next door for your Mass, Father? Will it do, do you think?'

Father Draycott nodded. 'Yes. That's the very place for it. I'll just get my stuff from the car...'

Bob opened the door for him. They both left the drawing room, followed by Father Freese. I heard the two priests' slow, tired footsteps on the stairs. Seconds later, Bob was back in the drawing room, ashen faced.

'The bedroom, quickly,' he said. He called down. 'Father Draycott! Father Freese! Hurry!'

The rest of us ran next door.

'Oh, Christ,' Nicholas breathed.

Dominic lay sprawled beside the Jacobean fireplace, tremors in his limbs, blood soaking his jerkin in two places and bubbling from his mouth. He was staring at the Jacobean ceiling in bewilderment. As everyone crowded round, I knelt, took him in my arms and cradled his dark, bleeding head in my lap. He saw me, gave me a grimace which might have been a smile.

Father Draycott raced in, fell to his knees beside him and spoke to him in Latin. Dominic replied, slurring, his head falling to one side. The priest made the sign of the cross over him. But by then there was nothing save a skull on my lap, and bones and faded rags on the floor.

EPILOGUE

WE GAVE Dominic a quiet, Catholic burial in the tiny, fourteenth century chapel attached to the retreat in Father Draycott's Somerset parish, where Giles had struggled to make sense of the twenty-first century. Father Draycott officiated, assisted by Father Freese. Besides the nuns, six of us who had known him attended, Nicholas, Alistair, Meta, Bob, Jack and me.

The burial proved to be one of Father Freese's last duties. Freya apart, he was the most affected of us all by the harrowing occurrences in the gatehouse. But he came out of retirement eight months later for my wedding to Nicholas, and he has promised to officiate at the Christening of our son, Dominic, who will be born in three months time. He was present, too, when Father Draycott exorcised the gatehouse without further incident. That represented a healing of sorts.

I no longer work in London. I am self employed and busy, working from a little room next to Nicholas's estate office in the manor house. Young Jack is thriving as a first year boarder at Alistair's school. Madogany is thriving too and baffling the vets, having never regained the stiffness of old age which he lost on that dreadful night in 1582. Alistair calls him Dogian Gray. Oddly enough, my ankle and bruises healed immediately too.

Freya, with this rejuvenated Madogany constantly at her side, has made progress beyond our hopes. It was heartbreakingly slow at first, and the psychological scars will always be there, but she no longer clings to Nicholas, has caught up with her schoolwork and, to my surprise, accepted me as a part of her father's life and her own. Her speech has returned and her hair is growing back.

We have managed to shield her from the press (the story got out – Elizabeth, who else?) and from the ghost hunters who visit periodically and whose fees help to fund the professional restoration work my father and brother have begun. Even if we were to tell the ghost hunters the truth – that they are wasting their time, that Deverell Gatehouse feels like a different, less cold, less oppressive place now – they wouldn't listen. Ordinary visitors too are flocking to us; the gatehouse, complete with updated guidebook, is these days booked out more than a year in advance.

Another trip to the sixteenth century appears mercifully unlikely. I would hate to go back again; sometimes I wake in the night, wondering whether I have, though it is only in nightmares now. But I cannot deny that alongside the cruelty and intolerance we witnessed, loyalty and courage were there too. We have no idea why Dominic came to die in our time, but instead of receiving a hasty, wretched and anonymous burial intended to conceal his murder, his bones lie in a place where he is honoured. The nuns at the retreat keep fresh flowers on his grave and remember him and Francis and Giles in their prayers.

So, attempting to make sense of it all, what conclusions have we reached?

I think the nearest we can get to the truth is to ask what would have happened had Giles known about Dominic's plans when he was interrogated by Topcliffe in 1582. Fresh from 1560, he knew nothing; Dominic's plans were in his future. Giles's suffering at Topcliffe's hands would have been appalling, he had no way to make it stop, but it may be that other lives were saved as a result of his ignorance. Before that, of course, Freya had been used as a messenger. So whatever Dominic's plans were, whoever else they involved, they had benefited twice over from the switch in time.

How did it happen? Our thoughts return to the Lady Chapel. Was the switch made there? Had it not happened, would Freya have died along with Sophia in that riding accident? We are haunted by a fear that she was meant to die and will only live another twenty-two years, the time taken from Giles. It's an irrational fear, perhaps, but we cherish her all the more because of it.

~ END ~

Thank you for reading a Pentalpha Publishing book.

Enjoyed *Deverell Gatehouse*?

Here's what you can do next.

If you loved the book and you'd like to help other readers find Pentalpha books, please write a short review on the website where you bought the book. Your help in spreading the word is much appreciated and reviews make a huge difference in helping new readers find good books.

Why not try books by other Pentalpha Publishing authors?

http://pentalphapublishing.weebly.com/

Also by Karen MacLeod:

THE WARBECK TRILOGY

DOUBTFUL BLOOD, which is based on real events, is the first book of ***THE WARBECK TRILOGY*** set between 1544 and 1559.

Winchester 1544. At a time of religious turmoil in England, a mysterious, fair haired boy is found in a Hampshire ditch with head injuries and memory loss by the Catholic Warden of Winchester College, John White, who gives him the name Jan and employs him in College. There, as his memory returns, Jan hides a dangerous secret concerning his birth and witnesses the tragic impact of the Reformation in College.

COUNTERFEIT and ***THORN MAKER*** follow on from ***DOUBTFUL BLOOD*** and complete the trilogy.

GARLANDS AND SHADOWS, also by Karen MacLeod is a romantic novel set in Scotland.

The above books are available as ebooks from Amazon sites worldwide and many other online bookshops including pentalphapublishing. weebly.com/.

Also from Pentalpha Publishing Edinburgh:

DELIRIUM: THE RIMBAUD DELUSION
by Barbara Scott Emmett.

1872: The explosive love affair between flamboyant French poets Arthur Rimbaud and Paul Verlaine rocks French society. They flee to London, abandoning the manuscript of *La Chasse Spirituelle* to Verlaine's scorned young wife. When a lawyer's clerk salvages it from a dusty deed box, the manuscript begins its journey down the decades, revealing the secrets and betrayals of its various keepers.

2004: Driven by her obsession with Rimbaud, Andrea Mann visits his grave at Charleville-Mézières. There she meets a beautiful young man who shows her a page from *La Chasse Spirituelle.*

Drawn into a manipulative relationship with the youth and his mentor, the mysterious Albert, she faces unwelcome truths. The closer she gets to the manuscript, the further she veers from reality.

But is Albert's copy genuine? And can *La Chasse Spirituelle* fill the void in Andrea's soul?

DELIRIUM: THE RIMBAUD DELUSION *is available in both paperback and ebook formats from Amazon sites worldwide and other online bookshops.*

For more books from **Pentalpha Publishing Edinburgh** *please visit:*

http://pentalphapublishing.weebly.com/book-info.html

Printed in Poland
by Amazon Fulfillment
Poland Sp. z o.o., Wrocław